THE DESERTER

A TALE OF THE FOREIGN LEGION

WAYNE TURMEL

ACHIS PRESS   LAS VEGAS, NV, USA

ISBN 78-0-9820377-8-2

Cover by Ruth Zakarian

Map by JJdraws

CONTENTS

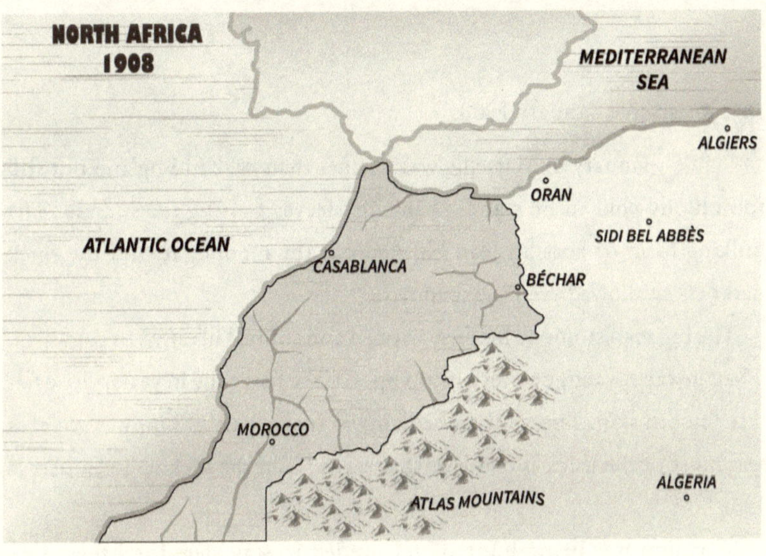

NORTH AFRICA
1908
MEDITERRANEAN
SEA
ALGIERS
ORAN
SIDI BEL ABBÈS
ATLANTIC OCEAN
CASABLANCA
BÉCHAR
MOROCCO
ALGERIA
ATLAS MOUNTAINS

CHAPTER 1

M arseille, January 1908

January in Marseille was warmer than back in England but still too bloody cold to be standing in shirtsleeves waiting for sunrise. The hulking form of Fort St. Jean blocked out the moonlight, and the thick darkness swallowed even the shadows.

The big man stomped his feet, slapped and rubbed his arms to get warm. Then he ran his tongue over his top lip. For the first time in years, all he felt was smooth skin. The moustache that was such a part of him was gone, as was most of the thick blond hair that earned him the nickname Gilbert le Lion.

This lion was being hunted and needed to stay alert for a few more hours if it wanted its freedom. A clean shirt, some underwear, and his good shaving razor were all he carried in a canvas rucksack slung over his shoulder. A second razor, the sharper one, hid tucked into his boot. For the hundredth time, Gil checked that the money was still in his pocket. It was.

For now.

The sound of footsteps shuffling from the narrow alley drove him against the wall. A figure emerged and looked around. The well-dressed man was smaller than Gil, but most Frenchmen were. He wore a thick coat with a sweater underneath, a wool beret and carried a walking stick. Anyone would think he was a merchant or a lawyer, out too late and easy pickings for street thugs. Gil knew better.

Alert to his surroundings, the man knew someone was there; he just wasn't sure who it was. He gave a simple, cautious nod and continued scanning the street. Gil smiled. Vincente didn't recognize him. With luck, nobody else would either.

"A guy could freeze his arse off waiting for you," Gil whispered in French. After all this time, he spoke the language well, but there was no hiding the North of England in his accent.

"*Mon Dieu*, I thought you were—" The older man froze, then took two tentative steps forward. "What in Christ's name did you do to yourself?" Vincente waved a finger at Gil's hairless face.

The Englishman took his friend's elbow and pulled him into a doorway. "I don't have much time, but I needed to see you."

"Has Colette seen this? She's not going to like it."

"She doesn't know. And she won't, because I'm leaving. This morning. That's why I needed to see you."

Gil shuddered and let out a breath, visible in the chilly night air. The older man instinctively offered his coat. The Englishman shook him off. "I'm fine. The sun'll be up soon."

"What do you mean you're leaving?"

Gil ignored the question. "How much do you owe The Belgian?"

Vincente sighed. "Too much. What is it now, a hundred thousand? Not enough to kill me for, too much to let it slide. He threatens. I ask for more time. It's a game."

Gil reached into his pocket and grabbed a wad of crumpled bills the size of his fist, wrapped in a rubber band. "A game you can't win. Get him off your back. My gift to you. For, well, for everything." He shoved it towards his friend.

Vincente recoiled. "What's that? Jesus, boy, where did that come from?"

Gil shrugged. "Does it matter?"

"Of course it matters."

Ignoring the protest, Gil grabbed his friend's wrist and placed the money in his palm, closing the fingers over it. "I'm done. For good. Just paying my debts."

The sky was becoming lighter over the Mediterranean. Four thirty maybe? He needed to stay invisible until eight thirty at most. Four long hours.

"You don't owe me anything," Vincente said.

"I owe you pretty much everything. Now we're square, and you can tell The Belgian to *embrasse ton cul*. With my compliments."

Somewhere on the next street, a door slammed, and a cat yowled as Marseille awoke. The city dawned grumpy and mean. "Where are you going?" Vincente asked.

"Away. From Marseille, from all this. I can't live like this anymore."

Vincente studied the younger man's face for far too long. Finally, he looked down and saw the bloodstains on the tail of Gil's shirt. "You're hurt."

Gil tucked the shirt in, hiding most of the blood. "It's not mine."

"Then whose?" Vincente stopped. His face and voice turned to stone. "The card game in La Barasse? That was you?" He turned away and checked for eavesdroppers down the alley. "Do they know?"

Gil held his palms up, pleading for him to be quiet. "By now? Probably. Likely. After today, it won't matter."

Vincente's eyes were watery. "What's that mean after today? You're not going to, you know. You promised never to do that again."

Gil remembered that last half-hearted attempt, and his thumb traced the scar on his left wrist unconsciously. Like everything he'd done since arriving in Marseille, the act was more messy than effective and laid a heavy burden on the few people who cared. Colette nursed him; Vincente gave him a place to recover and a job. No, he wouldn't do that to them again.

But he desperately needed to leave. Marseille. The petty hustles. The ever-present threat of childish, pointless violence. He needed order back in his life. Couldn't survive without it another day. There was still one place—and only one — he'd find it.

If he could make it to sunrise. The morning could not come fast enough.

While Gil was lost in thought, Vincente unwrapped the money and expertly thumbed through it. "Paying him back with his own money. You've got balls, I'll say that." He held two bills between his fingers and held them out. "There's too much. At least keep some for yourself. "

"Give it to Colette." The name stuck in his throat.

The older man tried shoving the hundred-franc notes into Gil's hand, but it was balled into an impenetrable fist. "You'll need it."

"Not where I'm going."

Vincente tried to look into his eyes. "And where's that, pray tell?"

Gil motioned with his head to the fort behind them. In the coming dawn, guards were visible, pacing on the parapet and in front of the giant wooden gate.

His friend squinted, confused. Then his eyes grew wide. "Bullshit."

Gil shrugged.

"It would be faster just to kill yourself."

"I need to do this."

"I don't get it," Vincente said, his voice full of fatherly concern.

"I know, mate."

The early-morning sounds and sights of the city filled the air. Water lapped against the boats at their moorings. Horses clip-clopped on stones, dragging squeaky carts. Gas lamps appeared in upper windows.

"Can I at least buy you breakfast?"

Gil smiled. "Probably the last decent meal I'm going to have for a long time. Sure. But somewhere dark."

Vincente slapped his fingers against the bloodstains on the big man's shirt. "You'll need a fresh shirt. Can't show up like that. Even they won't ignore something like that."

"Feed me first, then you can nag me."

Breakfast was delicious; the jam sweet, the croissants flaky and the air full of smoky bacon and companionable silence. They sat in the corner near the kitchen, smoking and drinking coffee. As old friends do, they avoided any talk of parting or where Gil was headed. It was the nicest morning Gil had experienced in far too long. And it would be the last of its kind.

Eventually, they stood on the sidewalk in front of the café. Gil looked everywhere but the port, while Vincente avoided looking him in the eye. Finally, the Englishman stuck his hand out. "Adieu, my friend. Thank you."

"Crazy bastard." Vincente stuck two notes into the offered hand, then shook it and pulled him in for a bear hug. "*Au revoir*, Gilles. "

Without dragging it out another second, Gil stuffed the money into his pocket, turned and walked with determination towards the port and Fort St. Jean. He felt Vincente watching, so he turned the corner a block too early just to be out of sight.

That nearly proved fatal. Two large goons stood at the top of the concrete stairs leading down to the docks. They smoked and watched the street, waiting for anyone trying to escape by boat. It was too much to hope The Belgian hadn't recognized him. Now he had to avoid these two gorillas.

It was just for a bit more. He could do it. He had to.

The clean shirt in his bag was identical to the one he had on, minus the obvious evidence of his crime. It wouldn't provide any sort of disguise. Everyone knew the Lion was a creature of habit, always wearing the same thing every day. Even half-shorn, they'd recognize him in an instant.

Gil considered the matter of his blood-stained shirt. He needed to change his appearance. Fast. Turning back a few blocks, leaned against a cold stone wall to think. The sound of retching drew his attention. A man just a little smaller than himself was puking into the gutter.

A drunken sailor was stumbling back to his ship from a night in one of Marseille's most decrepit brothels. The Italian snatched Gil's last twenty francs and swapped them for his watch cap and striped sweater. It was a size too small for Gil's sturdy frame, but would suffice.

As the man everyone knew as Gilbert le Lion pulled the fetid shirt on, he glimpsed his reflection in a bakery window. The sailor's shabby blouse bulged at the gut and stretched around Gil's thick neck and wrists. He'd never be caught wearing such rags, and his pursuers knew it. Perfect.

The morning dawned gray and chilly. Gilbert stood on the opposite side of the cobblestone street staring at the fort, then turned West away from the rising sun. For the last time, he took in the city that had been home but nearly destroyed him.

Out of a long-lost habit, he stiffened his back and marched with arms swinging to the small office building next to the fort. He lifted his leg and stomped to a halt. He studied the faded sign on the wall.

"La Légion Etrangère." The Foreign Legion.

Underneath it in smaller print, it simply said, *"Enrôlement."* Enlistment.

He reeked of failure, sweat, and another man's whore, but it couldn't be helped. Chin up and eyes clear, Gilbert tossed the cap in the gutter and stepped inside.

CHAPTER 2

British, French, it didn't matter. All military offices smelled the same. Because the windows were closed against the chilly wind coming off the harbor, the air was stale and dead. Tobacco smoke penetrated wooden walls like creosote and streaked the windows. The furniture smelled of sweat and flatulence, not to mention the desperation of those sitting on it. He took a deep breath, and his heart slowed a beat.

Two people looked up to watch him enter. One was a nervous-looking kid, maybe twenty years old. He wore working-man's clothes. At his feet was a brand-new travel bag. A gift from a worried parent? Gil had owned one just like it before he'd set off for the depot at seventeen. He couldn't help but feel a tinge of envy for the youngster and offered a friendly nod. Had he ever been so young and hopeful? He barely remembered sitting in that chair in Newcastle. Certainly, his old man hadn't given him luggage, just a black eye.

Across a trestle table, the second man tapped his pencil to get the young man's attention. The sergeant's pinched Gallic face scrunched as if a whiff of sulfur had just blown in. His perfect uniform was out of place in such a shabby room, but gave him an indisputable air of superiority. As intended. The way his left hand hung limply at his side explained his presence in France. He saw Gil and gestured with a pointed nose to a wooden chair against the far wall.

With a curt, "*Je m'excuse, sergent,*" Gil took the chair. He sat ramrod stiff, hands on his knees, staring straight ahead as expected of a good soldier. Three years of indolence and spitting at authority surrendered without a fight to muscle memory. He allowed himself a brief smile.

" Very well. All we need is for you to sign your name here, if you know how, and you are part of the Foreign Legion. It's all here; a term of five years. Five *centimes* a day, payable monthly, minus the cost of your uniform."

Gil flinched. Her Majesty's army paid new recruits a shilling a day, five times what he was being offered. He knew the Legion's pay was low, and in the depths of the desert, hard currency was practically useless. But after so much easy access to cash, he felt his guts tighten. Maybe because the kid was obviously green, and coming in at the lowest possible rank, Gil would get a better deal. The money was secondary, but a man had to eat.

"Sign here with your *nom de guerre*. You will only be known by this name and you will renounce your French citizenship for the first year."

"What's wrong with my real name?" Gil knew the question identified the kid as cannon fodder. He imagined that baby face covered in snot and tears the first time a sergeant bawled him out. Like his own had been. He'd survived. Maybe the kid would be alright. Maybe not.

"You want to be the same good little French boy you were when you walked in? Join the Army. In the Legion, you are not French, or anything other than a soldier. Odds are you won't live long enough to regret it. If you do, you'll earn your citizenship back. Sign or don't."

Gil flinched at the callous tone but watched intently. With shaking hands, the kid took a pen from the officer. He scrawled a new name across the paper, then dropped the pen.

The officer pulled the paper across the desk, read it, rose to his feet and extended his hand. "Private LaForce. Welcome to the Legion."

The newly minted LaForce gawked at the offered hand for a second, then grabbed it with unnecessary force. He squeezed hard, as he'd been taught, and pumped it once. As an afterthought, he gave a semblance of a salute.

"Do you have somewhere to stay tonight?"

"*Oui Sergent.* Sir... my uncle lives in town."

"We muster at dawn. Report to the fort with your papers and one bag of belongings."

LaForce stood there dumbly until the officer pointed to the door.

He nodded and picked up his bag. "Right. Of course. See you tomorrow. Sir."

The noncom sneered. "The hell you will. You think I'm going to that shithole with you? I will stay in France with the wine and white women. *Adieu.*"

The kid turned, then gave Gil a weak smile and stepped forward. "Jacques Manot."

"You mean LaForce." Gil enjoyed the confused look on the freckled face. "It's a good name. Calling yourself Strength. Ballsy. I like it. But you better get used to it. Try again."

A blush burned in his barely shaven cheeks. Christ, there's no way he'd ever been so young and innocent. "Of course. Jean LaForce. You are?"

"I don't know yet. In a few minutes, it won't matter." It sounded cold, but he'd had enough and hoped the kid would leave.

The youngster was stubborn. "I hope we're in the same unit. It will be good to have a friendly face."

Out of the corner of his eye, Gil saw the Sergeant point to the empty chair. "If you're done flirting, you're next."

Without sparing another look at the kid, Gil marched to the chair, stomped to a halt, then sat staring straight ahead.

Lighting his third cigarette since Gil had entered, the Sergeant studied him through the acrid smoke. He said nothing, daring the recruit to speak first. Gil knew the game, though. He sat staring back, hoping the legionnaire took it as a sign of strength and resolve.

The Sergeant waited an eternity and a half-finished cigarette before barking, "Well. Why are you here?"

Chin raised, Gil answered, "I wish to enlist in the Legion Étranger."

"You have military experience." It wasn't a question.

"Yes. Her Majesty's Army. Second Hampshire, Mobile Infantry. Three years, honorable discharge."

"Why not just go back?"

The lie came easily. "France is my home *now*."

The recruiter snorted and pulled a flake of tobacco from his lips. "Where did you serve?"

"South Africa. I was a Lance Corporal of Horse."

"You shoveled shit while others did the real fighting, is that it?" Gil furrowed his brow, but stayed calm. Recruiters always tried to winnow out the weak and uncommitted. It wasn't personal. In fact, he'd grown pretty good at the game. It was an acquired skill that came in handy when dealing with gangsters and others who preyed on the weak.

He straightened in his chair and returned the man's serious gaze. "I saw plenty of action. Paardeberg, for one. I'm a good man in a square." That inspired an unimpressed *hmph* from the Recruiter, so he continued. "Spent most of my time in the Orange." He felt himself relax. Speaking soldier-to-soldier always felt familiar.

The Frenchman raised an eyebrow. "You were at the camps?"

For the first time, he was tempted to lie, but the words burst from him before he could stop. "Sir. Bloemfontein."

Visions of dirty, hungry faces staring and filthy fingers clutching barbed wire flooded back for the first time in ages. Time and wine had banished such thoughts to the occasional nightmare.

The tap-tap-tap of a cigarette on a desk blotter dragged him back to the conversation. "An ugly business. Treating civilians—white people at that—like cattle. No work for proper soldiers."

"Well, we—" Gil snapped his mouth shut. The legionnaire stared at him like crap on a boot. What good would it do to justify himself? The French hated the English more than the Arabs. That was no reason to refuse him. Surely, they wouldn't reject him for doing his job? For following orders? He felt his plan crumbling at the edges, as they so often did. He willed himself to stay stoic.

The recruiter stubbed out the cigarette. "The Legion needs fighters. Real men. Not cowards who round up and starve women and children."

Gil's temples throbbed. A little desperately, he threw in, "My assignment was tending horses, not people. Sergeant." It took nearly three years of intense drinking and whoring and fighting to purge his mind of the memories. It took Vincente's friendship. And Colette. It took less than five minutes for unwanted memories to flood back. Gil tried not to panic, but wondered if he was truly screwed. There was no contingency plan. They had to take him.

The recruiter was speaking, but only brief snatches of it penetrated Gil's panicked brain. "What do you know about mules?"

"Mules, sir?" He'd never dealt with them, or even thought about them, if he was honest. A donkey fucks a horse, out comes something stupid and stubborn and ugly. The British Army ran on excellent horseflesh and marching men. What did he care about bloody mules?

"Horses are useless in the desert. That's why we let the officers prance around on them. We assign the real fighting men mules."

In his martial fantasies, Gil imagined himself as the hero of the squadron, slaughtering the enemy two for every one his platoon mates did. Leading the attack. Covering himself in glory, not manure.

"I can tend mules." He hoped the smile was convincing.

"*Bien.* We will take you as a private and see if we can make a real soldier of you."

A private? Starting all over? Like that punk kid? He looked down at the filthy sweater that crept up and showed his gut. He yanked it down, covering his belly.

"All we need is for you to sign your name here, and you are part of the Foreign Legion. It's all here; a term of five years. You're already not a citizen, so that's irrelevant. Five *centimes* a day, payable monthly, minus the cost of your uniform."

"Huh?"

"You can always return to England. Otherwise, we'll see if we can make a half-decent French soldier of you. Yes or no?" The legionnaire extended the pen across the desk.

With a heavy heart, Gil willed his hands to stop trembling he signed the paper. He hesitated just a moment as he wrote "Gil" in clear, precise schoolboy handwriting. He'd be damned if he gave up his first name, but he owed his father nothing. Instead, he claimed the name of someone more important to him.

He added "Vincente" to the page and handed it back.

The recruiter looked at it. "Gilles Vincente?"

"Gil. The English pronunciation."

The recruiter smirked. "Gill? Like the fish?" He wiggled his good hand on either side of his neck.

"As you say. Gil. Vincente. Sergeant."

The Frenchman stood and extended his hand. "Legionnaire Vincente, we muster at dawn. Bring your papers and one bag."

A jangly bell announced someone coming in. The door opened, and a thirty-year-old Turk entered. Next man into the sausage grinder.

Gil gestured to the bag at his feet. Then he shook the man's hand. He looked out the filthy window. The streets of Marseille had come to life while he was signing his life away. An unsavory-looking but unfamiliar character caught his eye. Somewhere out there, half the criminals in France were looking for him. He could only report tomorrow morning if he lived that long.

"I don't have an uncle here in town like that green kid. Is there somewhere I can stay until tomorrow?"

"There are quarters in the fort, but know that once you sign your contract, you can enter but may not leave until you board for Oran."

"And that's tomorrow morning?"

A curt nod and a wave out of the way to make room for the newcomer were the silent response.

Thank you." He picked up his canvas bag and flung it over a shoulder. His skin itched under the sailor's clothes, and he couldn't wait to change his shirt. The newly minted Gil Vincente stepped to the door and offered a salute, which the recruiter barely acknowledged. It didn't matter. Gil had a new name, a clean shirt, and steady pay. More importantly, he was finally free of Marseille, and the memory of Gilbert le Lion.

CHAPTER 3

Trouble came two hours out from Oran. Gil expected it, of course. Knowing soldiers as he did, the only surprise was the kettle took so long to boil.

The twenty or so recruits boarded *la Madelaine* at noon the day before, shuffling aboard, clutching one bag of whatever was worth bringing to the ass-end of the world. Some held creased, tear-stained pictures of sweethearts or mothers. A few had cash they'd brought for emergencies, but would no doubt lose to thieves or gamblers before they ever arrived at Sidi bel Abbès for training. Gil carried only his canvas sack, clean socks, and one last decent shirt. His sock held the few Franc notes and his razor. No mementos, no memories.

A *capitaine* shouted directions and insults while everyone picked their particular corner of the tub. It was going to be about twenty-four hours, depending on the whims of the January weather. Some made for the sleeping quarters to stake out the hammocks closest to the window or farthest from the latrine. Those already regretting their decision to enlist stood at the stern of the ship, clinging to the rusty, flaking taffrail. They stared at the fort and the last view of France they would have. The pessimistic among them were convinced it would be for the last time. The optimists hoped the vision would sustain them for five long years.

Gil was at the bow, his back turned to Marseille and his eyes on the horizon. Somewhere out there was Africa, which he thought he left forever. The wind felt cold on his shorn scalp and bare face. It smelled of salt, dead fish and diesel. He squatted beside a lifeboat, sheltered from the worst of the breeze, and rolled a cigarette, cursing as half the tobacco blew away before he could lick the paper closed around it.

From the corner of his eye, he watched his fellow future legionnaires. Just as at the depot in Newcastle years ago, It didn't take long for the recruits to form cliques. Those requiring conversation to quell their nerves quickly found each other and instantly indulged in introductions, boasting and outright lies. This was as good a chance as any to start living up to whatever *anonymat* and past they claimed.

Those preferring quiet quickly made themselves known, and the jabbering soldiers avoided them with suspicion. After all, if they were going to be in the same unit, they may as well be friendly. The friction kept building, and Gil did not want to be around when the spark ignited.

While seeking a quiet spot, he felt eyes on his back and the hair on the nape of his neck stood at attention. The razor in his boot was useless when not in his hand. He stopped and reached to tie a perfectly good shoelace. With the bone handle in his hand, he turned on a heel only to see the kid, LaForce, standing there with a shy smile on his spotty face.

"You look like you know what you're doing. Figured I'd follow you."

Had he ever been that young and naïve? "Jean, right? Looks are deceiving. I don't know much of nothing, and what I want is to be left alone. I'm not the one for anyone to be following."

Undeterred, he tried engaging Gil in conversation. "You're English, aren't you?"

"Used to be. Not anymore. I'm in the service of *la belle France*, ain't I? Go find someone else to play with, boy." He tried ignoring the crest-fallen look on the kid's face and walked off to an empty spot port side. He wasn't ready for companionship.

Jean LaForce was saved further embarrassment when someone yelled. "Look, dolphins." He immediately ran to the rail, a look of wonder in his eyes. Gil shook his head.

Gil's solitary little nest was fine for the first hours. When night fell, he went inside and grabbed the worst possible hammock, earning him the gratitude of some and the disdain of others. It was better to be underestimated and ignored at this point until he figured out who was who. Every bunkroom had a pecking order. He never wanted to be a leader. Too damned much responsibility, there. To be at the bottom of the heap meant bullying and unwanted attention from the non-coms. No, the middle of the pack was safest and gave him a chance to settle in with as little drama as possible.

It also allowed him to be across the room from the LaForce, who beckoned him over, having saved the spot beside him. Gil pretended not to see it and threw his sack into the canvas hammock and rolled up into it. He managed a few hours of fitful sleep before greeting the dawn back on deck.

Surprisingly, the hazy gray bump of Algeria was already visible through the haze when the inevitable happened. Men had been drifting forward for the last hour or more. The bigger men jostled the small and weak in the quest for a first view of their new home. In all the commotion, a small stack of folded bills fell from someone's pocket onto the deck.

Gil watched and winced as LaForce picked it up, looking around for the rightful owner.

"Hey, who dropped this?" He held the money up and looked around.

Gil saw the big ogre before the kid did. "Bloody wanker," he hissed.

The goon easily stood six feet and fourteen or fifteen stone. "That'd be mine. Thanks much," the big man grunted and ripped the bills from the kid's fingers.

LaForce tried to grab it back but missed. "Actually, I found it over there. I don't think-"whatever he planned to say was cut off by a cuff to the head that could have felled a tree. "Ow," he whined.

"You calling me a liar, you little pissant?" The two of them suddenly stood in an empty circle, surrounded by curious soldiers desperate for entertainment. Gil sighed and rolled his eyes.

Give the youngster his due. The boy drew himself up as tall as he could. "Didn't say that." He planted his feet and looked up at the bully. He flexed his small, pale fists. This was a kid used to taking a beating, but willing nonetheless.

"Kick his scrawny ass!" someone yelled from beside Gil. Before he could think, the Lion slammed the man against the railing.

"Shut your gob, "he hissed in English before remembering to say it again, in French and louder. The man considered arguing, but the stormy look in Gil's eyes dissuaded him.

He released the other fellow's shirtfront and turned back to the men in the circle, relishing the attention. LaForce had raised his fists and gone into a fighting crouch, preparing for a short, brutal, likely futile fight. The bigger, older man stood with his hands on his hips, grinning.

"Oh, you're a scrappy little bastard, aren't you?" He slipped the bills into his pocket and grinned a gap-toothed smile, shrugged his huge shoulders and stretched his neck until it cracked. "Okay, little brother. I'll give you the first shot."

It was an old bunkhouse trick. Get the least experienced, weaker man to throw the first punch. That not only let you gauge his ability, but justified whatever hell you rained down on him after that. After all, you were just protecting yourself. Gil had done it himself more than once. His stomach clenched, anticipating the mismatch ahead.

"Officer coming." The words bounced through the crowd, and the combatants stepped away from each other.

In a thick Prussian accent, a corporal barked, "What's going on?" He pointed at the larger man. "You. causing trouble?"

"This kid just found my money. He was returning it to me, and there was a misunderstanding."

The German turned to the red-faced, shaking LaForce.

"Is *zat* true?"

The pause was just a beat too long to be credible, but Jean LaForce unclenched his fists and nodded. "Yes sir. No problem at all."

"Good. Save that nonsense for the Arabs. There'll be fighting aplenty before you know it." He looked over the railing and pointed to the vague hills to the southwest. "Take a good look. Only two hours to your new home, if the tide's right. Try not to kill each other before we get there."

He took a long look at the group, appraised them, and sucked on his teeth. Gil wondered what he thought of the assembled riffraff. "As you were." With a clear look of disgust on his face, he shook his head and stomped back to the warmth of the wardroom.

The crowd became more interested in the approaching landfall than the aborted fight and scattered. Gil watched as the bigger man let out a belly laugh and almost put his hand right through the kid's backbone as he slapped him. "You did alright, kid."

He stuck a conciliatory hand out. "Auguste Dupre. Gus to my friends."

LaForce gripped the hand and tried squeezing hard enough to impress the giant. In a serious voice an octave lower than normal, he offered, "Jean. LaForce."

Another laugh burst from that barrel of a chest." Johnny Strong. I like it. Yup, you've got some balls on you." He made a playful jab between the kid's legs, just to watch the smaller man recoil.

LaForce turned away and drifted off, sparing a dirty look at Gil before accepting the praise of a gaggle of the younger men.

Gil watched him pass, then caught Dupre's eye. The two studied each other for a moment before offering curt nods of acknowledgement. They each had their eye on the other, but there was no real trouble there. Hopefully, there wouldn't be.

Gil approached the railing beside Dupre, who put his hands on the rusty metal. "You had his back, didn't you?"

Gil shook his head. "That boy is no concern of mine. I mind my own business." He looked at Dupre and motioned for one of his cigarettes. The big Frenchman held out the pack, then struck a match for the two of them. "I just don't like bullies."

"Just having a little fun. If we're gonna depend on each other, we should know what we're made of, don't you think?"

"And what did you learn?"

"Kid's got balls. I just hope he can shoot, cause he's gonna be bugger-all at close quarters."

Gil didn't disagree. He and Dupre smoked and watched the cliffs of Algeria draw nearer.

Chapter 4

"Recruits, form a line!" A corporal shouted from the makeshift gate on the rail.

Gil took his customary place in the middle of the pack. In front of him was a gangly Spaniard about a head taller than Gil. His first thought was this one would be an easy target for a sharpshooter. Behind him a stocky Nordic type, out of place and looking about as French as a strudel. Both stood at ease but alert. Real soldiers, at least.

It was easy to tell those who'd served in someone's army. About two-thirds of the men stiffened their spines, stood straight and stared into the neck of the person in front. The remaining half dozen or so kept swiveling their heads from side to side and elbowed each other, attempting to take in every fresh sight. They had also claimed the front of the line in their eagerness. Second from the front was Jean LaForce, naturally.

A crowd assembled on the wharf to meet the new arrivals. Most were mere rubberneckers, eager to check out the latest crop of legionnaires. A few women, a mix of officer's wives and vendors with baskets of fruit under their arms, jostled for position with old former war dogs and curious children.

A lieutenant with huge gin blossoms on each cheek spat on the deck. He studied the crowd, then looked at the line of men. "*Sapelard,*" I'll be damned if the first thing they see is you damned useless turnips." He grabbed a couple of ruffians and moved them into first and second positions. "There, let them think we're recruiting grown men instead of children."

A whine of protest was cut short by a withering stare. The men stood still and unsure of what to do until the ship shuddered to a halt and a gangplank snapped into place. The corporal pulled the wooden barrier to one side and addressed the crowd.

"You will follow me to the barracks. Do not fall out of line. Do not talk to anyone. Eyes straight ahead and march as if you know how. You are Legionnaires. Act like it, or, by God, we'll teach you so you'll never forget." With a salute to the Lieutenant, he spun on a worn heel and marched stiffly down the wooden ramp. Surefooted, he never missed a step or looked at his feet, despite the creaking and shaky planks.

Far more cautiously, the recruits followed. The crowd roared either their approval or disdain, depending on their mood. Most yelled, "Les bleues, les bleues!" It was their way of welcoming the newest members of the legion. A gaggle of old men yelled, "We're doomed if this is the best France can do. We'll have to give it back to the Arabs." They competed to see who could insult the new arrivals the worst while passing a brandy bottle back and forth.

Gil would have appreciated a railing on the gangway but managed to maintain his balance until his boots blessedly landed on the concrete pier. Somewhere behind him, he heard a shriek followed by a splash. The disaster was greeted with derisive hoots from the crowd. Gil fought the desire to see who fell, although a part of him hoped it was that idiot Dupre.

His first look at Algeria was a disappointment. Not that the city was ugly or seedy. To the contrary, Oran was a well-scrubbed town that looked more like Europe than the gateway to the Dark Continent. Mostly white faces lined the streets, cheering as the line of recruits passed by. Occasionally someone would yell, "Any news of Marseille?" "Who's from St Lo?"

A red-faced woman of about forty cupped her hands over her mouth and yelled, "Jacques Renault. Anyone know where the son of a bitch is? He said he'd come back five months ago."

A Dutchman shouted from somewhere in the line, "If you were prettier, I'd say I'm Jacques Renault."

The comedian exchanged grins with the soldier behind , pleased with himself until a sharp voice shouted, "Shut up, dog." The smile disappeared, and he continued marching in silence, the woman left behind screaming curses as the line passed.

After a few minutes, Gil allowed himself to take in his new surroundings. The briny petroleum smell of the docks was replaced by thick clay dust and the hint of lavender as the broad avenue turned inland. Flat-roofed, whitewashed houses gave way to warehouses and workshops. The parade spectators became less lily-white. A mix of Arab and black faces watched as they passed, the soldiers more interested in them than the other way around.

A brave, barefoot ten-year-old, at the instigation of his friends, ran to the side of the road and shouted, "Go home. Nobody wants you here." He then scurried behind a barrel to the laughing congratulations of his friends and the puzzlement of the corporal, who couldn't find the culprit. Gil smirked. He'd heard the same thing in Dutch and Zulu.

Out of nowhere, a voice began singing the marching song of the Legion.

We are crafty,
We are rogues,
Not ordinary guys,
We often have our dark moods
We are Legionnaires.

Many of the men knew the song and joined in. Gil knew the tune but continued listening to learn the words. It was a good marching tune, and he felt his feet adjust to the beat. The chorus began:

Hey, here's blood sausage, here's blood sausage, here's blood sausage.
For the Alsatians, the Swiss, and the Lorrains,
For the Belgians, there is none left,
For the Belgians, there is none left,

As he fell in, he couldn't help a sense of Victorian superiority. Just like the French, writing a fight song about food. A sausage, no less. In South Africa, the fusiliers sang" Marching to Pretoria," because that's what they bloody did.

Despite his smugness, by the end of the first mile Gil found himself singing along.

During our far-off campaigns,
Facing fever and fire,
Let us forget along with our sorrows,
Death, which forgets us so little.
We the Legion.

Then more about that bloody sausage. Begrudgingly, Gil had to hand it to the Legion. Just as La Marseillaise was bloodier and more belligerent than God Save the Queen, there was death and defiance in every line of the stupid song. And no, the Belgians weren't getting any damned sausages. Too bad for them.

Gil's stomach growled, and he hoped there was a lunch at the end of this trek.

The song faded to muttered conversation, and the stomping feet slowed as their home for the night came into view. The low, mud-brick, shockingly ugly Fort Ste Therese appeared.

Soldiers in clean blue uniform jackets and shockingly white pants paraded back and forth. The long cloths at the back of their *kepis* fluttered in the stiff breeze. Six sentries, armed with Lebel rifles, watched their new comrades approach and yelled through cupped hands. "*Les bleues....* The useless bastards are finally here."

The gate swung open slowly at first and then flew wide to welcome the newcomers. The corporal addressed the men.

"Don't get comfortable, you miserable animals. We are here for tonight only. Tomorrow you'll get your assignments and leave this paradise. Single file. March."

Amidst the good-natured jeers of their new compatriots, the newest legionnaires entered the fort. Arms swinging and still singing about that damned sausage, the recruits marched through the doors into a huge dusty square lined with uniformed soldiers.

The commandant marched out onto a balcony in his white dress uniform. The brim of his kepi shaded his hooded eyes, and a row of medals glinted in the Mediterranean sun. He was the direct antithesis of the sloppy, ragged, filthy men gathered below.

In a voice far too booming for his compact frame, he shouted, "Welcome, legionnaires. Don't imagine you are home yet. Tomorrow you will head to Sidi Bel Abbès and begin your lives as members of the greatest fighting force in the world. Tonight, you will eat, receive your regiment assignments and get a good night's sleep."

There was more, but Gil heard nothing after "eat." The growling in his stomach easily outranked the throbbing in his feet and the smell from his civilian clothes. He allowed himself a smile. He was still a soldier to his core. Stomach first.

CHAPTER 5

"What in Christ's name is that?" Dupre asked.

Gil poked at it with a spoon. "I think it's supposed to be soup. Either that or the laundry water went into the pot by mistake." The two men stared at the unappetizing mess in their tin bowls before being shooed along to make room for the next famished, and ultimately disappointed, recruits.

They sat at the first open bench, beside some Germans, who were too busy "ach"ing and "sheiss"ing to pay them any mind. The huge Frenchman took a chunk of the bread and while loudly chewing, said, "Bread's pretty good, though."

"It's alright," Gil grudgingly admitted, using it to sop up the gray broth along with a chunk of what he presumed to be gristly meat. With any luck, the boiling hot coffee would permanently cook his taste buds. If this is what they were eating at a well-stocked fort in peacetime, what horrors would he experience when they were on the march?

Gil couldn't help but remember that last breakfast with Vincente. As with most meals, the company seasoned the food, making it taste more delicious than it likely was. As he scooped up the last of the soup with the crust of bread, he thought dancing girls and his mum wouldn't help this slop.

"Hey," one of the Germans knocked on the table in front of Gil. In thickly accented French, asked, "Which regiment are you boys choosing?"

Gil mumbled into his spoon. "I've no bloody idea yet, mate. You?"

The German with the most teeth left in his head smiled broadly. "Ah, an English. John Bull, *ja*? Stick with us. I hear the Second has the most German officers. Old Prussians, most of them. That's the place to be."

"I'll think about it, thanks." He wouldn't. He may not enjoy it, but even knowing damn well he needed discipline, Prussians took it to extremes.

Dupre slapped Gil on the shoulder, nearly knocking him face-first into the soup bowl. "Nah. He's joining me in the *Troisième Régiment de Fusiliers.* Get in the thick of the action, kill as many sand wogs as we can. Isn't that right, *mon ami?*

A thin-lipped smile was the best Gil could muster. "Maybe, yeah. Haven't really thought much about it."

He looked around the mess hall at the mix of new recruits and experienced legionnaires. An assignment to an administrative group would keep him in Sidi Bel Abbès and safe, but he couldn't imagine how being trapped in a French city could be any better for him than Marseille. Even though he craved a return to real action, divisions like the Third Mounted had a lot of recently created openings, which didn't bode well for living to serve out his contract. He'd tried suicide once and failed. He was in no hurry to try again.

After dinner, he and Dupre, seemingly welded to Gil's side, walked around the fort, smoking and making small talk with the soldiers who tried to recruit them. Gil realized he had smoked more in the past two days than he had in a month. He threw the half-smoked butt onto the ground and crushed it under his boot. Dupre objected to the waste of tobacco, but the hell with him. It was a filthy habit. Worse, expensive. He'd be better off not smoking at all. As long as he was tossing old habits, this was a good place to start.

A grizzled Italian squeezed Dupre's arm and whistled. "Join us. A big guy like you would give me something to hide behind when the shooting starts."

The old Italian, who looked old enough to have fought with Garibaldi, was with a younger, peach-fuzzed Scot. "Good, ya kin quit using me for cover, ya old chickenshit." Gil smiled and felt himself tempted. He hadn't seen a single

Englishman, and if he wasn't too picky about the conversation, a Scotsman would do in a pinch.

"We'll think on it, yeah?"

Without planning it, Gil and Dupre found themselves on the parapet at sundown, looking south from the fort. They folded their arms on the brick wall and looked out at a drill yard and the whole of Africa beyond it.

In the fading light, they could make out a solitary figure scuffling in a circle around the yard. On his back was a bulging rucksack, and his feet had worn a deep rut in the sand. They didn't know how long he'd been out there, but it was getting harder for the poor bastard to remain upright. A sergeant ran alongside, yelling at the shuffling figure, "Fall and you start over, you worthless maggot."

"Christ, what do you suppose he did to deserve that?"

Dupre laughed. "Probably took a swing at some prick of a sergeant. Happens more than you'd think. That's been me more than once."

Gil's eyes widened. "If you did that in the Queen's army, it'd be the brig for sure."

Dupre laughed. "You *Anglais* must have had men to spare. Not a lot of jails in the desert, and we can't spare the bodies. There had to be witnesses, else the sergeant would have just beaten the crap out of him and let it go."

"Why'd you come back?"

The big man shrugged in the classic Gallic way. "Being a civilian is expensive, and I don't like bosses."

"Officers are just bosses."

"That's different." The way he said it implied there was a story there, but Gil declined to bite and the conversation ended.

A shaky bugle broke the night's silence, signaling lights out. The men made their way to the bunkhouse. Dupre glared at a skinny young recruit, who immediately found a cot further from the window, and the big soldier claimed the spot. Gil found an empty cot three rows away.

"Hey, Gil." The pimply face of Jean LaForce beamed at him from a sloppily made cot. "Decided which regiment to go with? Maybe we could—"

"Don't know yet. G'night." Gil passed without sparing the youngster another look. Whatever he decided, he hoped it wouldn't come with baggage or responsibility for anyone else. Even the good-natured but ever-present Dupre was becoming more company than he needed.

It took thirty seconds to expertly make up his cot. Geometrically perfect corners at one end, the blanket glass-smooth across the mattress with nary a crease to be seen. Then he folded his clothes on top of the footlocker, boots neatly set beside it. He looked around to see if anyone watched. Unnoticed, he slipped the razor out of his boot and under the putrid lump of feathers and canvas that served as a pillow. Off came his shirt and shoes, then in just his underclothes he laid on top of the blanket without disturbing it, enjoying the cool night air. Maybe morning would bring clarity about his next move.

It didn't.

The next morning came earlier than expected. After the first decent sleep he'd had since long before he left Marseille, reveille came as a shock. Old instincts kicked in. He was firmly on his feet by the time the sergeant began ripping blankets from lay-abouts and cursing those who couldn't remember how to stand at attention.

"Breakfast and registration. As soon as you've eaten, you'll get your billets and assignments. Everyone not staying here will be on board the train for Sidi Bel Abbès at noon, so pack your kits before you go. We haven't got all day. Move it."

Getting into the rhythm of things, Gil made his bed. The worn gray blanket was off-center, so he ripped it off the cot and took another stab at it. This time, the corners were perfect, and the line across the top of the bed could have been made with a plumb-line. Perfect. Orderly.

"I hear the General needs a new housemaid. You could apply for that duty." Gil turned, ready to say something involving the speaker's mother and her bed, when he stopped. A huge Corporal, missing an eyetooth but with shoulders a mile across, stood with his arms crossed.

"Sir."

"Just needs to be good, not perfect, and it likely won't matter since you're not staying. Who are you joining?"

"Don't know yet."

The corporal studied Gil head to toe. He pushed his Kepi back on his head and wiped a palm across his greasy forehead. "You're a soldier, if a bit prissy. They can use you in the Third."

"I'll remember that, corporal."

"See that you do. On with you, then." Gil saluted and trotted out to grab breakfast.

After a cup of putrid, tepid coffee and some shockingly adequate bread, Legionnaire third class Gil Vincente stood in line to await his fate.

One after another, the men gave their names to a clerk, who asked where they wanted to be assigned. He knew Dupre had been first in line to make sure of an assignment to the Third Rifles. Heated voices accompanied the two Germans, who were informed there were enough Prussians in the Second to retake Alsace. They wound up in the Third Rifles with a grinning Dupre, who bear-hugged them.

Gil approached the wooden plank that served as a desk. A bespectacled corporal, whose blue jacket was spotless, although his boots were worn so thin they were nearly transparent, barked but never looked up from his papers. "Name?"

"Vincente. Gil."

The clerk paid no attention to Gil but rummaged through some papers as he asked, "Which unit do you want to join?"

"The Second. Rifles. Sir." He had no reason for that response, only that he knew no one else who asked for it and it spilled out of his mouth. After studying a piece of paper, the corporal adjusted his glasses. "No. The Twenty-Fourth Mounted."

"Excuse me?"

The clerk waved a piece of paper. You've been requested for *the Vingt-Quatrième Régiment Monté*. Gille Vincente. You know horses?"

"Well, yes."

"Now you know mules. Next!" Gil took the paper waving in his face and stared at it. He didn't move.

"Uh, pardon. I thought we could choose our assignments."

"Oui. You chose. Then we decided. It comes with a raise to private second class, and eight centimes a week. Next."

Gil stared at the document and shuffled away. He'd never even met a mule and hated them already.

CHAPTER 6

Dupre grabbed the blue sash around Gil's waist and pulled until the air flew from his lungs. "There. Now you look like a real legionnaire."

"I feel like a horse's arse." Gil was still getting used to the uniform. It was very different from what he'd worn in South Africa, and most of the equipment, the sash included, made as much sense as a duck wearing a beret.

It had been a week since they arrived in Sidi Bel Abbès. All the recruits were going through basic training together. Since most of them served elsewhere before joining the legion, it was a mix of the very bored old-timers and terrified youngsters.

Gil tugged on the hem of his *capote*, the jacket a faded gray-blue. Uneven worn spots showed he wasn't its first occupant, but at least there were no bullet holes. He'd checked. Truth be told, he cut quite a dashing figure. If he didn't yet feel like Gil Vincente, legionnaire, he looked the part.

The kepi went on last. It was too snug on his oversized skull, and the stiff brim rode too high on his head. He looked at Dupre, with his hat already wrinkled and stained. it sat on his head at a jaunty angle. Dupre was a hand taller than he, and half again as broad in the shoulders, but his cap fit much better. Maybe it was the lack of brains that made the big oaf's head smaller.

Impractical as the headgear might be, the neck cloth hanging in back already proved its worth. By the third day, several of the more Nordic recruits were already blistered and peeling like paint on an old barn.

Dupre waved a finger at Gil's boots. "Umm, how do you get them so shiny?" They shone like church windows even though they, too, were previously worn by someone else. The big man's boots, several sizes larger, already had the look of someone who'd marched from Morocco, rather than several times around the parade grounds.

Gil gave a satisfied smile. "Pretty good, eh? Takes a lot of work. Can't just hawk a gob on them and rub twice."

"Stupid bloody waste of energy. Not like the Berbers are going to attack and go, 'wait a minute, their shoes are all shiny. Run for your lives!' Is it? I'm here to shoot'em, not dance with them."

They'd had this discussion before, and it wouldn't be the last time. There were two kinds of soldiers, in Gil's mind. Those who took care, and those who didn't. When Dupre saw how Gil made his cot, his boots polished to a high sheen, and gear stowed like a lady's hope chest, the teasing began. The last laugh was on him, though. Gil ate a long, comfy breakfast with the Germans as the rest did twenty laps of the parade ground the first morning for being sloppy.

Attention to detail was a mindset, and routine, life's guardrails. A well-made bed meant you were focused on your task. Take care of your boots, and it was a good bet you also took care of your socks, thus didn't get blisters. As a bonus, the lack of attention from the sergeants was worth a little ribbing from his bunkmates.

He'd forgotten that rule on arriving in France five years ago after mustering out. The freedom not to make his bed led to spending too long in it. Laziness in body led to taking the easy way out in the rest of his life. Every good habit devolved into a bad one until he couldn't remember the last time he had dusted his rooms or changed his sheets. A belief that rules were for others meant not getting a proper job, or at least keeping one, and to the streets of Marseille. He grew to loathe his life there. That final bloody night in La Barasse was a logical extension of a breakdown of discipline when left to his own devices. Rumpled sheets and water-spotted boots were the path to destruction, but that was secret knowledge, not a conversation to be had with anyone.

A thumb unconsciously rubbed at the scars on his wrist. Let them laugh. Gil Hawkins, or Gil Vincente, or whoever he was these days, needed sharp corners and shiny boots to survive, and that was no lie. His big friend—and Auguste Dupre was fast becoming at least a barracks-buddy—would never understand, and didn't have to.

After breakfast, the men gathered in the parade yard, muttering as they stood in the sun, waiting for today's version of hell. Gil's stomach was full and his mind at ease.

At last, the corporal he'd met yesterday marched stiffly to the front of the group and looked them up and down. He stared at them; they stared back. After Christ only knew how long, one or two of the younger men began shuffling back and forth, switching weight from one leg to the next. The corporal gave a missing-toothed smile.

"Sergeant!"

A sergeant saluted. "Yes, Corporal." Gil chuckled at the staged performance, wondering what sort of mummery was about to take place.

The big non-com pointed to the fidgeting recruits. "The men are eager today." He stopped, took off his kepi, and wiped a forearm across his brow. "It's a lovely day. Take them for a walk."

Gil heard Dupre groan beside him. He whispered to the big man, "How far do you figure?"

From the corner of his mouth, Dupre whispered, "The first time? Twenty miles." Gil felt the weight of his rucksack and his not-quite-new Lebel rifle, bayonet and ammo pouch. Twenty miles under the winter sun wouldn't be pleasant, but not awful.

The puppet show between the non-coms continued. "And make sure they pack enough for the trip, will you?"

"Sir." The sergeant marched up to poor LaForce, who struggled to look straight ahead and not at the grinning man two inches from his nose. "What's on your back, boy?"

"My pack. Sir." Gil felt an unreasonable pride in how the kid kept the quiver from his voice. He was toughening up. Maybe there was hope for him.

The sergeant laughed and slapped Jean on the back, so hard he nearly lost balance. "That's not a pack for walking in the desert. Might as well carry a picnic basket. No, that isn't your pack."

He pointed to a line of oversized, bulging backpacks lining the parade ground wall. "Those are a legionnaire's packs. You will all go claim one. That will be your pack from this day on. Learn to love it. It will save your life. Or kill you if you're not man enough. Go. Grab one. Move!"

They looked huge and grew bigger as the men approached them at a trot. Besides a tightly wound bedroll, they contained long poles on either side that would form a tent. The material for the tent was wrapped around the pack. A canteen, a *bidon,* hung from the side of the pack in a mesh bag called a *capote.* Add what was already in their pack. It probably came to sixty pounds or so. Adding rations for a long march that could last days, the pack would be over a hundred.

A hundred pounds on one's back. In the sun, on the soft footing of the desert. For twenty miles. More than one of the recruits muttered, *"Oh, allez. Baise-moi."* One forgot to say it quietly enough and got a large rock added to his pack for his troubles. Everyone shut up after that.

Gil struggled into his pack and turned to Dupre. "Well, do I look as foolish as I feel?"

"Not yet, Englishman." He roughly unbuttoned Gil's jacket and pulled it open, clumsy fingers fastening each flap to a button sewn into the side of the *capote.* What little breeze there was filled the coat and dropped his temperature. "There. Now you won't roast."

The Sergeant barked, "Fill your canteens turd form single file. Move." The men obeyed. In his hurry to obey, one of the Germans tripped and fell face-first into the dusty courtyard. Jean LaForce offered a hand up.

"No. Let him do it. Any man who can't keep up is a danger to you all. Stragglers get left behind for the scorpions and the Arabs. This is the Legion. You march, or you die." The young Alsatian soldier gulped, thought twice, and returned to attention. The German nodded his thanks and struggled to his feet, carefully maintaining his balance. "Thanks," he said. "Wilmer."

"Jean LaForce," said the young man. They nodded to each other and fell in line.

With Gil safely buried in the middle of the line, the Corporal nodded to the Sergeant. "Enjoy your walk in the countryside, gentlemen."

While the sergeant counted off, they marched through the southern gate of the fort. Gil winced as they started again with that stupid sausage song.

CHAPTER 7

F ive years of civilian life made him soft, and he hated it.

Rocks. Gravel. Scrub brush. That's all Gil saw for miles once Fort Ste. Terese disappeared behind the hills. The singing had long since stopped, replaced by the low-level grumbling of soldiers on the march. They reached the top of a low rise that felt mountainous. When the call for a five-minute break came, he could barely speak. His tongue felt two sizes too big for his mouth and dry as jerked beef.

Gil reached for his canteen, but Dupre's big hand stopped him. "Not yet."

"Come on, mate. I'm dry as a nun's—"

"When he drinks, you drink." They watched as Sergeant Martineau stood with hands on hips, eyes darting around, assessing the men. "He knows how far we're going and how to make it last. Not like them." Dupre nodded to the rear of the line. They saw several of the men gulping from their canteens. The paler they were, Prussians, Germans, Swedes, the redder their faces and the more they chugged the warm water until the precious fluid dripped down their chins.

"The two Prussians, or whatever they are, will be out of water before we reach the turnaround. You need to be smart, right?" Dupre reached down and picked up a small, round pebble. Taking it between two thick fingers, he rubbed some of the loose dirt on his johnet, then popped it in his mouth and moved it around with his tongue. He waved his hand under his chin. "Gets the spit going. See?"

With a mouth that felt lined with gauze, Gil obeyed. He placed the pebble into his mouth and swished it around with his tongue. His reward was a single drop of moisture that he greedily sucked down, coughing as the stone almost went down his throat with it.

The rocky ground reflected the sun's heat back up at them. Good boots made the marching manageable, but it was so very different from the hot but grassy expanses of the African Veldt. The tall Spaniard, Gomez, put his hands on his knees, panting. "I expected, I don't know. More sand?"

Dupre laughed and pointed south. "Keep walking about two days that way. You'll get all the sand you could ever want. Stretches for hundreds of miles in either direction. It goes up your nose, down your boots, up the crack of your arse. Marching in it is no damn fun. Tell you that."

Jean LaForce whined. "How far have we gone?"

"Ten miles or so, I imagine," Gomez.

Gil shielded his eyes and looked at the sun's position. Then he shook his head. "They said twenty miles, so we turn around at mile ten, and we're not there yet. We've been out about, what, two hours? I figure three, four miles an hour, right?" Dupre nodded, and Gomez groaned from the bottom of his soul. Proud of his calculations, he had to rub it in. "We've gone seven miles at best."

The perfectly pressed and infuriatingly fresh-looking sergeant shouted, "On your feet. We're getting to the hard part, so be ready."

Gil watched as Wilmer opened his canteen and looked inside, sloshing what little remained around. His eyes widened, and he put the lid back on. "Getting to *ze* hard part? What in Christ's name have we been doing?"

Dupre laughed. "Just getting started, you pretty little cornflower."

The sergeant spun the lid off his canteen and took one solid gulp, then replaced the cap. Gil and Dupre mimicked him. "I think he's half camel," Gil muttered.

Dupre stood straight and adjusted the pack on his shoulders. "The front half is a camel. The rest of him's a horse's arse. *Allons-nous.*"

With hands on his hips, the sergeant's lips curled into a fake smile. "We are a little behind, my brave ones, so now we march double-time. *Non?*" He turned and, without looking behind him, set off at a faster clip than before.

"*Oui*, Sergeant." The group let out a collective groan and followed, struggling to keep pace. A feeble attempt at "Le Boudin" led to a good-natured threat on the singer's life.

Gil closed his eyes and took three cleansing breaths. He allowed himself to think about nothing but the tromping of boots on gravel and keeping himself upright. In his mind, he counted the beats of leather on stone. His brain shut out everything but the blue jacket at the front of the line. The reverie distracted him from the heat and sweat and the flies it attracted.

HUP, hup, hup, hup, HUP, hup hup, hup.

He scarcely noticed the increase in grade as the path grew steeper. In his dreamlike state, his mind opened to a kaleidoscope of visions. The blue of the Indian Ocean at Capetown. The endless sea of green and brown that was Boer farmland until they'd reclaimed it for Her Majesty. He even allowed himself a rare thought of Colette.

It wasn't one of the lusty fever dreams she often inspired. The way he had been waking up the last few mornings, he would need to find privacy and do something about that soon. This vision was of the soft hazel of her eyes and the smooth touch on his forehead. He smiled at the memory and marched. *HUP, hup, hup, hup. HUP, hup, hup, hup.*

"Hey, watch where you're going."

He almost mowed Dupre down before realizing everyone had stopped. What he hoped and prayed was the halfway mark was a circle of stones at the top of a hill, allowing for a panoramic view of miles and miles of nothing. The center, tamped hard stone and dirt, was littered with packs and the bodies of panting, moaning soldiers.

Gil looked around and felt something wasn't right. Bad enough that nothing living could be seen besides the troop of weakened soldiers. With a soldier's trained eye, he spotted half a dozen places someone could set up to fire at them without being seen themselves. Without a conscious thought, he picked his pack off the ground and set it upright against a rock, his Lebel within arm's reach. He looked up to see an approving nod from the sergeant.

"Hungry, my brave ones? A lovely spot for a picnic, don't you think? Eat. Eat."

The men fell on their packs like locusts on a wheatfield. They pulled out the hard loaves of bread and dried dates. Only when they had taken huge bites of the crusty loaves did they realize the joke that had been played on them. It was impossible to choke down dry bread when the surrounding desert held more moisture than their mouths. The sounds of gagging and choking filled the air. Gil watched as the sergeant took small chunks of the bread and ate them with a pinch of date, then took a small sip from his canteen. He smiled and chewed, assessing the men in the circle.

The sun was just past its peak when the order to march rang out. Wilmer and an older Frenchman, Martin, stared at their already-empty canteens. Any hope in their eyes vanished. Gil watched as the kid, LaForce, took the lid off his canteen and gestured to Wilmer.

"Stop!" Their commander's voice echoed across the distant hills. "What do you think you're doing, sonny boy?"

LaForce was genuinely confused. "Giving a fellow soldier some water. Sir."

The sergeant marched over and grabbed Wilmer's canteen, opened it and held it upside down. One lone, sad drop fell to the ground. He threw the container at the blond soldier with a sneer, then turned on the youngster. "You're not giving one drop to this useless *Boche* bastard. He's been drinking like a sot in a saloon while the rest of us marched like soldiers. Let this teach him a lesson."

Then he waved a finger in LaForce's red, angry face. "Your mother did an excellent job with you. Caring for others is all well and good. You want to take care of your fellow soldiers. It's admirable, but this is not a schoolyard. A troop is only as strong as its weakest member. If he can't control himself, do you think he'd hesitate to drink your water when he needed it? No. He'd leave you shriveling like a raisin to save himself. Let the dog learn from this. Or die. His choice."

Gil felt for the kid, still green as when he first saw him in the recruiter's office. He worried for a moment when he saw Jean draw himself up to say something, but the younger man saw Dupre shake his head and swallowed his outrage before it could spill out. His eyes burned with a hatred that was impressive. It usually took years of experience to hate an officer that much. The sergeant glared back at him, daring the kid to open his mouth. Neither man spoke.

"LaForce, march with us." The words were out of Gil's mouth before he could stop them. Damn his eyes. He knew better than to get involved. Jean picked up his pack and tottered over to Gil and Dupre.

The giant slapped him on the back. "March with the adults for a while. Try to stay out of trouble." With a look back at Wilmer, red-faced and whimpering, Jean LaForce stood at attention and fell in with the others.

They were two or three miles from the fort when it happened. Gil was lost in a marching trance when he heard a body hit the ground at the rear. Someone yelled, "Man down!" Of course it was Wilmer.

His first instinct was to help. His second was to grab the baby-faced LaForce by the arm.

"Leave him."

Sergeant Martineau's eyes burned like a magnifying glass in the sun, and they settled on Jean LaForce. "Did I tell you to stop? I have dinner to get to and a woman in town waiting for me. If this useless *saloparde* wants to get home, he will. And next time he won't be such a pig with his water."

Wilmer squatted on the ground, weeping. "Come on, comrade. Just a drop." The men spared him one last look and set out again, leaving him where he sat. Gil waited a few minutes before daring a look back. The German soldier somehow staggered to his feet and hefted his pack. A couple of stuttering steps and he fell to a knee but rose once more.

"No one's going to wait for him?" LaForce asked.

Dupre shook his head. "Eyes front, boy. It's only a mile or two. He'll make it."

"But what if the Arabs get him?"

"Anyone within twenty miles of the base is on our side. Besides, take a look." He pointed to a nearby rock outcrop where a blue-coated legionnaire sat watching their approach. He waved to the soldier, who half-heartedly waved back.

Gil, Dupre and Jean looked back. There was no sign of Wilmer, but the tracks of twenty marching men were plain in the dusty soil, clear as road signs. Gil allowed himself the last of his water. "Between the sunstroke and the thirst, he's going to be bloody useless tomorrow."

Dupre grunted. "Not much use to us at the moment, is he?" LaForce looked like he wanted to say something, then clenched his jaw and nodded. In silence, they and the rest of the troop marched back to the fort.

Gil ignored the thirst and the burning on the back of his neck. First, he tried re-conjuring the vision of Colette, but she was gone. He settled into his rhythmic chant.

HUP, hup, hup, hup. HUP, hup, hup, hup.

Chapter 8

To a legionnaire, the bayonet is always named Rosalie. After taking his turn in line, Gil pulled his blade out of the straw-filled canvas dummy. He wondered idly who the first Rosalie was, and whether naming something so wicked after a woman was supposed to be a compliment. She couldn't have been like his Colette, sweet as sugarcane and nearly chaste. Too good for him indeed. Some women could be lethal. Not her.

"Next. Again." Sergeant Martineau yelled, and Gil stepped aside, making way for the next trainee to charge. He watched Wilmer lower his rifle and run at the bag. The blond kid's feet stuttered a bit, and the point of his personal Rosalie entered only a couple of inches into the target while his body slammed into the structure, almost knocking it over.

Wilmer rolled onto his back, spitting dirt from his mouth. Martineau grabbed the Lebel from the boy's hands, held it aloft and shouted to the crowd. "The bayonet has killed more Arabs than bullets ever will. The Lebel magazine holds eight shots, with one in the hold and one in the chamber. By the time you get a second shot off, the devils will be on you with their swords and knives.

"Sir, don't they have guns too?" Gomez asked.

Martineau nodded. "Yes. They steal a lot of weapons, but they have no ammo. They can't afford to waste it practicing, so they shoot like blind men. And they'd as soon gut you so they can see the look in your eye."

The sergeant used one hand on the blade to poke at the straw man. The tip barely penetrated the burlap cover. "And you can't poke it like fingering your girlfriend back home. You thrust like you're trying to see it come out the other end. And you don't stab at the heart… aim for the gut, where there are no bones."

He turned, took both hands and let out a shout that echoed around the training yard. Rosalie sank to the hilt in the dummy's midsection. The rest of the rifle hung there, vibrating. With a nod from the sergeant, Wilmer retrieved his rifle. He had to put a foot on the wooden stand for balance in order to pull it from the pretend Arab's belly.

As he trudged back to the line, Gil remembered his first time.. Her Majesty's Army had more faith in the bullet than did the Legion, so they spent less time in bayonet drill, but it was a tough lesson nonetheless. The human body was surprisingly hard to stop with a pointy object.

Running thumb over the blade, he realized he'd have to sharpen it tonight. He still hadn't gotten any demerits from bed check and had no intention of receiving any. It was inevitable, of course. The non-coms would make sure not to play favorites, and they would want to see how he'd react. For now, he was a model soldier. His chest puffed a bit. As he did nearly every day, he reminded himself that Gil Vincente was in the right place. The Lion was dead and gone.

He returned to the end of the line where the others waited for their turn. Dupre was wildly gesticulating at Jean LaForce. The kid finally found someone he could follow around like a puppy. Dupre loved the attention. He was such a mediocre soldier that the big galoot took delight in being a role model. LaForce hung on every word like a sermon from Christ Himself. Good. Gil had himself to look after.

At last, it was the kid's turn. Dupre slapped him on the back and said something. Jean's face turned into a mask of rage, and he charged the dummy with a scream. The shout was full of rage and venom, and Gil's eyes widened. The slim soldier buried Rosalie muzzle-deep into the midsection, then screamed, his eyes as wide as his mouth.

Martineau grunted in appreciation. "*Bien*. We may make a soldier of you yet." LaForce yanked his bayonet free and trotted back to Dupre and Gil, sticking his tongue out with an enigmatic grin on his face.

"Good Christ, what did you tell him?" Gil asked out of the side of his mouth.

"I told him it was his chance to kill the person he hated most."

"I'd hate to be that poor bastard, whoever he was."

"The little pansy has more in him than we thought. Tell you that. Good job, kid." Dupre patted the grinning soldier on his slim shoulder.

LaForce smiled and turned to Gil. "How did you do on your first drill?"

Gil smiled. "Terrible, but then I never hated anyone that much. Who were you thinking of?"

He was sure a cloud passed over Jean LaForce's eyes. The kid turned away without answering and took his place in line, eager to kill whoever it was all over again.

"Gus, did he ever tell you why he enlisted?"

Dupre shrugged, put a finger to his nose and blew a sand-filled snot ball to the ground. "Never asked. I know better. But sure as sunrise in the East, it had something to do with whoever he just stabbed."

Gil said, "I don't think anyone's hated me that much. Even the Boers." A vision of young, bloodshot eyes staring at him through barbed wire flashed in his head, then disappeared. Maybe he was wrong. None of them had the chance to act on their rage.

"You've only been in the Legion a week. Give it time."

The sun was low when the grumbling soldiers could finally lower their weapons and trudge back to the fort for dinner. Gil and Gomez were at the end of the line when a sentry on the parapet waved his arms and let out a shout. "Party incoming. Send help!"

Sergeant Martineau pointed at the two stragglers. "You two, come with me."

Gil's stomach protested, but he kept a stoic face and turned on his heel. Gomez groaned. "We'll be late for supper."

"It's not like that slop's going to get cold—it's never hot anyway. And you don't look like you eat much of anything."

Gomez said something in Spanish that was likely foul. They marched to the Sergeant and saluted.

"Go give whoever it is a hand."

"*Oui, Sergeant,*" they replied in unison.

Gomez and Gil walked quickly to the rear gate. The wood creaked as the last of the men passed through and closed behind them.

They raised hands to their eyes, scanning the stony bleakness. Far down the boot-tamped gravel road were two figures headed their way.

Gil squinted as the blurry shapes came into focus. He'd been wrong. There were three figures. In the lead was a legionnaire, an officer judging by the braid on his filthy white kepi. He led an ugly gray mule by the reins. The third blob was the limp body hanging over its saddle.

Gomez crossed himself and sprinted towards the incoming party, Gil on his heels. A canteen bounced on his hip as he ran and he hoped there was enough water that he could offer some to the stranger. Or strangers. There was no way to know if the figure on the mule was alive or dead.

The Capitain, Gil could make out the rank now, took his hat off and rubbed a sleeve over a stubbly, bald head. He nodded to the two soldiers. They snapped to attention and saluted. He responded with a vague wave of his hand across his forehead.

"*Capitaine* Pavel Orel," he said.

Gil's eyes went to the body over the mule's back but responded, "Privates Gomez and Vincente, Captain." He fumbled for his canteen and offered it to the officer, who accepted it as his due and took a long, warm swig from it.

He nodded gratefully. "*Merci*, private."

Meanwhile, Gomez approached the skittish mule. It took two steps away and brayed. Then it snapped huge square teeth at his outstretched hand. The Spaniard pulled his hands to his chest. "What was that for, *pendejo*? I wasn't going to hurt you."

Orel turned to the mule, raised a calming hand and went, "Shush. It's okay, Anya." The mule shook its head but allowed the tall soldier to reach out to the soldier across its back.

"He's alive," Gomez said and reached for his own canteen, opened it, and poured a few drops across the figure's blistered, dried lips.

Orel gave the slightest grin. "Huh. I thought I'd lost him an hour ago."

"Who is he?" Gil asked before adding, "Sir."

Orel handed the reins to Gil. "A deserter. *Sale et sans valeur.* DuPage, from the Fourteenth. Took me three days to find him." He spoke French with a thick Slavic accent. Russian? Hungarian? Gil couldn't place where it was from, and it took a second to translate into his English mind.

He looked at the reins in his hand and gave a slight tug. The ugly beast refused to move. Without looking, the Captain whistled through his teeth and the ugly beast meekly followed. This was the first mule Gil had ever encountered and was so far unimpressed.

As they neared the fort, Gil couldn't help looking over his shoulder as the limp form of the deserter bounced, dead weight on the mule's back. Gomez asked, "What did he do?"

Without looking back, Orel marched towards the opening wooden gates. "This piece of crap snuck out at Constantine. If he'd run off during a battle, I could have just shot him where I found him. But no. Instead, I have to bring him back here to face court martial."

"Why did he run?" Gil knew the question was impertinent, but the captain didn't seem to mind.

"Why do any of them run? He's a coward, and an idiot, and a traitor to his comrades. There's nothing lower than a deserter. Or dumber. That's why they're so easy to catch."

Gil didn't disagree with the sentiment. Nor could he match the passion in the man's voice. He'd never given deserters a single thought. Pavel Orel, on the other hand, clearly hated nothing in this world like someone who'd run out on his duty.

Switching the subject, Orel asked, "Am I too late for supper?"

"They were just serving it when the guard spotted you, sir."

"Ah good. We'll drop off this worthless cargo, and you can join me. You're better company than... that." He gestured with his thumb over his shoulder. "First, help me put Anya to bed."

The mule honked at the mention of her name.

CHAPTER 9

Two orderlies helped Gomez remove DuPage's body, put it on a litter and haul it to the infirmary, the dutiful Spaniard following. As soon as they were done, Orel spat on the ground, looked at Gil and motioned with his head for him to follow. He obeyed, holding Anya's leather reins as the mule tossed its head and locked its legs. Gil nearly tripped when the animal stopped so suddenly.

Captain Orel walked ahead a few paces, then turned with a grin. "Anya, don't be a bitch." The creature relaxed its locked knees, lowered its head and followed. The officer whistled between his teeth as they walked around the back of the fort.

Before they'd even rounded the turn into the stables, Orel shouted, "Thibault, get off your arse. We're home."

Gil heard a rustling and a grunt from the tack room. Out hobbled a short, wiry corporal with a limp that made him rock side to side as he hustled out. In a high yet raspy voice, the stable master, and Gil could only assume he was Thibault, waved to them and greeted the officer with a most casual and inappropriate grin. "Did you get him?" No salute or sir. The captain didn't seem to mind.

"Bah. Is take a day more than should have." Orel's accent was more Russian than French, but Thibault didn't seem to struggle with it like Gil did. They clearly had a history with each other. "He dug in like badger, and I had to wait him out."

Gil's jaw tightened. The bald officer was casually talking about hunting down soldiers—his own soldiers, no less. What kind of man did that? He hoped no one noticed his discomfort.

Old Thibault took the reins from Gil, and the mule meekly followed. He waved Gil over. "Help me cool her down and we can all get dinner." Gil tried not to show his distaste and obeyed.

As they removed the saddle and gear from Anya's narrow back, the wizened man and the captain chatted like old friends.

"Why'd this one do it?" Thibault asked as he unbuckled the breast collar.

Orel lit up a factory-rolled cigarette. Officers made more money than the infantry and didn't care who knew it. "Same as most. *La cafard*."

Gil wrinkled his brow as he tried to follow the conversation. Even though he'd mostly spoken French for the past four years, between the unfamiliar word and Orel's accent, he must have misunderstood. "I'm sorry, corporal, did he say the cockroach?"

Orel tried to explain, miming something with a lot of legs. "*La cafard*. It digs into the brain. It's... it makes men... agggh, you tell it."

Thibault had been standing with the heavy saddle in his hands as though it was nothing. He finally threw it over a wooden sawhorse, landing with a heavy *whoomph*. "You're right, it means cockroach, but it's also the word for a sickness of the mind. Like the bug has dug in there and made you crazy. A terrible sadness. You *Anglais* call it the Black Dog."

The scars on his wrists suddenly itched. Yes, he was familiar with the Black Dog. It had a lot of names: depression, melancholy. Lack of pluck, to hear his father tell it. "What, he was sad, so he just walked away?"

Thibault threw a towel to Gil. "Dry her off and I'll comb her." Anya looked at him suspiciously as he wiped the sweat from her coat. Thibault prattled on, "The desert makes people crazy. You'll see. You spend too long with the sand in your asscrack. There are no women but whores- and there aren't enough of those. Everyone not in a uniform wants you dead. A few can't take it and snap.

Some plan their escape. Some just walk out and keep walking til the Arabs get them. Or the scorpions."

"Or I do." Orel added.

"*Oui*. Or you do. The fearsome Capitaine Eagle." Thibault snapped to attention and offered an exaggerated salute. Orel chuckled and returned the salute with two fingers as the old man curried the mule's rear legs. "His *anonymat*. It's Russian for Eagle. Can see for miles and is a superb hunter." Then he lowered his voice, "and a little snooty. Heh."

The officer shrugged. Gil was doing more listening than currying now, as Thibault continued his nonstop narration. It wasn't unusual for men who spent their time with animals to talk way too much when they had a human audience. "Heh, heh. Remember that poor idiot from Oued? Just stripped off his clothes and walked into the desert."

Orel sucked at his bottom lip. "That one I didn't get in time."

Gil couldn't help himself. "What happened to him?"

Thibault's mood darkened just a little. He looked at the officer, then back at Gil. "You ever see what happens when the Arabs catch a legionnaire alone? They hand him over to their women. Hoo boy."

Gil grinned. "That doesn't sound so awful."

Thibault wasn't smiling. "First, they cut his balls and cock off. Then they really hurt him."

Gil's guts churned, and he shivered. He would expect that kind of thing from the Zulus, savages that they were, although he saw nothing like that himself. He'd always assumed the Arabs were more civilized than other Africans. Children of the book and all that.

Orel crushed his cigarette butt out on the stable floor. "By the time I found him, they'd flayed him like a side of beef. Only knew it was him because he had a beard and a tattoo. Just buried what was left and hotfooted it home before they got me, too."

Thibault led Anya to a stall and bowed low, waving her in. The mule high-stepped in like a princess. Gil could swear she nodded her head at the groom.

"Hey, it's none of my business, but... the *captain,* he's an officer. Why doesn't he get a horse?"

The corporal followed the dappled mule into the stall and gently lifted her front leg to inspect the hoof. "Doesn't want one. You know mules?" Gil shook his head. "You will. They're good desert animals. Can carry twice what a horse can on half the water. Smarter than a camel and most legionnaires."

Gil hung up the bridle and other leather tack as they spoke. "I've always worked with horses. Like them better than people, mostly. Don't know a damn thing about mules, other than they're half donkey and half horse."

Thibault lowered the hoof and lifted the left leg, checking it over. "Heh, heh. You'll see. They are better than both."

Gil sniffed. "If you say so. You don't shoe them?"

"If they're going to stay in town, or on paved roads, we do. Don't bother if they're going to be in the desert. What would you do if they threw a shoe in the middle of nowhere? No farriers around. Plus, mules like to feel the ground under their feet. Makes them better than horses in the mountains and rugged ground."

Gil thought about the cavalry mounts he looked after in the veldt. Broken legs from rocks and holes were far too common. The notion of beautiful animals put down because of poor riders or stupidity on uneven terrain turned his stomach. Maybe these ugly critters were more suited for the desert. And who'd miss them if something happened? And the Russian seemed particularly attached to Anya. God only knew why.

One of Anya's back hooves had a stone in it, and the stable master used a hooked knife to dislodge it. "Poor baby. That'll feel better." He gently lowered her leg and patted her skinny behind.

"Is this his personal animal?" Gil asked.

"May as well be. I make sure nobody else rides her, and she's always ready if he has to head out on one of his manhunts. Those two are like an old married couple. I think she understands Russian. Better than I do, for sure."

"How often does he need to, uh, hunt deserters?"

"More than you'd think. If someone deserts in wartime or in battle, it's the firing squad. Assuming they make it back, which, heh heh, most of them don't. Otherwise, he brings them back for prison duty. They get sent to the Zephyrs. Then they wish he'd shot them."

Orel cleared his throat impatiently. "Don't you ever stop talking, Thibault? I'm starving." The two enlisted men locked the stall behind them.

"Sir? I think they've already served the soup." Gil's stomach wasn't happy about it, either.

Orel laughed. "Oh, I think they'll make an exception. You're with me. Come on."

The three men turned to leave the barn. Anya let out a bellowing honk. A child-like grin crossed the rugged officer's face. Without turning around, he waved and shouted, "Good night, *moya kokhana*."

Gil didn't speak Russian, but he couldn't remember the last time anyone had spoken to him with that much affection. Not even Colette.

The men entered the empty mess hall. The cooks were nearly done with their cleanup, but a word from Thibault and a withering glare from Orel had them rustling up some sausages, bread and hard cheese. When the kitchen help wasn't looking, Thibault pulled out a flask and poured brandy into his tin cup, then the captain's. He held it up for Gil.

Figuring what the hell, he looked at the officer, then shrugged. The old soldier poured a healthy shot. The men toasted each other and took a sip. It was surprisingly good, and the first booze he'd tasted since leaving Marseille.

Orel's voice intruded on his thoughts. "So, private. Why are you here? You're old for a recruit. What are you, thirty?"

"Thereabouts. Sir." Gil scrambled for a reason that would make sense without revealing more than necessary. "I was in South Africa and thought I was done with the military. Spent some time kicking around France, and decided I was, um, better off here."

Orel was already on his second brandy, to Thibault's unspoken distress. He wiped a hand across his stubbly head. "Being a soldier, it's a good thing. Noble."

Gil wasn't so sure about that and looked at Thibault. The old man sucked his lip. He looked from the officer back to Gil. The smirk on his grizzled face seemed to say, "Here we go."

Orel noticed none of this, just continued speaking. "My people. Cossacks. Go back a thousand years as soldiers. A real man's life."

Those raptor eyes focused on something over Gil's shoulder as he continued, "Soon as I could, I joined the Tsar's army. We were great then. Before. Well, before."

"Vladivostok," Thibault explained, filling in the gaps. Clearly not the first time he'd heard this tale.

Another shot from Thibault's flask splashed into the officer's cup. "Da, Vladivostok. Nineteen and four. Five? Anyway, we were fighting those little yellow monkeys. Tough little bastards, you'd never know it to look at them."

Gil knew little about the Russian-Japanese war except that it was particularly bloody and took international intervention to stop the killing. It had been a massive embarrassment to Russia. He set down his cup to listen.

Orel droned on, only partly addressing Gil. "The Russian army should have mowed them down, but then the desertions began. First one soldier, then a couple more. Soon even the officers began retreating-with or without permission-leaving us there. Cowards. I was captured. When peace came, they let me go."

Finding himself more interested than he would have expected, Gil asked, "Why the Legion? What about being Russian? Weren't you fighting for the Tsar?"

Orel's speech became thicker, slower. His French grew worse, making him harder to understand, but the anger on his face spoke clearly. "Tsars. Kaisers. Kings. Your Queen Victoria. It's all bullshit. We fight for our families. Our land. Our comrades." He gestured to the two legionnaires. "This is why we fight. For each other. To fail... to fail your fellows is to not be a real man."

Gil watched as Thibault picked up his flask and surreptitiously sneaked it off the table to save the officer from more temptation.

"Countries don't matter anymore. Only armies. The Army of Russia is a joke. The British are losing their colonies. La Legion... this is the last bastion of real men." Gil wasn't sure he deserved to be included, but couldn't help feel a touch of pride swell in his chest.

At last, the captain had vented his anger on deserters, treacherous officers and useless bureaucrats. He stood unsteadily, nodded and wished the men good night.

Gil returned to his bunk, warm with drink, and dreamt of mules and dead cowards. He woke up only once, when one of the dead wore his face.

CHAPTER 10

Wilmer couldn't march worth a damn and was crap with a bayonet. But Gil had to admit the Prussian son of a bitch could shoot. Prone, kneeling, or standing, he could empty a ten-round magazine dead center in any target from almost any distance.

"Maybe he's not completely useless after all," Dupre muttered out the side of his mouth. Gil shrugged. He'd always considered himself a decent shot, and a good man when a square was called for, and it bothered the hell out of him that this otherwise useless, much younger boy was outdoing all of them. Wilmer looked arrogant, like all Prussians, as he accepted everyone's congratulations as his due. It was uncharitable of Gil to think that, after screwing up so badly all week, a little humility might be called for. But again, Prussians.

As for his own marksmanship, Gil was still getting used to the Lebel after using a Lee-Enfield all those years. The French weapon could hold up to ten cartridges, as opposed to five, and the bolt action was slicker and didn't interfere with the sight as much. Grudgingly, he gave that round to the French. He stood with everyone else as Wilmer finished up his last targets.

Cleanup went faster than usual, and the men scrambled to pick up shell casings and check for trash. Tonight was the first night of liberty they'd been granted since arriving in Sidi Bel Abbès. Dupre, as the only person in the class who'd been there before, promised to show off all the sights worth seeing. They teased each other about who was going to drink the most, lose the most money, or teach the Algerian whores what a real Frenchman (or German, or Pole) could do. Gil picked up his brass and played along.

He looked forward to discovering a new town. It was unlikely that either the best or worst places would match Gil's experience of Marseille. Drinking bad wine and flirting with whores one couldn't afford weren't novelties. No, what he really wanted to experience was something new. Exotic. The famed temptations of the Arab quarter called to him, although wandering in alone and ignorant wouldn't be the smartest thing for a legionnaire to do. Maybe in time.

It was like the last time he was in South Africa. His fellow soldiers were tolerable company, but he hadn't traveled halfway around the world just to play Crown and Anchor, drinking warm beer. The Boers offered little in the way of entertainment. Dutchmen, particularly of the religious variety, seldom provided much of interest, and certainly not fun.

That's why when the others were occupied, he'd sneak off to see the real Africa. The Zulu and Bantu porters had their own quarters, and at night their campfires rocked with the beat of drums, the ululations of voices, male and female, and the casual sexuality of the women. Not that he'd brought himself to sink so low as to be with a local girl. No, he was too much the Englishman for that, but he was intrigued and stood off to the side. He stood rapt, watching, learning, occasionally coming so close to surrendering to temptation that his skin itched and burned, but always pulling back at the last moment. He relived the sights and sounds and smells when he was alone, and no one could see his shame.

Best to take things slowly, he supposed, and stay with his mates. Besides the big oaf Dupre, he hadn't yet made real friends. Other than Vincente or Colette, he could count on one hand the number of proper companions he had. What was the point? People disappointed. They disappeared or got killed, which amounted to the same thing. Sure, LaForce was always hanging around like an annoying little brother eager to play the big boy's games. Harmless but irritating. There certainly wasn't much to recommend Wilmer and the other German, Hans Richter, who turned out to be Bavarian, not that there was a pinch of snuff's difference between the two. Gomez, with his talk of a sweetheart back in Valencia, was just dull but took all the jokes about his height with good humor.

The men hustled to stow their gear, and gather and get ready. Kepis slapped against knees to get rid of most of the grime. Boots were spat on and rubbed more-or-less clean. Gil focused on sharpening his bayonet before leaving. He'd been unhappy with his last round of practice and taken a fair amount of abuse from Sergeant Martineau over it. He was determined to continue his unbroken inspection streak.

At last he was satisfied that Rosalie's knife edge was honed to perfection. He stood and buttoned his capote. Not bad if he said so himself. As a last touch, he did what he'd done since the day he left South Africa. He slipped the bone-handled razor into his boot.

The air thrummed with anticipation, like the last minutes before the school bell. Twenty or so men champed at the bit to taste a night of freedom. Dupre was already in the doorway, waving him on. "Quit stalling. You'll never be as pretty as me, and the women will all find officers if we don't hurry."

Gil snapped to attention and stomped a boot on the ground. "Sir. Yes, sir," he barked, while offering the most exaggerated salute possible.

A harsh voice yelled from behind him. "Vincente, what the hell is this mess?"

It was Becker. Until now, Gil had avoided running afoul of the Austrian. This time the barrel-shaped, moss-bearded sergeant stopped pulling the wings off flies and frying scorpions with a magnifying glass long enough to do bunk inspection. Gil forced a neutral look onto his face and spun on his heel.

"Sergeant?"

The hulking figure glared at him, pointing to Gil's bunk. At the foot of the cot, one corner was hanging loose and sloppy. Clearly, someone had simply pulled the perfect corner loose. "You call this bed properly made?"

Gil strangled the response before it rose in his throat. He knew he'd made his usual precise corners. The sheet had been tight as a drumhead. Heat rushed from his chest to his cheeks, and he hoped it wasn't visible. This was not personal, he reminded himself. It was just his turn. As calmly as he could, he responded, "No, sergeant."

Richter shouted from the doorway. "What? Private Perfect screwed up? Even Wilmer can make a bed." Wilmer slapped his friend on the back of the head a little harder than necessary. Gil stood silent, ignoring the red-faced idiot. Richter was on a roll, though, and considered himself quite the comedian. "What happened? Forgot to make your bed? Naughty, naughty."

Gil had plenty of practice remaining calm in the face of a blustering, bullying superior. It was part of the game. Taking crap from someone like Richter was a different sport entirely. Without looking away from Becker, he said, "Didn't have time to make my bed. I couldn't get your fat mother to leave."

That's all it took. A week of close quarters and jangly nerves, smart-ass barbs and minor grievances burst like a blister. Until now, it was dampened by the prospect of a night out. Now it gave way to a small but bloody donnybrook. Richter rushed Gil, only to be met by Dupre's hairy forearm, clothes-lining him, knocking him to the bunkhouse floor. Wilmer felt obliged to defend Teutonic honor and Gomez, of all people, clocked him with an uppercut. Soon everyone was shouting, swearing, or punching. Those who hadn't picked a side grabbed and held on to somebody else, so they appeared to be doing their part without choosing sides.

Gil bit the inside of his cheek and maintained his position, eyes locked on Sergeant Becker. The Austrian waited just long enough to notice who could fight, who pretended, and who got their asses kicked before blowing an old, tin whistle.

"*Arretez*, you animals. Arab girls fight harder than you lot. I should cancel your liberty and assign you to barracks."

A wave of tortured groans met this statement. Gil remained at attention as Becker sniffed and rocked on his heels. He pointed at Gil, then at the bed. "Fix this poor excuse for a rack."

"Oui, sergeant." Gil immediately obeyed, making sure the creases were exact, and looked up to see Becker give a curt nod, as if the whole unnecessary charade hadn't happened. It had been a test, and he passed.

Becker sneered at the men. "As for the rest of you, if we didn't need a break from your whining and bullshit. I'd keep you here, but we need a rest worse than you do. Try not to get arrested or killed. Dismissed." He allowed himself a quick grin as the men scrambled for freedom.

Dupre grabbed Gil's arm, and LaForce took hold of the big man's capote, tugging like a dog on a sock. "Come on, before he changes his mind."

CHAPTER 11

The headquarters of *Le Legion Etrangere* in Sidi Bel Abbès opened up onto the west end of the Rue Tlemcen. It was named for the quiet street in the Twentieth Arrondissement of Paris, where the bureaucracy that ran the Republic insisted on replicating itself in the colonies. It was a broad avenue, lined with the finest homes and most modern businesses and architecture. The façade of a miniature Paris became less convincing with each street and alley leading east until the neighborhoods in the northeast and southeast became a warren of dark dead-ends that maintained only the slimmest veneer of civilization. Of course, that's where they headed.

Barely inside the Port de Mascara, the easternmost gate leading out to the real Algeria, was a cluster of dark, smoky cafes offering cheap wine and only slightly more expensive companionship. It was far enough out to discourage officers and the high prices their salaries and positions commanded, while being a straight, easy stagger home even in the darkest hours of the night.

Gil slightly regretted giving Vincente all his money as he stared at the small glass of red wine on the rickety table in front of him. On an eight centimes a day salary, and three centimes a glass, he would be broke before he was too drunk to care. Of course, it was his first night out in a new town. Best to keep his wits about him.

His foot pressed against the table leg and felt the comforting press of the razor in his boot. A tinny piano fought with the roars of laughter, boasting and threats coming from ten tables of soldiers in varying stages of drunkenness.

The men had entered together and sat as a group, laughing about the dustup back at the barracks and either blaming or congratulating Richter for starting the trouble. Eventually, conversations with nearby clumps of men revealed someone came from someone else's village, or offered conversation in their own language instead of stilted French that got worse as liquor thickened tongues. Germans, Prussians and Austrians formed white-haired groups at one end of the long smoky room. Poles, Russians and Hungarians gathered closest to the bar. The true French, with the occasional Italian and Spaniard thrown in, took their rightful spot at five tables in the dead center.

Gil sat on the fringe of the French cluster, idly wondering why so few Englishmen joined the Legion. Maybe it was the national aversion to the French. Most likely, it was because if you wanted to see the world and kill people, only Her Majesty's government offered more opportunities.

Leaning back in his chair, he joined in a toast to all the lonely women in France, weeping inconsolably now that all the good men were in Africa. Needing to conserve his wine, Gil pretended to sip and slapped his palm on the table along with all the rest. Gomez, already deep in his cups, was passing around pictures of his beloved Isobel and tearfully extolling her virtues. Jean LaForce, bless him, politely praised her beauty and wished him the best. The kid never thought to ask why someone would sign up for five years away from such a paragon, unless she had already tossed him aside. Twenty francs said the dark-eyed tart in the sepia photo was already married and popping out someone else's babies, despite the Spaniard's whining protests to the contrary.

His eyes fell on a dark corner of the room where an officer sat by himself with his chair leaning back against a smoke-stained wall. The red and blue cap and dark blue capote stood out in the hazy air, as did the bottle of cognac in front of him. The man removed his kepi to wipe a sweaty brow, and Gil recognized the clean-shaven head. It was Captain Orel.

The captain's head jerked up, as if sensing Gil's eyes on him. His head tilted to the right, and those dark raptor eyes locked on the Englishman's gaze. He lifted his cognac glass in a silent toast, surprising Gil, who had never had an officer acknowledge his presence without a damned good reason.

He fleetingly wondered why the infamous tracker would choose to sit in the lowest-caste place in town rather than with his fellows, but didn't dwell on it. Gil's desire for novelty and the exotic made anyone not in uniform far more fascinating. Like a naturalist, he studied the fauna of his new surroundings.

The piano player was the first truly dark-skinned African he'd seen since arriving on the continent. The man wore a red fez and a white dinner jacket, and his long fingers hammered hard on the keys, usually the correct ones. Gil winced at the clinkers.

The barmaid had to be the owner's wife. No self-respecting saloon keeper would hire such an old, toothless biddy when the goal was to attract male trade. Her Gypsy-brown cleavage dipped almost to her waist, long saggy breasts contained by a tight cotton vest. The wear and tear did little to discourage the ass pinches and vulgar offers offered by the customers. She took no offense. Her tongue was as sharp as Gi's razor, much to the hilarity of everyone not on the receiving end.

Arab pimps and hustlers ducked between tables. They were small, thin bees, buzzing from group to group, offering everything from opium to dead soldiers' equipment and uniforms. Losing equipment and replacing worn uniforms was expensive, and there was a thriving trade in replacement gear, as long as one didn't inquire into the source. Not surprisingly, every single entrepreneur had a sister or cousin who would just love to meet a big, brave legionnaire.

After brushing aside the third or fourth such offer, Gil felt the call of nature. With a nod to his companions, he hustled through the crowded bar and out the back door. The rank odor of stale liquor and urine filled his nose as he stepped to the curb and unbuttoned his pants. He threw his head back in relief as the stream splashed into the deep gutter, running along the plank sidewalk.

The trouble began as a low thunder-like rumble from inside the Café le Chat Noir and grew louder until the chaos spilled out into the alley. The rolling body of an old bearded legionnaire nearly took Gil behind the knees, staggering him, almost sending him toppling into the gutter.

"Oi, watch it," he yelled in English before correcting himself and shouting it again in French. Before he could get off the ground, another soldier stepped on the old man, then a third. A quick look told him to leap over the gutter to the other side, creating a barrier between himself and the madness.

Shouted voices and a moment alone to observe the action identified the source of the problem. Some of the older men decided to take the piss out of the fresh meat. Once he knew what the fight was about, he was happy to do his part. Just like old times.

One of the first soldiers he hit was a wiry old codger with the thickest whiskers Gil had ever seen. The man jumped like a monkey onto Dupre's back and was cuffing his ears. Roaring like a bull, the big man tried to rub him off against the wall. The bearded soldier was like a burr on a sock, not painful but annoying and unshakeable. Gil grabbed the man's capote with his left hand and yanked him off his friend and flung him to the ground. Gil knelt low over him and threw a single punch. That was all it took to put the old drunk out of the game.

Dupre grinned and gave a thumbs up. He yelled, "Thank you. But there's more of the bastards," then turned to swing at any soldier who wasn't a bunkmate. Gil stood back-to-back with him, looking for the next target.

A warm rush of adrenaline ran through Gil's body. He realized he was grinning as he blocked a wide haymaker from a corporal. Hitting someone one grade up wasn't a punishable offense like clocking an officer, so he let his fist fly, reveling in the familiar ache of bone on flesh and the buzz of sensation up his arm. He shook his hand and chuckled. God help him, he'd missed this.

From the corner of his eye, he saw something was wrong. A middle-aged legionnaire had Richter up against the wall with an elbow across his chest. That wasn't the problem. In his other hand, metal glinted in the gaslight. Gil felt himself growl deep in his throat. The rules of bar fights were clear in every army on the planet. There was nothing wrong with a good donnybrook. Fists and chairs were within the rules, but knives were an escalation and forbidden.

Much as he hated Richter, this couldn't stand. Before he knew it, his razor was in his fist. Leading with his left elbow, he knocked the stranger off Richter and against the wall. In less than a second they were nose-to-nose, the bone handle in his hand, the finely honed blade pressed to the older man's throat.

"You pull a knife on my friend, you *salopard?* Maybe I'll shave that beard off for you." The other man's eyes widened. Heat ran through Gil's body. It was that old feeling. He knew exactly what his opponent saw. His eyes bulged, the madness behind them unmistakable. The stranger let out a whimper and opened his hand, the knife clattering to the ground.

"Vincente, don't." Richter's voice filled his ears.

Gil stepped back and snapped his razor shut with a single well-practiced motion. He snarled at the other soldier and nodded his head. The man took off while Gil stood, panting and sweating.

"*Danke,*" Richter said.

Gil's head cleared. He looked around and realized the fight was all but over. Men on both sides of the fracas watched open-mouthed. The moment blades were drawn, the fun was sucked out of the air and everyone sobered up.

Gil spat, then wiped his mouth. "Doesn't mean we're friends. I still think you're an arsehole. But you're my arsehole. Understand?"

Putting his hands on his knees, Gil breathed deeply and allowed the fury coursing through him to abate. Dupre slapped him on the back. He leaned low and whispered in Gil's ear, "What the hell was that?"

Gil ignored the question and walked in small circles, sucking in air, attempting to calm down. When he was back to himself, he looked at the back door of the bar. Captain Oral stood stone-faced, looking right at him.

With a single nod, the officer disappeared back inside.

"What the hell was that?" Gil wondered.

With the air out of the balloon, the men decided it was time to go back to barracks. They trudged or staggered, depending on their level of inebriation or their wounds, up the long Rue de Mascara, past the Place Carnot to the Rue de Tlemcen. They were met at the gate by sentries who bluffed anger at their condition, then burst into laughter and slapped them on the back as they shuffled off to bed.

In the bunkroom, Gil had enough sense to carefully store his uniform, strip and slide into his rack. The blanket was perfectly taut in the corners, and he slipped inside as if it was a cocoon, careful not to disturb the creases. He let out an audible sigh as the material wrapped around him tightly. Screw Becker. His bed was made correctly. Gil lay on his back, swaddled in cloth, and took several long, slow breaths. Immediately, he fell into a deep sleep.

Chapter 12

I t was the second afternoon of a four-day march, and Gil was too tired and focused on marching to notice the tiny speck on the horizon. LaForce was the first to acknowledge it.

"Sergeant," he shouted. "Someone's hailing us."

Everyone snapped to. The notion of another living creature was noteworthy. Since leaving the base, they'd seen four fennec foxes, eight snakes and a herd of antelope too scrawny to bother shooting. Wild dogs and the insects that serenaded them between attempts at eating the men alive.

Sergeant Becker gave the order to halt. He removed his cap, wiped his forehead and squinted toward the figure staggering their way. The sun was directly behind the man, so he was an indistinct blur until he drew nearer, but it was clear he was a legionnaire, and in trouble.

"Wilmer, Richter. Get on that high ground and keep a sharp eye out." The two sharpshooters dropped their packs and picked up their rifles, ammo bags and canteens and hustled to a boulder rising a few feet above the stony desert floor.

Gil briefly wondered if this was a setup, or some kind of drill, but a close look at the stumbling, panicky scarecrow staggering their way set him right.

It was a lieutenant, judging by what remained of the cord on his kepi. He was still yards away when he began shouting, "Bandits! "

Sergeant Becker was all business. He cupped his hands to his mouth and yelled, "When? Who was it?"

The man could not answer until he'd taken two huge gulps of water and fell to his knees. "Yesterday. The payroll for the men at Flatters. We lost five men."

"Any taken alive?" Becker asked. Gil held his breath. Thibault's tale of what happened to captured soldiers still haunted him.

The lieutenant, Gaspard, shook his head. "I had stepped off to shoot a gazelle for meat and…" His voice quavered and cracked. His body shook as he told the tale. "I heard the shots. And the screams. By the time I returned…" This time, his whole body convulsed with dry sobs.

The sergeant was having none of that. He grabbed the lieutenant's collar. "How many? Where did they come from?" The young officer sputtered, trying to spit out the desired answers.

Gil had enough experience to know that the line of questioning wasn't cruelty but necessity. Cutthroats willing to attack one armed platoon wouldn't hesitate to take a second bite of that apple. And they needed to know how many and where they might be if the Legion was to get its pound of flesh.

The lieutenant sobbed uncontrollably, ignoring the sergeant's questions. At the end of his rope, Becker pulled the man to his feet. He put his bulbous nose an inch from the officer's face and barked, "Enough! Was it al-Bereb's men?"

The shock of a noncom yelling at him snapped Gaspard back to his senses. He gave a loud, wet sniff. "No. They weren't from the village. They were brigands, maybe six or eight of them. Nobody knew them. On camels."

"How far out?"

The lieutenant looked up at the sun. "Three, maybe four hours?"

A whispering wave passed through the men. Most of them had never seen a camel before, and it gave the thieves an aura of mystery, as if they might go up against magical genies and flying carpet riders rather than mere marauders.

Becker turned and shouted to the sentries up on the rock. "Anything?"

Richter answered, "*Rien.* Nothing."

The sergeant looked at the men. His lips moved silently, counting the number of soldiers at his command. There were twenty raw recruits already halfway through a four-day march, with limited water, food, ammunition and training.

No one doubted how the arithmetic worked. Most of the men were already picking up their packs and checking ammo bags when the sergeant drew himself up and called, "Attention!"

The men, weary and shabby as they were, clenched their jaws and felt their blood warm. They were soldiers, and this is what they were here for. Weeks of training had prepared them for this moment. The few with no prior military experience, and Gil couldn't help but notice this included LaForce, nervously checked with each other. The youngsters stood taller and straighter than the rest, hoping they looked brave, eager, and that no one saw their eyes bulging out of their heads.

The large sergeant buttoned his capote despite the late afternoon heat and stood tall. He addressed the men at full volume. "Listen up. You finally have the chance to make yourselves useful. These bandits think they can attack the Legion without consequences. We're going to prove them wrong, *non*?

"*Oui*, Sergeant." Twenty voices, including his own, shouted back. Gil felt his blood rush through his body. Well-made beds and regular meals were fine, but this is what he'd enlisted for. Soldiers fought. A long-forgotten tingle ran up his spine. His mouth pulled into a tight smile.

He wasn't alone. Dupre's jaw tightened, making him look more frightening than oafish. Others bit their lips and steeled themselves. The men with military experience allowed muscle memory to take charge. The younger, greener soldiers mimicked their older comrades. Becker looked them over, moderately satisfied with what he saw. After a month of practice and playacting, they resembled an actual unit.

Two of the older, slower soldiers were assigned the task of helping Gaspard back to Sidi Bel Abbès to report. They didn't look unhappy with the assignment. The more ancient of the two offered his canteen to the lieutenant, then they nodded at each other and the three of them set off as quickly as they could, one of the lieutenant's arms draped over their shoulders.

Martineau barked out an order that echoed off the desert rocks and followed Lieutenant Gaspard's footsteps off the path and into the wild track of the Algerian wilderness.

HUP hup hup hup. About an hour into the march, Gil's mind was pleasantly vacant except for a growing need to pee. He briefly thought of finding the first coarse bush, but an inner voice told him to stay in the middle of the closely bunched marchers. His rapidly filling bladder interfered with the calm he'd imposed on his mind.

He wasn't alone. Most of the men were growing nervous. Idle conversation had long ceased, and the sweat staining their shirts was only partly because of the weather. Without thinking about it, the group bunched closer together. Outliers were easy pickings.

They were on a flat plain, probably an old riverbed. It twisted between two jagged outcrops of red rock. The hair on Gil's neck stood straight up. This was the perfect place for an ambush.

Gomez shouted, "There!" Something brightly glinted in the afternoon sunlight. Metal? Glass? Everyone turned to the east, trying to see for themselves. From the north came a sound somewhere between a donkey's bray and a dented bugle.

"That's a camel," Dupre said just before a shot rang out, the sound reverberating from hill to hill. A sharp crack and a puff of dust flew up five feet in front of Gil, where a bullet struck rock.

Amid curses and demands to know where the shot came from, the men threw their packs down and grabbed their Lebels amid the click of magazines snapping into place and bolts being thrown.

Someone shouted, "Where are they?"

Someone standing behind Becker responded. "Both sides, up high. Look alive."

Gil crouched low, wishing there was an outcrop, a log or even a bigger soldier he could hide behind. He sighted down his rifle, scanning the rocky hill for a clue as to their assailant's whereabouts.

He was so focused on his prey, Gil nearly screamed when a huge hand gripped his shoulder hard. It was Becker. The sergeant's eyes blazed with the hint of a smile under that giant moustache.

Pointing at Gil and Dupre, he said, "You two, find the bastard over there. You—" A huge finger pointed to Gomez and Wilmer. "Take the other way. Find them. The rest of you *solapardes*, cover these men. There are only six of them and sixteen of us. Even you can't lose with those odds!"

Gil was sure Gaspard had said eight, but the legionnaires still outnumbered them, even if they held the worst possible ground. They were sitting ducks there on the flats, but about fifty yards ahead was a granite boulder sticking out of the ground. It would have to do.

The soldiers formed a loose square and sporadically fired back, trying not to waste ammunition but to draw out their hidden opponents.

Dupre slapped the back of his hand across Gil's gut and silently pointed to the rocks. They nodded and set off as fast as they could, duckwalking for the relative safety of the big rock. They fell to their bellies in its shadow just as a bullet pinged off the top of the boulder. Sand and stone chips flew into the air and showered down on them. His kepi kept grit from going down the back of his uniform.

Halfway up the hill, Gil glimpsed light-colored cloth billowing in the breeze. The man wearing baggy cotton breeches and a sloppy turban stood out against the rock just long enough for Dupre to waste a shot. There was no way to accurately aim while shooting uphill from this far away.

From behind, the men fired in uneven bursts, hoping to flush out the bandits. Gil squinted, happy the sun was sinking behind him. The good news was it lit up the hill, but it wouldn't last long. Night fell fast in the desert.

He asked Dupre, "How many do you see?"

The big man held up three fingers. "Two right, one up high to the left." Gil thanked God for the colossal idiot. He'd only counted two of the bandits.

"We need to get closer," Gil said with more bravado than he felt.

"I thought you said Englishmen were smarter than the French." Dupre gave a gap-toothed grin.

Gil grinned back. "We are, but I'm a Frenchman now, remember?"

"Not yet, you're not. You need to kill a couple of sand wogs first."

Gil made sure he had a full clip and slid the bolt into place." What are we waiting for, then?" With a deep breath, he took off at a run, headed for the stones at the foot of the hill. Dupre's heavy feet tromped behind him. Zigzagging across the desert floor, he saw a bullet strike the ground where he'd been only a second before.

After several seconds that felt like an eternity, he belly-flopped to the pebbly ground. Dupre grunted and landed beside him. His bladder screamed for relief.

Gil put his back against the rock. "So far, so good, mate." Two shots echoed off the hills above in quick succession. He flinched as a pebble flew up and nearly took out his eye. Frantically, his hand checked his face for blood, but found none. "What the hell? I thought they didn't have modern weapons?"

Dupre grunted. "Bastards are using our own rifles against us. That's cheating. At least they shoot worse than you do."

On the hill above, one figure crouched low, trying to find a better angle to fire at them. Another followed too quickly and wobbled, nearly losing his footing. Gil caught his breath, feeling a moment of sympathy until the figure regained its balance.

The firing stopped for a moment, both sides either needing to regroup or simply reload. He watched as one bandit scampered towards them. Good a time as any, Gil thought, and ran to the base of the hill.

Firing on the run was futile, but it allowed him time to find cover. He pointed his rifle roughly in the direction of the enemy and fired, hoping at least it would keep their opponents off balance. He found shelter and slipped the bolt, sending used brass flying, and felt the next shell enter the chamber.

In training, the weapons masters said you'd get two shots at most before the enemy would be on you with knives slashing. He wasn't wrong. Gil had only just gotten off a second shot when he heard Dupre shout, "Beside you!"

In his peripheral vision, he saw a tan blur fly towards him. Gil rolled to his right and brown, sandaled feet landed in the spot he vacated. The Berber glared at Gil. He wore a loose tunic over breeches and had a beard like black steel wool. His breath smelled like a vulture's ass as he panted inches from Gil's face. None of that mattered. Gil's focus was on the wicked curved blade in the man's fist.

"Bloody hell." Gil's footing was shaky and off balance, so his bayonet thrust was met with a stream of Arabic curses and a countering slash from the bandit. The blade sliced a hole in the sleeve of his capote but didn't draw blood. He staggered two steps back, raised his weapon, and fired.

The bandit dropped into the dust, crimson staining his tunic. Gil knew instantly he was dead and felt nothing but the terrifying knowledge that the fight wasn't over yet. He wheeled around to see Dupre wrestling with his own opponent. Scrambling over the rocks with his rifle in his left hand, he found it nearly impossible to make out what was happening elsewhere.

Not daring to fire with his comrade in such close quarters to the target, Gil lowered his weapon and charged, with Rosalie leading the way. Dupre saw him coming and summoned the strength to push the bandit far enough away from him that he could drop and roll to the side.

Gil charged the confused fighter, screaming from the depths of his belly. The man rose, maybe to fight, maybe to run. His bayonet struck the Arab square in the back, knocking him forward and off balance. It was a piss-poor thrust, Gil realized. The bandit screamed, bleeding but still alive. He writhed on the ground, cursing at Gil or calling on Allah. There was no telling which.

Gil stabbed the man again and again, thrusting down and cursing. Finally, he pointed the weapon and fired, catching the squirming man in the face. Blood, bone and brains splattered the rock and his own uniform. "Take that, you motherless prick!" he yelled.

Dupre wiped his sleeve across his mouth and let out a whoop. He smiled at Gil, who collapsed on a rock while checking himself for damage.

Gil allowed himself a last giddy kick at the lifeless body. That was far too close. "I'm crap with a bayonet."

"Any fight you walk away from is a good one, no? Well, we each got one." Gil sat beside him, both panting and feeling proud of themselves. A chill ran through him as a thought cut through the fog of relief. His face fell.

There were three of them out there. They'd only killed one apiece.

The third fighter screamed and dropped onto Gil from above. The weight knocked all the air out of his body, leaving him helplessly prone. He squirmed on the ground, desperate to escape, but the attacker straddled his chest, knees pinning his arms to the stony ground. Summoning what strength he could, Gil weakly shoved the attacker off him. Legs scrambling, he scooted backwards to give himself room, but the Arab was on him again. Gil somehow grabbed the smaller man's wrist, barely keeping the curved blade from penetrating his eyeball.

Unable to do anything else, the men locked eyes and screamed at each other. Gil tensed, waiting for the inevitable end. This wasn't how it was supposed to end. It was too soon. He closed his eyes, hoping it would come quickly and not hurt too much.

Rather than cold steel, Gil felt hot liquid against his face. He opened one eye to see his opponent frozen in shock, his mouth open, eyes rolling up at the sky. The sharp tip of a legionnaire's bayonet poked through a bloody gash in his throat.

The man fell dead at Gil's feet. He looked up at Jean LaForce's panting, wide-eyed, ashen face.

Dupre dropped both his hands on the kid's shoulders and pulled him into a bear hug. "Mother of Christ, kid. Where'd you come from?"

LaForce couldn't speak. He stood staring at the dead bandit over Dupre's shoulder and pointed behind him. His mouth moved twice before he could summon the words. "Over there," was all he could manage.

Dupre continued manhandling LaForce, squeezing the air and life from him, dancing around in circles and whooping like a savage. Gil stood staring down at the body of the man who'd damn near killed him.

Next to the lifeless hand was the man's knife. It had ornate Arabic writing etched into the handle and a curved blade. This was a weapon made for slashing throats, not sticking people. He bent to pick it up, balancing it in his hand, and admired the workmanship. Without thinking, Gil stuck it in the blue sash that served as a belt.

"We... we should get back," LaForce somehow squeaked out between bear hugs.

Gil nodded. Then he said, "Oh, Jesus, I forgot. I really need to pee."

CHAPTER 13

Two days after the fight with the bandits, Le Chat Noir was packed past its meager capacity. Even though it was a Thursday night, the men felt entitled to blow off steam. Training in the morning would be brutal, but sod it. Gil and his cohorts had barely made it through the fort gates when they were bombarded with demands to tell their story. As soon as everyone stowed his gear, and into town they went. Such tales were never best told sober. The sergeants would likely understand. In fact, Gil was a little surprised they weren't there already, commandeering the best tables.

Hours later, the air was thick with smoke and bullshit. Gil had long reached that pleasant state where his blood was warm and he could sit quietly, picking up conversations around him and eavesdropping or allowing others to do the talking. Occasionally, he was called on to chime in with some detail of the fight as one gaggle of soldiers after another demanded the story.

He settled on a few details that were mostly true, and only exaggerated enough to make it interesting. The bandit he killed was further away, meaning he must have made one hell of a shot. The one LaForce bayoneted in the throat was a foot taller and thirty pounds heavier than the absolute truth dictated. By making him larger, the fight was more dramatic, the risk to his life higher, and LaForce's deed more impressive. Let the kid look like even more of a hero. He earned it.

Unlike Dupre, Gil kept his version of the story plausible. It discouraged follow-up questions and shifted the burden of conversation to more amusing storytellers. The big man was glad to play the role of raconteur. The Arabs were evil and massive, not to mention more plentiful and bloodthirsty with each telling.

It didn't take long for him to realize Gil would not be better company, so he shifted down the table and put his huge, hairy arm around Jean LaForce.

"And this kid. Damn near decapitated the bastard, didn't you?" LaForce squirmed under the scrutiny of so many of the soldiers, most of whom he didn't know. He tried waving off the attention.

Dupre was relentless. "Oh no. Don't play shy. You're the hero. The Englishman here would have been cut to ribbons without you and Rosalie, huh? Speaking of..." The big man slapped the table so hard drinks sloshed out of glasses. He turned his bleary eyes to Gil.

"I hope you bought the kid a proper drink." Gil winced. He'd hoped nobody would notice he hadn't yet sprung for a round. Money was still tight, and the kid already looked a little the worse for drink.

It was easier just to comply while everyone was watching. Gil beckoned the owner's wife over. "Brandy, for the handsome lad in the corner." She gave him a brown-toothed smile and an extra glimpse down her top and hurried off to comply.

She returned in five minutes and set the glass down in front of Gil. "No, no, madame. The hero on the end there. The pretty one."

She scooped up the brandy and placed it in front of LaForce, giving him a quick rub with her breasts across his shoulders. "What's the occasion?"

Dupre had assumed the master of ceremonies duties. He stood and waved his glass at the lad while slurring, "The occasion, madame, is that this one became a man out there. He not only saved that gloomy bastard's life," he pointed to Gil. "But he lost his cherry. Killed his first man. Like a real soldier, huh? Come on, you slugs, drink up."

He put the drink into LaForce's hand and stood unsteadily, addressing the group. "Here's to... Hey Vincente, what did you say the kid's name was in English?"

Gil grinned. "Strong. Johnny Strong."

Those who had a smattering of English laughed at the obvious discrepancy between the words and the shy, fidgeting lad. Those who didn't thought it sounded just fine, or at least easy to pronounce. Everyone had their drinks lifted and shouted, "To Johnny Strong!"

LaForce blushed to his boots. Dupre stared at him until he drained his glass in one and a half awkward gulps. For a moment it looked as though it might come back up, but he kept it down and slammed the glass on the table to the applause of his tablemates.

Dupre slumped into the chair next to him. "Congratulations kid. You popped your cherry. Now you're a killer, like a real legionnaire." Dupre leaned back and eyed the boy, one eyebrow lifted quizzically. "You have popped your other cherry, right? I mean, you've been with a woman?"

LaForce couldn't meet the big man's eyes. "Course I have." He looked to Gil for help.

"Gus, you've had your fun. Leave the lad alone."

Dupre was drunk on bad wine and all the attention. "No, this will not stand. I won't fight alongside a virgin."

"I'm not—" but the lad's words went unheard. Dupre was already digging into his pockets. "Come on, men. We owe it to our comrade here to make him a man. Can't have him die in a state of chastity, can we?"

He pulled a franc from his pocket and placed it on the table. "Gomez, you're saving yourself for that lovely lady in the picture. You won't be spending the money anytime soon." Dupre glared at him until he shrugged. Reluctantly, the tall Spaniard pulled a couple of coins from his pocket and handed them over while muttering into his moustache.

Wilmer and Richter thought it was hysterical and added to the kitty. "Come on Englishman, it was your neck he saved."

Gil cursed under his breath. He dug into his pocket, careful only to pull out a couple of the smaller coins and scooted them across the table. "Best I can do."

"Remind me never to save your life, you cheap prick." Dupre bellowed as he looked around the room. His eye caught a hard-looking woman with coal-black hair. She ignored him until he gathered the money in his giant fist and waved it at her. She was at the table in seconds.

"Up for a good time, private?" She ran a red-nailed hand down Dupre's chest.

"Not for me, my darling. It's for our young Achilles here. His name's Johnny Strong." Dupre laughed at his own joke. She didn't even bother pretending she got it.

LaForce sat like a mouse trapped in a snake's gaze. His eyes were huge white circles, and he shook his head from side to side.

Her face softened a little, and she allowed herself a hint of a smile. "Oooh, a young one. I like virgins. Can't catch anything from them."

"No, thank you, madame," LaForce sputtered. "And I'm not a virgin."

"Not anymore, you're not." Dupre roared like a bull and hoisted the young man out of his chair and over his shoulder. "Which room, your highness?"

The woman laughed and pointed with her chin. "Number three, up the stairs."

LaForce kicked his feet uselessly and pounded on Dupre's back. Flung over the bigger man's shoulders made his complaints sound weak and his attempts to escape futile. Gil felt bad for the kid and hated that he chuckled a little at the kid's predicament.

Gil had seen the woman before. He thought her name was Rose, but legionnaires weren't the only people in Algeria using *anonymats*. She scooped up the handful of francs from the table, her lips moving as she gave it a quick count. With a shrug and a crooked-toothed smile at Gil, she followed Dupre up the stairs, led by Jean LaForce's drunken protests.

Things calmed down for a while after that. The men broke into their usual cliques, although now that the new recruits had been properly tested, they were allowed to sit among more experienced soldiers. The group scattered to other tables, probably to tell their own versions of the battle with the bandits, expanding their own roles considerably.

Gil enjoyed the relative solitude and, against his better judgement, ordered another drink. The rough camaraderie of fighting men differed from that of the ruffians in Marseille. No smarter or more enlightened, but real trust could be earned and respected. There was no honor among thieves, while there was at least a thin patina of it with soldiers. Gil smiled and took the first sip.

Thirty minutes later, he was ready to leave. The evening's excitement had worn off, and he suddenly needed nothing more than his snug, safe cot. Nobody else was ready to call it a night, and he wasn't too disappointed. Gil picked up his kepi from the table and headed for the door.

From his usual table, Captain Orel gave Gil a nod, which was returned with a sloppy but well-intentioned salute. Gil opened the door, and the cool night air embraced him. A half-moon hung over the gaslit streets.

He nearly bumped into the woman who he presumed was still upstairs with LaForce. "Oh, I'm sorry, love. Rose is it?"

She took a drag of her thin cheroot and nodded. "*Oui*. Rose, yes."

Gil studied her. He'd misjudged her age by half a decade, at least. Her eyes were deep-set and bloodshot; the first signs of crow's feet extended from the corners no matter how hard shed tried to spackle them with makeup. The way she leaned her head back against the brick wall exposed a short, puffy neck. It sported a dark, angry hickey. It looked fresh.

She caught Gil looking at it and pulled her collar up to cover the mark. "Your friend. The young one? Not as innocent as you think."

"Did he... did he hurt you?" Gil's voice couldn't hide the surprise.

Rose shrugged. "Nothing out of the usual, just surprised me, is all."

Not knowing what to say, Gil tipped his kepi. "You have a good night. Stay safe."

"You too. Any chance you will pay me a visit soon?"

Gil preferred his women softer and more innocent. Like young Colette. At least he told himself he did, but this was Sidi Bel Abbès, and he'd already been here a month. "It's entirely likely."

She flipped the stub of her cheroot into the street. "Good," she said and went inside, leaving him on the sidewalk by himself.

He took a deep breath of desert air and headed up the Rue de Ecoles towards the fort. He was thinking of nothing in particular when his ears detected the rustle of clothing and a light sniff. Someone sat on the edge of a horse trough. It took a minute for him to recognize Jean LaForce.

"Oh, Johnny, didn't see you there."

The young man stared up the street at nothing in particular. "Don't call me that. It's Jean. LaForce." There was a faraway, melancholy look in his eyes.

"Right then. You okay, mate?" He got no answer. "Come on, let's go back to barracks. You've had a hell of a couple of days."

LaForce stood up, almost losing his balance. Gil was afraid the kid might fall into the water, but righted himself.

"Have a good time?" Jean LaForce didn't look like someone who'd had a pleasant evening, but Gil was eager to get home and didn't figure the kid should be on his own.

"I wasn't a virgin, you know. He wouldn't listen."

"Didn't think you were, but Dupre's not as smart as I am." That didn't elicit the expected smile. "Screw it. Come on."

Gil walked in silence. Occasionally LaForce would mumble under his breath, most of it inaudible. "Stupid bastard. Didn't need his pity fuck." Clear as a bell, he added, "That wasn't my first woman."

More quietly, he added, "Not the first man I killed, either."

Gil took his elbow and kept walking. "If you say so, mate."

CHAPTER 14

"About time they gave me some help around here. Welcome to the *Régiment Monté*." Thibault held a square-nosed shovel like a rifle to his shoulder and offered it to Gil.

He reluctantly accepted the gift. "Piss-poor weapon for a real soldier."

Thibault just laughed at him. "Heh heh, maybe. But it doesn't take training and never misfires. I presume you know what to do with that?"

"I can figure it out. Why am I here? I should be out with the *Troisieme*." Most of his compatriots were still in Sidi Bel Abbès but were now assigned to various groups, especially the Third. None of them were currently seeing any action.

From somewhere beside them came the high-pitched scraping sound of sawing on wood, followed by hammering and the occasional curse. The mules skittered in their stalls. Several of them offered their opinions by dropping brown balls of crap into the filthy straw.

"Think you're too good for this, soldier?" The bandy-legged old man glared at him, chewing his thin bottom lip. Gil was sure he caught the scent of cheap brandy in the air.

"No, nothing like that, corporal. But the mobile squads have done no real work in months."

Thibault pointed to a dozen empty stalls. "Little birdie tells me that's about to change. A dozen of these beauties are arriving next week, and I only got two hands."

Gil leaned on the shovel. "That many? What's that mean?"

Thibault laughed and kicked the head of the shovel, nearly toppling Gil off-balance. "Word of advice. Never let the officers catch you leaning on a shovel. Means there's a mobilization coming. Morocco most likely. We need to get them saddle-broken and ready. Get to work."

Gil flinched as more banging came from the woodworking shop next door. Thibault shook his head. "Too many men in the fort these days. Stuff gets broken more often. Gauthier has his hands full these days just replacing doors and tables you idiots smash up, playing like schoolboys. We need to point you at the enemy, or you'll bring the whole damned place down around our ears."

Gil may as well have been back in South Africa. Empty the foul contents of the stalls into a wheelbarrow, wheel it out to the midden heap behind the fort without spilling and dump it all over the place, then pitch fresh straw onto the floor. Repeat.

After an hour, his nose adjusted to the reek and clouds of huge, ravenous flies. His mind fell into the comforting rhythm of routine tasks. Thinking about most of his bunkmates marching through an empty desert for no apparent reason, maybe he was the lucky one after all.

All afternoon, the clamorous banging and quiet singing from the carpentry shop accompanied his grunts and the mules' braying. The mysterious Gauthier had a pleasant enough voice. Eventually, Gil's curiosity got the better of him.

Thibault had wandered off somewhere, likely to get a drink. Gil thought it was the older soldier's limp that got him assigned barn duty. Now he wondered if a less physical condition wasn't responsible.

He stroked Anya on the nose. She bowed her head quietly, accepting the tribute from a lesser being. The black john mule in the next stall stomped a hoof on the ground. "Oh, you want some too?" His hands were sore with new calluses, but gave the animal's velvety nose a vigorous rub. The mule shook its head and took a vicious nip at Gil's fingers with teeth the size of piano keys.

"Ah, you stupid git," he yelled in English. The john snorted, and Gil could swear the beast chuckled at him. "Frigging mules." He wiped his hands on his pants, checking that all his digits were accounted for. He picked his kepi off the workbench and decided he needed a break.

There was still no sign of Thibault, so he left after making sure all the stalls were locked and the shovels and pitchforks neatly wiped clean and lined up against the wall.

The afternoon sun was pleasant, not too warm. The wood shop doors were thrown wide open to catch the light and the clean, cool air. The scratching of a broom on the floor nearly drowned out the soft, sad voice.

Gil recognized the song. He'd heard it from an Apache dancer in Marseille a few months ago. That version had been loud and impassioned for peak drama in a noisy nightclub and the amusement of a rough crowd. This was slower, quieter. Sadder. A slim man of about forty carefully swept the floor, taking three or four passes to get every flake of sawdust.

With his back to the door, the man Gil assumed was Gauthier, the carpenter softly crooned. "*There is no more moon dancer. He died in a shroud of mist...*"

Gil looked around the carpenter shop with awe. He'd never seen a workplace so spotless. The tools hung on the wall in order of function and size. Lumber was piled neatly against the back wall, again in perfect rows. Even the sawhorses were stacked one atop the other. In his manure-streaked uniform, he felt unworthy to be there.

Guilt at spying on a stranger in such an intimate moment caused him a moment of slight panic. He waited until the carpenter finished his song with, "*The sky is almost bare, and no one saw a thing.*"

The singer let out a heavy sigh, and Gil took that moment to rap on the doorjamb. "*Allo?*"

Startled, Gauthier wheeled around, clutching the broom to his chest. "Who are you?" The man was clearly nervous, perhaps embarrassed at being caught out.

"I'm Vincente. Gil Vincente. I work in the—" he jerked his thumb in the direction of the stables.

"Guy Gauthier. What do you want? "

The question caught Gil aback. "Oh nothing. I just heard you singing and thought I would say hello."

The man looked blankly at him. "Hello."

Gil took a step inside the spacious workshop and looked around. He let out a whistle. "I am impressed. This place is, I don't know. Lovely. Everything in its place. Perfect." Something in his brain warmed to the sight of all that order and neatness.

Gauthier cocked his head, suspicious. "Perfect? I don't know about that, but I try. Most people don't seem to care about order. They just want wood cut and nails hammered, but I can't work in chaos."

"You're an artist."

The man demurred, but was obviously pleased with the compliment. "No, merely a craftsman who cares about his work."

Gil shook his head and pointed to the workbench. "No, I mean it. A genuine artist. What's that?" On the bench, one leg clamped to the tabletop, was an unfinished three-legged stool. The seat was smooth and shaped like a saddle. Two of the legs had intricate figures carved in it.

Stepping nearer, Gil saw one leg showed a viper, winding its way down from seat to foot. The figure was carefully whittled; the detail stunning. A second leg displayed a fennec fox, its pointed ears brushing the stool's seat bottom. The third leg was bare, caught in the clamp, waiting for its maker to finish the job. A wood chisel and paring knife gleamed in the sunbeams streaming through the door. Even his tools were immaculate.

Gauthier hustled between Gil and the bench. "It's... it's not ready yet."

"It's fine work. I mean, I don't know anything about woodworking, but it looks really good. Who's it for?"

Gautier shrugged. "Me, I suppose. I needed a stool, and this is what I came up with."

In the calm of the wood shop, Gil studied the bookish-looking carpenter. The corporal had it as good as one can have in an army. No troops relying on him. His workspace in perfect order. Useful work at that. He never thought he'd envy another soldier, but he was awfully close at that moment.

"I thought maybe you were making it for the commandant or one of the officers."

The voice that responded sounded nothing like the mild-mannered corporal Gil had just met. "I'll chop it into kindling first."

"Whoa, mate. That seems a bit much." Gil tried laughing off the answer, but he'd kicked over a hornet's nest and there was no putting the stinging bastards back.

"They're sending us—all of us—to that dung heap in the mountains."

It took a minute to decipher what that meant. "Morocco?"

"Did you know that? What am I going to do out there except die like a dog? I'm good with a hammer, absolute *merde* with a rifle. It took a month just to get this place in order, but nobody cares about that. No. No officer is getting this." The calm, crooning craftsman had vanished, and in his place was a red-faced, sweaty Breton who spit when he spoke.

Gil shifted his feet. "Well, nice meeting you. I have to go now."

Gauthier just sniffed and waved his hand dismissively. "Fine. Yes, go."

Leaving the barn, he took one last look for Thibault, but the old sot was nowhere to be seen. Giving the woodworking shop a wide berth, he headed back to the barracks. Gil couldn't help but wonder what was stuck in Gauthier's gullet. If he had to report to that place every day, he'd gladly work, sleep and eat there.

Speaking of which, the sun was low in the sky now and the bugle just rang for supper. Just as well, this was the second time Morocco had come up and there was no better place to catch up on the scuttlebutt than a mess hall full of bored legionnaires.

CHAPTER 15

The rumors were true, or at least true enough. A *harka*, a war party of Berber tribes in the Atlas Mountains over the border in Morocco, was raining holy hell on the fort at Béchar. Yet another crazy religious fanatic claiming to be the Mahdi, no doubt. It seemed there was a new descendant of Muhammad claiming to be the Messiah every few months. The Germans were also poking their greedy, arrogant noses into the cities of Casablanca and Rabat, but they were the politicians' problem.

The objective was three hundred and fifty miles away, and no train ran through the trackless desert. As Thibault predicted, it was going to take mules, boot leather, and a lot of walking cannon fodder to put the crazy buggers back into their place.

The next morning, Gil and half a dozen others arrived at the stable. He eyeballed his compatriots. They came from several smaller troops. Some he recognized from Le Chat Noir, and he offered them a friendly nod. Others came from God only knew where. From the looks of them, he couldn't decide if they'd been handpicked for talent or evicted by their peers for being useless. Time would tell.

Thibault, on the other hand, was in his glory. He wore a completely clean uniform, his kepi at a jaunty angle. "Alright, you've heard. We have a hundred new beauties coming in, twenty at a time, at the end of the week. The empty stables need prepping, and we have to make sure there's enough quality tack for every mount." Then he gave one of his dry laughs. "Heh heh, I hope you don't mind the smell of grease."

Mounts. It was hard for Gil to imagine anyone actually riding these ugly monsters. The huge john that tried to bite Gil's hand off the day before let out a bellowing honk, and the wet plop of manure on straw gave everyone a chuckle. Seconds later, they waved their hands in front of their noses. A couple of them gagged. City boys, then. They'd best not expect him to pick up their slack.

As for the grease, it was mostly tallow. That made the leather stronger and more supple, but since it was primarily animal fat, attracted crowds of flies that seemed to think soldiers made a delightful change from their usual diet of mule crap and sweat.

The prospect of action has always inspired soldiers, and Gil's companions were no different. For most of the afternoon, there was a lot of fly-swatting, friendly conversation, and accomplishing a little more than the bare minimum. Most of the men were Hungarian or Serbian. Their thick accents, remnants of the Austro-Hungarian Empire, made it hard for Gil to understand their grammatically butchered French. It wasn't a loss. He wasn't much for conversation anyway. Still, it was a pretty good clue as to how they got this assignment.

Each mount required a simple saddle, a breast collar, and two belly-straps. The animals needed to carry a soldier, baggage, the man's rations and its own feed. That was a lot of leather, metal rings, bits and saddlebags to prepare. Gil grunted and laughed when required. Otherwise, he kept his head down and willed his fingers to remember their training. By noon, his knuckles ached, and grease burned into every crack in his skin.

At the lunch break, Gil needed to stretch his legs and setout for a quick walk, only to get caught in the pounding rain. It was the first precipitation he'd seen since arriving in Africa and was shocked how cold it felt on his skin. At least it dampened the reek of tallow and chased the flies away.

He ducked into the shelter of the wood shop door, not intending to do anything more than get dry. Gauthier saw him and waved him in. "Get out of the wet. I've got something you'll want to see."

His voice was friendly, and Gil recognized the mild-mannered corporal he had met before the sudden mood change. Gauthier had his back to the door and was busy putting the tools on their allotted hooks, humming to himself.

A little wary, Gil stepped inside. "What's that?" he asked.

With a smug maître d's smile, Gauthier bent and pulled something from under the workbench. He put it on the bench and then gave an exaggerated bow and flourish. "*Et voila.*"

The stool was finished. Not only was the carving complete, but he'd used something — linseed oil maybe—to polish the wood until it was a golden brown that gleamed in the gray light of the shop.

Gil stepped closer and ran a hand over the slick surface. "It's beautiful. Really. I said you were an artist. A real Rodin."

The carpenter puffed a little at the praise, although his stiff smile got no bigger. "I decided to do a camel on the third leg. See here?" A callused finger lovingly traced the lines of the hump, long neck and thick-lipped face. "The scale is a little off, but it's not bad."

"No, it's great. What are you going to do with it?"

Gauthier shrugged. "I don't know. Do you want it? You appreciate craftsmanship, at least."

Gil stammered and shook his head. "No, I mean thank you, but it's yours." What would he ever do with such a thing in the barracks, never mind in a tent in the desert? He imagined the beautiful piece of woodwork strapped to a mule beside the feedbags and cartridge boxes. "You should keep it somewhere nice."

"They're shipping me out in three days. It won't last a week out there. Neither will I."

Gil waved his hands frantically. "Jesus, mate. Don't say that. It's bad luck. I mean, I know you don't think of yourself as much of a soldier, but you can't—"

"I know what I know," Gauthier said, then held the stool by one leg and examined it. "Maybe I can sell it in town."

That sounded more positive. Gil smiled with false enthusiasm. "Absolutely. It'll fetch a pretty penny. At least enough for a decent bottle of cognac, no? Set off in style."

The carpenter lovingly caressed the stool's saddle-like top. "Perhaps, yes." Gauthier paused, and Gil thought he detected a tear. "Stupid of me to do anything beautiful in his horrible place."

"No, no. Don't be like that. What's life without nice things?" His mind flashed to the foolishly ornate razor he kept in his boot, or the Berber knife with the Arabic markings. A little ornamentation could make even the most mundane item—or the most wicked—worth owning. "Cheer up. You might even live to enjoy it yet."

The man chortled and put the stool back under the workbench, giving it one last loving stroke. He looked so sad and alone, Gil couldn't help himself. "Come on, join me for dinner tonight."

Thankfully, Gauthier waved off the suggestion. "Bah." That was all he said, then acted as if Gil wasn't standing there.

After an uncomfortable few seconds, Gil said, "Right then. Have a good night. See you tomorrow." Gauthier gave him a look he couldn't decipher, then simply shrugged dismissively. Gil turned, shaking his head. Some people made no damned sense.

The next morning came cool but clear. The bright rising sun sent long shadows across the fort. Gil made a point of staying in the sun because it felt so good on his face. It was going to be another long day of greasing tack and trying to understand a cursed word his Slavic workmates said.

He passed the woodworking shop. The door was ajar, although not open all the way as usual. He listened for the usual sounds of sweeping, or sawing, or singing. He heard nothing. The hair on the back of his neck stood up. It was never wrong when it came to sensing trouble. He put his fingers on the door and opened it wide enough to enter. Everything was perfectly in place. Nothing seemed wrong.

"Hey, Michelangelo. You in there?"

There was no answer. "Gauthier?" He shouted loudly enough to hear in the back room and listened. He heard nothing but the distant training of men in the yard and the braying of mules. His stomach clenched the moment he recognized a faint sound. The rhythmic creak of rope against wood.

The carpenter hung from the ceiling, with an elaborate, perfect noose under his chin. Gauthier's tongue lolled from the corner of his lips. His face was almost as blue as the dress uniform he wore. The body swayed side to side like a sad metronome. The reek of urine filled the air, and Gil saw he'd suffered one final indignity. He'd pissed himself.

A few feet away, his beautiful new stool lay on its side where it landed when Gauthier kicked it out from under himself. Dusty boot prints marred the shiny surface.

"God dammit." He pulled the razor from his boot and slashed at the rope, while yelling for help. "*Au secours.* Somebody help!" The cheap hemp rope unraveled as he hacked at it, and Gauthier's corpse fell to the ground in a heap.

Gil hurried to him and checked with little hope for a sign of life. "What the hell were you thinking, you stupid bastard?" He pressed fingers to the cold neck for a pulse. When he finally admitted it was futile, he cradled the Breton's head in his lap.

Sergeant Thibault's head popped through the door. "What are you yelling about? Oh, *merde.*" The man crossed himself twice and stepped forward with eyes wide. There was no need to ask if the carpenter would live, so no need to rush.

Gil held back unbidden tears and punched a fist into his own leg. "Why would he do something like this?"

Thibault put a hand on Gil's shoulder. "*Le cafard,* I suppose. At least Orel didn't have to chase this one down."

It was a rhetorical question. Gil knew all too well why men attempted suicide. Some were more determined than others.

Maybe braver.

He half-heartedly joined Thibault in crossing himself, then walked over, picked up the stool, and dusted it off. After running his fingers over the fox, the snake and the camel one last time, he held it out to the stable master.

"Here. We can use this in the tack room."

CHAPTER 16

Every time Gil closed his eyes, his treacherous brain showed him images of death and chaos. It wasn't just Gauthier's blue, lifeless face, although that was awful enough. As he lay in the quiet bunkroom, he saw comrades long dead in the dusty fields of the Transvaal conflated with those of Dutch civilians visible through barbed wire. Colette's face as she nursed him, and his own ragged scarred wrists completed the stereopticon horror show.

Long before reveille, Gil tossed in his bunk, unable to tune out the snores, farts and occasional nightmare moans of the other soldiers. Bloodshot eyes traced every crack and bubble in the whitewashed ceiling as if the answer to why Gauthier did it, or why he cared, would reveal itself and silence the demons in his head.

Before the first bugle note finished, he was on his feet. If he didn't get active, the rest of the day he'd be thinking about... well, things that didn't bear thinking about. He threw on his uniform and then made his bed as usual. It took three tries to get the bottom corners exactly right. He couldn't quite get the creases as sharp as they should be. That didn't bode well for the rest of the day, and he refused to leave until they met his standards. His cot was as neat and perfect as Gauthier's workshop.

Gomez watched in amazement as Gil ran his fingers over the blanket and finally grunted approval. "What is it with you and the blankets?"

Unaware he was being watched, Gil blinked and turned to him. "What?"

"The blankets. Everything is just so. I've never seen anyone so worried about their rack."

Gil knew the real answer would make no sense and wasn't worth the time. You either understood or you didn't, and most people clearly did not. He offered a rote response. "Do one job half-arsed, they all get done half-arsed. Details matter."

"Some do. Some don't."

Gil shrugged. "If you say so. By the way, you buttoned your shirt wrong."

The Spaniard checked the buttons, cursed, and refastened them. "It's just a bed, *amigo*. It's not like your weapon or your woman," but Gil was already out the barracks door.

After choking down a quick breakfast, Gil hot-stepped to the stables. Today, the first twenty mules were scheduled to arrive. They needed to be broken, outfitted and assigned to Captain Maury's Twenty-fourth Mounted Company, First Regiment. Once that batch set out for Morocco, the next would arrive. Then the next batch. And the next. Upwards of a thousand men and three hundred and fifty mules were being sent to the middle of God knew where, to accomplish only God knew what.

As usual, he was the first to arrive. Thibault nodded a greeting, but that was all. The way he limped from the tack room, muttering a stream of curses, Gil knew the stable master was in the grip of a monster hangover, and to steer as clear of him as he could.

Gradually, the others filtered in. As usual, they spoke in a maelstrom of Hungarian, Serbian and bad French, excluding Gil from the conversation unless absolutely necessary. That was fine with him.

He felt an unexpected sharp twist in his gut as Thibault took the beautiful hand-carved stool and jumped on it with filthy boots, whistling through his teeth for attention.

"Listen up. In a bit, we'll have twenty new animals coming in. Don't muck around; just herd them into the stable, and get each one in a stall. And don't let any of the silly bastards get away."

A barrel-chested Hungarian snickered. The bandy-legged Thibault glared at him. "Something funny, Private?"

The Hungarian, whose name was Kovacs, smirked. He towered over Thibault, even standing on the stool. "I think we can manage a few stupid animals."

"I'll remember you said that. One of them gets loose, it's your arse'll be chasing it all over town."

The meeting was broken up by a series of loud shouts and whistles from outside. Thibault jumped down from the stool and clapped his hands twice. "*Bien.* Get them in here. *Allons-y.*"

Whooping and laughing, the half dozen soldiers trotted out to meet their new charges. Even Gil felt himself caught up in the excitement as he trotted into the courtyard.

Through a cloud of dust, he saw two fat, sun-baked Frenchmen on horseback, shouting and waving coiled whips over their heads. Twenty of the mangiest, ugliest mules ever spawned brayed in response to the shouting and chaos trotted in every direction. A half dozen older Arab men and three young, raggedy boys fanned out behind the mob, keeping the herd together. They wildly waved their arms and shouted in a mix of French, Arabic, and the local patois.

Thibault watched all this with a smile, then turned to the soldiers. "Alright, *mes braves.* Do as I do and don't let any of the whoresons get away from you." He strode forward, a coiled rope in his hands. He revealed a large loop at one end of the rope. Emitting a stream of "shh-shh-shh" noises, the little stable master held up a callused hand.

Whether bewitched or amused by the man's performance, the gray mule stopped dead in his tracks and showed its teeth. The moment it planted its feet, Thibault sprung forward and passed the loop over its head and long ears. For a second, the beast shook its head. Then, aware of what was happening, its black eyes widened and it let out a panicky honk, bent forward and kicked backwards with both hind legs, nearly decapitating one of the Serbs to the amusement of his friends.

Gil watched, fixated, as Thibault gripped the rope and slowly wrapped it around his forearm, drawing closer and closer. The animal kicked again and yanked hard, but the corporal held his ground. The tighter the rope became, and the less it could swing its head, the more stoic the animal became.

With a slow, sure hand, Thibault reached out to caress the animal's face, carefully avoiding its mouth. Then he gave the rope a tug, then another. On the third pull, the mule took a tentative step towards the man. By the second step, it followed meekly, as if there had never been a problem.

Triumphantly, Thibault shouted, "See this? It's simple. Now you do it and let's get them inside!"

Each of the men ran to grab coils of rope, making sure the loops on the end would hold, then picked an animal and charged. Gil knew better than to run or make any solid movements. Horses, mules or people—nothing enjoyed being chased and startled.

Weighing the rope in his hand, he spotted the smallest, least panicky mule. With short, calm steps, he increased the loop until it would pass easily over the head and ears. The suspicious mule shuffled its hooves and took four steps back as the Englishman approached.

"Alright, darlin'. Let's not do anything stupid." Gil swung the loop in his right hand as his left reached out towards the animal. Big dark eyes followed the empty hand, making it easy for the left hand to toss the loop around its neck. Reefing on the rope, the loop tightened, and Gil braced for the reaction.

Almost instantly, the mule honked and tossed its head with surprising strength. Gil nearly left his feet but replanted in the dust and held on as the gray beast stomped and snorted, finally running out of steam. Gil could swear it pouted as he wrapped the lead around his fist, tugged the rope and led it back to the stables.

Thibault cackled with delight as Gil slammed the stable gate. "Good job, Englishman. Only eighteen more to go." Gil offered a half-hearted wave and headed back to the yard, recoiling the rope in his fist.

Not everyone was as successful. Kovacs, never the brightest member of the team, was swinging the loop around his head like an American cowboy. He was too far away, and every attempt to lasso an animal resulted in the limp rope smacking the beast across the nose and falling to the ground.

Lucic, a young Serbian, was becoming frustrated at his own inability to snare any of the mules. "Hold still, goddammit," he yelled as a black molly ran past him. Exasperated, he reached out to smack the animal's flank as it ran past him, then turned to find another target.

Gil had a second animal under control and was heading to the stable when he saw Lucic ignore Thibault's most basic rule. For two days, the old man had drummed into their heads, "Never turn your back on a mule. Always look the same way they're looking." Now, after smacking the animal's rump, the kid was facing the wrong way, complaining to the others.

A moment was all it took. Whether it took umbrage at being smacked, or simply didn't like the young soldier, the black mule dipped its head, tightened its shoulders and snorted. Then it kicked with one leg, catching Lucic square in the back.

The Serb flew three feet and landed face-down in the courtyard. Everyone stopped and watched as he thrashed on the ground. The man's panicky, shallow gasps rose above the chaos. Lucic flailed, unable to breathe, his nostrils flaring, face rapidly turning blue. Blood sprayed from his lips with every attempted breath.

Gil knew the signs of a collapsed lung. The kick had probably fractured a rib or two, causing internal damage. That's if it didn't break the young man's spine. A sergeant cupped his hands to his mouth and yelled, "Medic! Get a medic!" Horrified, Gil watched. Knowing what was wrong wasn't the same as doing bugger-all about it.

A strong hand smacked him across the chest. Thibault glared at Gil and barked. "Get back to work. They'll take care of him. And don't turn your back on these bastards." It took a second swat to get him moving. He led the second mule to the stables, sparing a long look over his shoulder for his wounded comrade.

By the time he'd returned, Lucic had been carried off to safety. Whether he'd live or not was a different question. Eventually, and without any further damage, the men got the mules to their new homes. It was deathly silent in the courtyard.

Gil watched as Thibault conferred with one of the Frenchmen on horseback. They shook hands, and the man gave a sharp whistle. His men offered quick, obsequious salaams to the soldiers and filed out.

Kovacs kicked at the ground. "What a disaster."

Thibault shook his head. "Yes. And we get to do it all again in three days. Good work, gentlemen."

Three days. A hundred mules in all. Gil wasn't sure he could do this four more times, but what choice did he have?

CHAPTER 17

By the end of the second week, most of the mules were greeted, housed and equipped. Two of them had to be shot for going lame. Animals that had come fifty miles across rocky, bandit-infested desert led by ignorant, thirteen-year-olds arrived without harm only to be crippled by clumsy legionnaires.

Two killed. It was nearly three.

Gil was leaving the stalls, slapping his hands on his pants and trying to avoid inhaling the dust and bugs. It was a glorious day, sunny and warm, made more so by the fact that these were the last of the mules. Half had already been shipped out to Béchar, with the Twenty-Fourth reinforcing the men already there. Gil also felt a satisfied glow in his gut. He'd handled more animals than anyone in his cohort, nearly two to one. The Serbs and Hungarians could handle the rest.

That's when he heard an animal's high-pitched scream. Kovacs, because who else would it be, had buggered up the rope. It was over the mule's nose but caught behind one of its ears. The raw hemp rope sawed against one long ear and rubbed it raw. In protest, the molly tossed her head and stomped wildly. As chewed up as the courtyard became over the last week, it was a matter of time until it caught a hoof on the edge of a hole and did itself serious injury.

The Hungarian was yanking on the rope and uttering a stream of frustrated profanity. The friction created a nasty wound at the base of the ear. Blood streamed into its eye, making it panic even more.

Chalk it up to those years working with horses in the Transvaal, or his own time growing up in the North, but Gil found he had more room in his heart for people acting like crap to other people. Anyone who ever met another human knew it was to be expected. In wartime, it might even be a necessity. But mistreating an animal, whether it be a dog, horse, or ignorant monstrosities like these, was worth a bloody nose at the least.

"Oy, what the hell are you doing, you daft idiot?" Gil shouted in English, but Kovacs spoke terrible French, anyway. The tone and violence in the shout were warning enough to make him yell back over his shoulder.

Whatever he said, it wasn't in French, but "piss off" sounds the same in every language.

Blood pounded in his temples, and rage overtook good sense. Gil grabbed the rope above Kovac's wrist and yanked up. The rope burned the other man's palm, and the Hungarian let go with a shout, waving his hands and blowing on the crimson line across his palm.

"You bohunk piece of shite. Get out of here." Gil then turned his attention to the wide-eyed animal, *shh-shhing* to calm it down. He slipped the rope off its head, and for his pains the mule head-butted him and trotted away to become someone else's problem.

His pride as injured as his hand, Kovacs let out an ursine roar and threw a punch. It nearly missed, barely clipping Gil on the side of the head.

Anger replaced any good sense he had. First, he reached down his leg only to realize his razor was safely back in his footlocker. Given the level of fury, it was just as well. He grabbed Kovacs by the shirtfront, glared at him and let out a lion-like roar. Then he smashed his forehead directly into the man's nose. He was rewarded with a crunch and a gush of blood. The bigger man fell to the ground, hands covering his face as he rolled back and forth in the dust.

Only Corporal Thibault's intercession kept Gil from more than one night in the stockade. Hard as he'd hit the big dolt, it would have been easy to send him away or even assign him to work detail with the Zephyrs. They mostly built roads and did grunt work in the hottest part of the desert at the peak of summer, with little chance of redemption. At least, that wasn't going to happen. The old soldier gave Gil a wink and a pat on the back as he yelled at the guards to "take this troublemaker to jail and let him cool off."

The Englishman slept the sleep of the just on that concrete slab that passed for a cot. His back ached, but at least he was alone. Early spring in Algeria was cool and pleasant, with wind blowing through the barred window above his head. More importantly, the lack of a straw mattress kept the fleas that infested the barracks away. A sore back was a fair price to pay.

Had he really hurt Kovacs, the price would have been higher. Real trouble could land a soldier in jail for a while, or to the Zephyrs. Worse yet, banishment to the Zouaves. They were the native troops all colonial powers created. In Turkey, it was the Janissaries. In India, the Sepoys. Because the Queen wouldn't have blacks wearing her scarlet uniform, the Native Trackers in South Africa were visually indistinct from the locals but just as indispensable. No self-respecting white man wanted that duty, to be associated with them, even if they fought like demons.

As he lay there, he recalled that in a strange way, the Zouaves were the reason he decided to join the Legion. In his first year in Marseille, pockets full of cash for the first time and slightly drunk, he'd splurged and watched the Lumiere brothers' exhibition of moving pictures. He even remembered the title, "Le train des Zouaves." It was just a flickering film showing Zouave troops, with their dark faces and glittering smiles in full dress uniform, disembarking at a train station, heading to the capital for a parade.

The pride on the men's faces, compared to his own mild embarrassment at how disheveled he'd become, made him nostalgic. For the first time since mustering out, he missed the army. Any army. The regimen. The uniform. Most of all it was the look in people's eyes he missed. The awe he inspired in some and fear in others was a drug whose embrace he missed. It took five years of intemperance and petty crime to realize that he couldn't attain that high through his own efforts.

Indeed, here he was. He caught himself running his thumb over the bumpy scar on his left wrist and immediately willed himself to stop touching it. The past didn't matter. Gilbert the Lion was gone. Gil Vincente was where he belonged. Safe from the world. And himself.

The first thing he saw as he left the stockade the next morning was Thibault. The old soldier stood, bandy-legged, arms crossed, and a mostly sober grin on that leathery face. "How'd you sleep?"

"Great. Nobody was snoring to keep me awake."

"Glad you enjoyed it. It's the last good night you'll have for a week or two."

Gil was rested, but hadn't yet had his coffee. "What do you mean?"

"The Moustache wants the last of the Twenty-Fourth in Béchar right away." The Moustache was the whispered nickname of Marshal Hubert Lyautey.

"What's that got to do with me? You love having me around." Gil hoped charm would keep him out of trouble.

"The troops are nothing but green peas. I need someone who knows the animals to make sure these cretins don't kill them before they get where they're going. You're the lucky winner."

Gil knew there was something Thibault wasn't saying, so he said it. "And away from Kovacs."

"That too. I'd rather keep you and send him, but half the animals would die before getting there. Probably a bunch of legionnaires, too. How the Habsburgs keep an empire with oafs like him, I'll never know, but he's our problem now."

"How long do I have?"

Thibault laughed. "Heh, heh. About an hour, so you'd better get some breakfast and grab your kit.

"Bloody hell."

Thibault's face tightened. "Excuse me?"

Gil caught his mistake and straightened, then offered a quick salute.

Thibault smirked. "Better. Go eat. This is the last fresh bread you'll see for a bit."

Two hours later, Gil was the second man through the gate for the nearly three hundred and seventy-five-mile trek to the fort at Béchar. His back was still sore from sleeping in the cell, and the nearly hundred pounds of gear on his back didn't help. He marched on one side of the unnamed john. A very blond and granite-jawed Alsatian named Meier was on the other. He was a truculent young man, and Gil was grateful for the lack of conversation.

HUP-hup-hup-hup.

It was still too early to ride. After the first fifteen miles or so, they'd take turns riding for an hour while the other partner walked, then switch. The mule didn't get a vote and didn't seem to care much. As they trudged along, Gil held the reins loosely, in case a clump of grass or a desiccated bush proved too tempting to the animal.

About an hour out of Sidi, a commotion broke out near the end of the line. The lieutenant rolled his eyes and lifted his hand to call a halt. He pointed at Gil, then gestured down the line with his thumb.

Gil plastered a fake smile on his face and saluted. Nobody had made him the boss, and he didn't want the responsibility. Why couldn't people just do their bloody jobs?

He handed the reins to Meier. "Don't hold it too tight, but don't let the silly bugger wander off. I'll be right back."

Without waiting for an answer, he set his jaw and marched down the line of men and mules until the source of the problem became clear.

A circle of laughing men formed a rough circle. A lone, panicky voice shouted, "Stop, you motherless whore. Stop it."

In the center of the makeshift ring, a stocky soldier bounced atop a mule that took objection to his presence. The animal spun in a circle and kicked, while the terrified legionnaire clung to the reins, and whatever cargo he could lay hands on.

Gil pushed his way through the men. He felt the same disgust in his gut that incompetence always caused. Without a word, he strode forward and grabbed the mule by the bit, prepared for the force of the animal's tossing head. Surprised to see its progress halted, the animal stopped spinning and tried to take a chunk out of Gil's hand instead. Holding the bit where he did, the terrifying teeth clicked together impotently.

The soldier was still on the animal's back, panting. His red, jowly cheeks puffed in and out, and he clung to a tent pole so he wouldn't fall off.

Gil snapped, "What are you waiting for, you ignorant bastard? Get down."

The soldier obeyed, landing in a heap to the amusement of the others. He staggered to his feet, smacking the dust from his uniform and trying to find the remaining shreds of his dignity.

Gil spent a few moments stroking the mule's velvety nose and looking into its eyes, willing it to calm down. When it appeared that both man and beast had calmed down, he barked a question at the soldier. "What happened?"

"I... I wanted to take my turn riding, and the cursed thing went crazy."

Gil took a second to take a swig from his canteen so he wouldn't take the man's head off. "First, we've only been out an hour or so. It's too early to put that burden on the mule."

"I'm not that fat, you Limey bastard."

"It's not the size of your arse. But think about the animal. It's already carrying twice what you are with half the bitching about it." Gil stopped and grabbed for the man, pulling him out of the way and barely avoiding a foul-tempered kick. "And stay beside him; don't ever stand behind him."

He waited an extra second before asking, "Are you okay?" The man's partner, a bearded giant stopped laughing long enough to answer. "He'll live. You will live, right?" The chubby soldier offered a sharp, "Piss off." He'd be fine.

Three dozen sets of eyes watched him as he turned without another word to return to his own blessedly silent partner and well-behaved animal. Eyes straight ahead, he ignored pleas for help.

"Hey, is this breast buckle on right?"

"English, Can you check this for me?"

Gil just marched on, not deigning to look at the speaker. "I'm not your bloody sergeant. Figure it out."

Without a word, Gil marched back to his spot near the front of the line. He felt the sergeant and the lieutenant studying him as he walked. He avoided their gaze and muttered to himself. "Don't bloody think of promoting me. I don't need the aggravation."

As night fell, the men fell out and made camp. Without realizing it, Gil oversaw the staking down of the mules. He answered questions, and the men obeyed without a question. A little disgusted with himself, he found a spot by himself on a rock, cut some sausage and bread from his stash, and washed it down with just enough water to make it digestible. All he wanted was to be a soldier, a part of the machine without the responsibility of rank or privilege. Was that so hard to understand?

He dipped inside the tent to sleep, only to find Meier already there. Neither said a word as Gil did a quick check for scorpions and snakes, then lay down and closed his eyes. His tentmate offered a terse, "Good night," and those were the last words exchanged until morning.

Chapter 18

*H*UP *hup hup hup.*

For two more days, they marched. On the second, Gil and Meier pulled the first watch. Normally, Gil Vincente didn't mind. After all, that was a real man's duty- not playing nursemaid for a bunch of stubborn animals. It was the part of the job that made him a soldier. Plus, he'd still get four hours of shut-eye before the next day's march to the oasis marking the midpoint of the trek to the fort at Béchar.

His taciturn partner would be no help in staying awake after such a long walk. While useless chatter usually annoyed him, there was a modicum of basic human interaction one could expect. All he'd learned so far of Meier, his mule-mate, was that he was from the village of Colmar in Alsace and that French sausages were crap. Gil didn't give a damn about the first point and wasn't about to argue the second.

He stood up to stretch his legs and wandered around the outside of the encampment, looking up at the stars. After so long in Marseille, with its smoke and lights, he couldn't help but be dazzled by the infinite pinpricks of light stretching from one horizon to the other. Even a backwater outpost like Sidi created enough competing illumination that it was only in the depths of the desert the stellar show reached its zenith.

Busy wool-gathering and looking up, Gil never saw the wooden peg sticking out of the ground until he kicked it and tumbled onto his belly. "God dammit. What the Christ was that?"

His eyes were sufficiently adjusted to the dark so he recognized it as a grazing anchor. There should have been a mule attached to it so the animal could have its supper without wandering off. So far, none of the beasts had been reported lost. Each pair of legionnaires should have their mules staked for the night. An empty peg meant one of the critters had wandered off. Or worse.

Bending low, he cursed then struck a match, hoping it wouldn't attract snipers. Legion-issued boots and unshod mules trampled the ground. Thankfully, there were no strange tracks or sandal marks indicating thieves. A line of paired hoofprints led off to the West. It wasn't bandits, then. Some lazy idiot hadn't secured the reins, and the mule simply wandered off.

Which of the others hadn't been paying attention? If he had to guess, it was the lazy lard-ass. If it was him, there's be hell to pay. Then Gil shook his head. Not his problem, but finding the mule was.

He shook the match out and stood, giving a soft whistle. Meier trudged over, his eyebrows expressing the question he couldn't be bothered to ask.

"One of these daft creatures buggered off. It can't have gone too far." Gil pointed away from the camp.

"So?" Meier clearly wasn't any more proactive than he was chatty.

"Let's see if we can catch it."

Meier shrugged. After alerting the two legionnaires patrolling the other side of the camp, they set off, following the tracks. The moon and stars provided enough light that it was simple work. Gil spent the time imagining the tongue-lashing he'd give the careless soldier. He didn't have the foggiest clue what was going on in his partner's mind.

After ten minutes, he felt the nagging itch in his scalp. They were supposed to be watching the camp, and it was almost time for the next watch. He was about to give up when he heard a soft, lonely-sounding honk.

"There you are, my beauty. Come on now." He whistled between his teeth, hoping the animal was scared or bored enough to return on its own. At a second honk, a little closer this time, he and Meier picked up speed.

Yards ahead, a dark shape loomed. Gil motioned for Meier to halt, then scuffled forward with his hand extended. "Shh, shh. That's it. Time to go home." The mule shook its head and stomped its feet. He kept turning its narrow face over his shoulder, looking at something Gil couldn't see.

With one last look back, the mule trotted forward. Gil grabbed the reins that should have anchored it to the peg, but now dragged uselessly in the dirt. After cursing whoever had been so sloppy, he rubbed a hand over the beast's nose. The mule shook its head and brushed past him. Its eyes were wide, and it looked in a hurry to get home, which was fine with Gil.

Then he heard it. A low rumbling cough. Something was out there.

Gil squinted, trying to figure out which particular murderous beast was now hunting whoever interfered with its dinner. A second sound, a little to the north, answered it. Whatever was out there was circling them.

"What is it?" Meier hissed.

Gil held up a hand, hoping in the dark his partner could see his plea for silence. He'd heard something like that once before. On the veldt. Thousands of miles to the south.

"A lion."

Even in the dark, the whites of Meier's eyes shone in the dark. "*Verdammt.*"

The mule took it upon itself to trot back to camp faster, leaving the two men alone in the dark. Meier started chasing it, but Gil whispered harshly, "Stay still. Don't move."

A four-legged figure crouched low in the darkness at the edge of his vision. It was moving inexorably clockwise. The rumble grew closer. He knew the Barbary lion was smaller than its southern cousin, but no less lethal. Something in the back of his mind told him he was forgetting something important, but he couldn't summon the thought. He kept hoping the beast would show itself so he could get a shot off.

As quietly as he could, Gil unslung his rifle, motioning for Meier to do the same. He bolted a cartridge into place and raised the muzzle, desperately seeking the source of that hellish noise. He thought he located it and took a breath when there was a second, higher sound nearly behind him. That's when Gil remembered what he'd forgotten.

Lions hunt in packs. Pairs at least.

He spun in time to see a lioness twenty yards away and closing fast. Her teeth were bared as she emitted a roar that shook him to the core. He felt his sphincter tighten and bladder threaten to let go.

A shot rang out, and the animal tumbled head over tail, shrieking. Meier hit the target, but clearly didn't kill it. There was a quick "click" of a bolt, and a second shot caught the animal under the chin. The lioness dropped to the stony sand, a bloody mess, its fangs still snapping at empty air.

As Meier relaxed, Gil raised his own weapon. The Alsatian turned his back on the male to kill its mate. The male now charged at the man's unprotected back.

Gil barked, "Get down! Now!" Meier dropped to a knee and Gil fired over him, catching the beast in the shoulder. It howled in outrage and spun away, limping. The big male left its mate to the desert.

The two men turned and sprinted for the camp, pausing every fifty yards to look around for more predators.

"There they are!" A voice rang out, and half a dozen soldiers, led by the sergeant, hailed them.

Gil turned to his partner. "Thank you, *mon ami.* I owe you one."

Meier shrugged and kept walking. He remained quiet as Gil answered all the shouted questions. By the time they reached the camp, the place was abuzz, and everyone was awake. There'd be no more sleep tonight, so the men began packing up.

The lieutenant slapped him on the back. "Are you alright?"

Gil nodded. "I thought we'd killed all the lions in these parts," he said.

The lieutenant grinned. "I guess we missed some. Good job out there. Do you need anything?"

He paused and then gritted his teeth. "The name of the arsehole who can't tie a decent knot."

CHAPTER 19

Three days later, they were still a day's march from Béchar. They were somewhere in the *Oran Sudanais,* but nobody could really tell. The scenery hadn't changed in two days. Everything was the same gray and brown pebble-strewn expanse except the flat valley turning to gently sloping hills and at the top of each rise, the hazy serrated tops of the Atlas Mountains to the west grew more distinct.

The heat increased as well. It was late March now, and the cool ocean breezes that somehow reached Sidi Bel Abbès died long before reaching this far inland. Gil watched as the silent Meier stopped, took his canteen and poured a couple of precious mouthfuls of water onto the neckcloth of his kepi., then hustled to catch back up with Gil and the mule. Neither had given it a name.

At the sensation of the wet cloth against his sunburnt neck, Meier let out a grateful sigh. Gil quickly followed suit. "Good idea," he said as he wadded the material under the water, then licked his fingers dry.

"Is this Morocco? Certainly glad we walked all this way to see it." Gil couldn't decide if he was more shocked that Meier made a joke, or that he spoke at all. Either way, he rewarded the effort with a chuckle.

Gil's surprise continued as the Alsatian spoke two sentences in a row. "Doesn't look like much, does it? Why do the French want it?"

"La gloire de la République Troisième," Gil said, in an effeminate Parisienne accent. He didn't really know the reason, but "The glory of the Third Republic" was the government's reason for everything.

Meier nodded. "Damned politicians."

Gil asked, "Why do the French and the Prussians keep fighting over Alsace? Every other year you're taken over by one or the other?"

Meier spit. "Like I said, damned politicians."

Gil thought that said all that needed saying, so patted the mule's rump and gave it an affectionate rub, then caught himself and withdrew his hand. He savored the feel of a damp cloth on his neck and kept walking.

"What's that?" A voice called out.

Dozens of eyes scanned the horizon. Sure enough, to the north and south, black dots appeared over the rocky hills, then vanished only to reappear a few yards ahead. Maybe half a dozen of them, but it was hard to tell.

"Those ours?" someone asked from near the front of the line.

"Berbers," barked the Sergeant. "Eyes sharp. The locals will be everywhere now. Still think this is their country, poor deluded bastards. Stay alert and keep marching."

Now that he knew they were there, Gil couldn't not see them- or imagine he did at least. For a while he tried counting the turbaned heads as they popped up over the rocks, but there was no telling them apart.

It should have been worrisome, but signs of a human enemy after walking through the sandy void energized the men. Chatter grew louder, laughter more common, and without being aware of it, they picked up the pace.

There were maybe three hours of daylight left before they made camp. With an early enough start, they could be at Béchar by noon tomorrow. That meant two more hours of wasted boot leather before settling in. Gil allowed himself the luxury of climbing astride their nameless john mule. He couldn't resist giving those big leathery ears a good scratching. Meier, of course, said nothing but walked alongside, his eyes darting to the periphery for signs of the enemy.

As the mountains became less hazy and more solid, Gil thought he saw more teams of enemy scouts. The farther into the wilderness and the closer to the frontier, the more the danger increased. There hadn't been any attacks on military caravans in weeks. The Berbers and their *harkas* were more than content to let the French sit in their forts and marinate, but that didn't mean some local chieftain wouldn't try his luck.

Word was that there would be an offensive as early as mid-April, only a week or two away. That was part of the reason for bringing this bunch of misfits up now, and why he had to return right away. The main force would come up shortly. Gil studied the hills and licked his dry lips. Marching through enemy territory in a troop was risky, but nothing compared to the idea of going back alone or with only a couple of others. It wasn't the first time he cursed Kovacs and wished he'd hit him harder. Then he'd be in a nice comfy cell in Sidi Bel Abbès.

No sense dwelling on past mistakes, as his mentor Vincente used to say. There'll be plenty more to make tomorrow. *HUP-hup-hup-hup.*

They made camp in a surprisingly green valley with good water. Meier and Gil struck their tent using the poles they'd carried on mule-back. The canvas would provide enough shade for the little daylight that remained and shelter them from the chilly night breezes. Gil was still getting used to the drastic temperature drop in the desert from day to night. Another change from the weather in South Africa, which now, with the help of his selective memory, always seemed pleasant. Or at least warm. If he wanted the cold, he'd have stayed in England.

It was an hour before dawn Gil heard a distant voice shout, "Who goes there?" His brain barely registered the question, but the shot that followed jolted him upright before the echo vanished into the enveloping darkness.

Meier's pants were already half on before Gil was even out of his bedroll. He held a rifle up and asked, "Yours or mine?"

Gil squinted and reached to the right, where he felt the cold metal of a gun barrel. "Yours." His Lebel was on his right, where he always kept it. How could someone not know where their weapon was? Routine was the essence of organization, and organization could save your life. The high opinion he'd formed of Meier dropped a peg.

Their tent was in the second ring around the central fire. He ducked out through the flap, already sliding the bolt, loading a cartridge into the chamber. The fat legionnaire he'd chewed out on the first day shouted, "Try to steal my mule, huh?" and fired into the darkness.

Gil shouted to Meier, "The animals. Come with me." They ran to where the mules were pegged down. After ensuring every peg and its animal were accounted for, he stood and tried to make sense of the chaos all around him.

From a distance, the whinnying of horses and the *"you-la-you-la-you-la"* cries of the tribesmen filled the air to the west of the camp. Most of the men ran in that direction, while Gil and Meier joined Lard-Ass and his partner in trying to calm the mounts.

Braying from the far edge of the makeshift corral caught Meier's attention. "What's that?" they trotted over, Gil following, swinging his rifle side to side, watching his partner's back. Before he clocked what was going on, he watched Meier bolt for the edge of the circle and let out a shout.

A black form popped its head up and ran as quickly as it could. It was a young man, a kid really. Maybe fifteen years old. He was barefoot and ragged, and no match for a grown man in full flight. Meier grabbed the boy's shabby robe at the neck, and a ripping sound filled the night. The boy screamed in Berber, and the older man's momentum drove them both to the ground.

"Hold still, you filthy bugger," Meier said, spitting sand out of his mouth as he spoke. The young man kicked wildly, and when the soldier took a bare heel to the chin, stumbled to his feet and kicked again, hitting nothing but air.

Unfortunately for the would-be mule thief, Gil was behind him and wrapped him in a bear hug hard enough to drive the air from his young lungs. The thief was nothing but skin and bone. Gil felt his ribs through the dusty, filthy tunic.

"Hey, stop. Just stop. I'm not going to hurt you." The boy either didn't speak French or didn't believe a word of it. He thrashed harder. Gil felt his grip slipping, so gave the wriggling Berber a cuff across the ear. This elicited a full-blown scream, but the lad stopped fighting.

In the distant firelight, Gil got a look at him. He looked younger than before; small , but then his type usually was. Snot and dust covered his face, along with a bruise on his left eye. The puffy skin around it looked green and yellow. Whatever caused that happened days ago.

"What do we have here?" The Lieutenant strode over, looking to Gil for an answer.

Lard-ass spoke first. "Caught someone poking among the mules. Chased away the one on the horse, but this one tried to take my Dandelion." It took both Gil and the officer a moment to realize he'd named the animal. It seemed they'd bonded after all.

But Dandelion? Jesus Christ.

The Lieutenant looked to the sergeant, who joined the party. "What should we do with him?"

"Shoot him and be done with it. An example to the rest of the thieving vermin." Lard-ass was red-faced, growing more excitable by the minute. He reached out and grabbed a handful of brown hair. The boy shrieked and kicked at him.

The Sergeant barked, "Enough." The fat legionnaire immediately stepped back, his eyes cast to the ground. The rest of the camp turned instantly silent.

The lieutenant got down on one knee so he was more or less eye to eye with the boy. He stammered a few words in the local language. The lad's eyes widened. The boy opened his mouth, then snapped his jaws together, determined to be brave and stay silent. After a few more attempts, the officer stood, wiped his knees clean of dust, and sighed.

The sergeant said, "Sir, we can let him go or take him with us. Not much other choice, is there?"

The Berber lad's eyes followed the conversation, uncomprehending. Gil knew the look of a local who'd been told horror tales of what soldiers would do to him if caught. Which war didn't really matter. The campfire talks were always the same, and many of them weren't far from the truth.

The lieutenant looked uncertain. The Sergeant coughed. "If I may, Sir. It's only a couple of hours to Béchar. Command at the fort will probably know which clan he belongs to, and that should tell us who this lot was. Might prove useful.

Lard-Ass reached for the nape of the boy's neck. "Leave him to me. I'll—"

Gil backed away. Now that the mules were safe, he felt no compunction about getting further involved. He looked out into the empty desert beyond the camp. The stars were a pale white awning, extending from the mountains in the west to the flat horizon East. He yawned and allowed himself a relaxing stretch.

Suddenly a dozen voices shouted behind him, and he turned just in time to hear the sergeant yell, "Halt!" Rapid footsteps on gravel headed into the darkness. A gruff voice cursed, then two shots rang out. By the time he and Meier reached the rest of the troop, it was over.

Maybe twenty-five yards away, the boy lay face down, a dark wet pool forming on the back of his tunic. The fat prick had a service pistol in his hand.

"Told you we should have just shot the thieving bastard." He held a hand to his swollen eye, pulling it away every few seconds to check for blood.

The lieutenant muttered something to himself, then straightened his spine and barked. "Collect the body. Maybe someone knows who he is. The rest of you get some sleep. We march at dawn."

Meier's last words for the night were, "Damn it. And I was sleeping so well, too."

CHAPTER 20

The mule with the dead teen slumped across its back led the troop the last few hours, with the run rising behind them. Long shadows pointed the way due west towards Morocco, although Fort Béchar was on the Algerian side of the border. Exhausted men trudged behind them, clumsily attempting to catch up.

To Gil's surprise, the glorified goat path they marched on had become a true road. He wasn't sure when it happened, but the surface was flat and graded. The mules made better time and the men's boots were blessedly pebble-free. Romans, Brits and the French conquerors always made it easy to get from A to B.

The ringing of pickaxes greeted them as they came over the rise about four miles from their destination. The French government was taking full advantage of the Zephyrs, the prison detail. Legionnaires found guilty of stealing from the barracks, or striking an officer, or being aggressively fond of their bunkmates were put to better use building roads, forts and way-stations. Just because you were useless to the Legion didn't mean France was done with you. That five-year commitment was still a contract. Assuming of course, you lived to see it out.

He studied the shirtless, scruffy men, swinging picks high or shoveling stone into barrows. For five days, Gil had carried a grudge the size of his backpack for Thibault sending him on this mission, but watching the prisoners at work, it changed to a form of gratitude. If he'd really hurt Kovacs, that could be him out there. Shame burned in his cheeks at his lack of control. He knew better. He'd do better. The alternative was too awful to contemplate.

"Poor bastards," Meier said from the other side of the mule.

"Their fault. If they can't keep their heads straight, do you want them fighting next to you?" He was surprised to hear Captain Orel's voice in his head as he said it.

His mule-mate gave him a look Gil couldn't interpret, but as usual didn't say a word and kept walking.

The whole unit fell silent as they passed the work crew. The two sets of men stared at each other. The prisoners finally broke into a mocking chorus of "le Boudin" and saluted the legionnaires with big, mostly missing-teeth grins.

Gil wondered if having to sing that damned sausage song was part of their sentences. Gritting his teeth, the marching soldiers sang back and mouthed the words. Screw the Belgians. They'd done nothing to or for him.

He didn't have high expectations of what the base at Béchar would look like, but was disappointed anyway. At first, their destination was indistinguishable from the sandstone hill it sat on, and practically invisible against the higher mountain behind it. Eventually he made out the embrasures, the man-high brick blocks with the crenelles in between that allowed the defenders to fire down into the valley below. One round turret, higher than the rest of the structure by a good forty feet, formed the front of the edifice. The gates and medieval-looking wooden portcullis opened at its feet. Otherwise, it was a square, drab, sand-blasted block.

"Hardly seems worth the trip, does it?" Meier said as they marched forward.

Men, mules and tents littered the valley floor. Individual platoons had staked out their piece of ground with plenty of space in between.

A trio of officers rode out on Arab horses to meet them. The Lieutenant and Sergeant snapped to dusty, bedraggled attention while the Captain and two Lieutenants saluted from their spotless brown steeds.

The lieutenant coughed the dust from his throat, then smiled. "Sir, brought forty men, mules and equipment from Sidi . We sure would appreciate a hot meal and a decent bed."

A freshly shaven lieutenant shook his head. "Afraid not. We're already bursting at the seams. Commandant Lyautey is bringing in a few new troops for an offensive in a couple of weeks. Find a piece of ground and have at it. We'll bring water and fresh food out, best we can do." He pretended not to hear the groans of the soldiers at the front of the pack who'd heard the entire exchange.

Gil looked out over the valley, counting the canvas structures. With two or three men per tent, there were already forty or more men outside the fort, never mind how many were already inside. Their unit made the total over fourscore. Add the eighty mules and twice that number of men yet to come, and there'd be over two hundred men camped at a brick box made for thirty at best.

Someone was expecting trouble, and not the minor skirmishes they'd been told were coming. Gil wondered what other lies they'd been told. No, not lies, he reminded himself, incomplete information.

Individual locals wandered through the camp. Gil tensed, then slowly released a breath he'd held trapped in his chest. There was nothing to fear. They were mostly women with tanned, rough hands and dark sad eyes, the only body parts visible under long scarves and dresses. Gil did not know what you called them, but they dragged in the sand. Young boys, old enough to do the work and carry goods, accompanied them, male but not old enough to present a threat. They'd stop at a group of soldiers, salaam politely, then mime eating and combing mules while talking a thousand words a minute in their language. It didn't sound like Arabic, so must have been the local dialect.

Usually, the locals got sent packing. Occasionally, a soldier would hand over a coin and receive fresh bread or dried fruit. He'd good-naturedly try to bow back, eliciting polite head bobs from the women and raucous laughter from the boys, at least until their mothers cuffed them upside the head.

"Pardon me, sirs. But is that wise? Giving them the run of the camp?" Gil's lieutenant, a self-important youngster named Coste, asked the officers.

This brought a chuckle from the captain. "Relax. These are our people. We protect them from the maniacs out in the desert. They're smart. Don't like the rebels any more than we do. They know where their bread is buttered." Gil thought he sounded far more confident than he looked saying it.

The sun reached its peak, and what little shade was available seemed to be to the north, in the turret's lee. The sergeant pointed and asked, "How's that spot over there?" It would be close enough to the fort for supplies and aid, but not on the longest, flattest part of the valley floor. If there were an attack, enemies would have to cut through the rest of the soldiers first.

That was fine with Gil. He wouldn't be here long, dropping off the mules and heading back. The trip back to Sidi Bel Abbès, bandits or no bandits, seemed a lot more appealing than sitting outside in the baking sun waiting for God knows what to happen.

An hour later, he and Meier were set up and their mule fed and watered. Gil considered a quick nap, but before he could dip into the relative shade of the canvas, a voice rang out, "Well, Vincente, isn't it? What are you doing here?"

He looked up to see a familiar bald-headed officer and an even more familiar mule.

He remembered to salute. "Captain Orel." The Russian moved his arm casually, as much of a salute as he could bother with. "What are you doing here, sir?"

Orel removed his kepi and wiped a sleeve over the sweaty top of his clean-shaven head. "The usual. Two men deserted yesterday."

"Do you know where they went, sir?"

The Russian shrugged. "The closer we get to Morocco, the more cowards will try to run. Something tells me it will only get worse." The officer sucked at his bottom lip, thinking and studying Gil. Then he gave a glance at Meier. "I could use some help. Come with me."

Gil looked around. As much as he didn't want to stay doing bugger all in the heat, he wasn't sure chasing fellow soldiers, and maybe killing them, held much appeal. "Sir? I would have to check with my commander. I'm supposed to be heading back to Sidi right away."

"Bah, Sidi . There's real work to be done. Anya can't wait, can you, girl?" Orel affectionately patted the mule's nose and was rewarded with an enormous head rubbing against him so hard it nearly knocked him off balance. Then he gestured to the other mule. "Who's your friend?"

"He doesn't have a name. He—"

"Fritz, sir," Meier piped up. "His name is Fritz."

Gil turned to his tent-mate. "Fritz? When did you name him?"

"The day we left." Gil gawked at him. Meier didn't talk much, but one would think he'd mention this.

"Why didn't you tell me?"

"You never asked, and you wouldn't have liked it if you had."

Orel chuckled. "I like him. Both of you report to me at fourteen hundred hours."

"Yes, sir!" They saluted, Meier with more gusto than his bewildered tent mate. Or was the quiet blond now his partner?

CHAPTER 21

The three men, along with the fort's commandant, sat on splintering wooden chairs in a hot, windowless wardroom that smelled of cheap tobacco, sweat, and boredom. Oil lamps gave off a little smoky, creosote-scented illumination.

A thick finger stabbed at a mountain pass on a map. "They likely headed here." Orel looked at the two privates. "And probably didn't get much farther. If they're even still alive," he added casually. Meier's stony face asked the obvious question. Orel sucked his chapped bottom lip. "It's only logical. The fastest way out of Morocco is through Casablanca."

Gil could read maps a little. There were coastal towns closer. In fact, someone determined enough could even slip down the coast to the Spanish cities of Ceuta and Melilla in the Western Sahara Territories, which were technically French but entirely uncivilized. "Sir? Why Casablanca?"

Orel stood and put his hands on his hips, stretching out muscles shaped by too much time on Anya's back. He sucked air through his teeth, then said, "It's a big port, lots of boats. But mostly, the Germans have been playing their little games there. They're trying to ingratiate themselves with the King. And they're helping deserters get out of the country."

His raptor eyes focused on Meier's face. The young man shuffled his feet uncomfortably, but said nothing. "Meier, is it?"

"Yes. Sir. But I'm French, well Alsatian so…"

"Alsace and Lorain, yes? Every few years, you change sides. You're French; now you're German. So, this week you're French. *Bon.*" Orel took the edge of the map and started rolling it shut.

Gil put his hand on the parchment. "If I may, sir? Why do you say they won't get much farther? I heard the roads through the mountains are good." He hadn't stopped thinking about the Zephyrs since he saw them the other day, doing nothing but breaking and grading rock all day in the heat. Not honest work for soldiers, but they were quickly transforming the desert into something navigable. He shuddered at the idea of being one of them. He'd rather die.

"The Mahdi, or whatever they're calling him this week, has men everywhere. Thick as fleas on a dog's ass. Two men alone won't get far." Orel sat back, looking very confident and pleased with himself.

By Gil's calculation, they were only three themselves. Their odds couldn't be that much better, but the Russian didn't seem concerned, just eager to get on the road. There was no blaming him for that. Conditions inside were far from ideal.

Fort Béchar itself was crammed past capacity, which explained the tents scattered across the valley floor. Twenty-five men originally posted there had gone from the intense boredom of being an understaffed backwater troop, there to justify the land claim, to being crowded out by rowdy, oblivious men with no idea of what was coming. The incumbents resented the intrusion on their peaceful lives and knew that with each new arrival, the chances of a full-blown fight ballooned. Dusty brick walls vibrated with escalating tension. The desert air was certainly fresher.

The Commandant was a fifty-ish man with a walrus moustache darker than the hair on his head. His uniform was sweat-stained and had cigarette ashes dusting up and down the front of his blue jacket. "I can give you food and water for three days, but as you can see, we're rather stretched."

Orel nodded. "That's all we'll need. With luck, we'll bring back two more mouths for you to feed."

The walrus peered over his pince-nez glasses. "Don't work too hard on that score. We have plenty of cowards and thieves here already."

Orel pursed his lips and nodded. "As you say."

Gil and Meier exchanged raised eyebrows but kept mum.

Orel turned to the two privates. "Be ready in an hour. Get your Fritz ready to go for a walk."

"Sir." They both saluted and left the wardroom, grateful for the relatively fresh air of the courtyard.

Two hours later, they began the climb into the foothills. The three men and two mules followed an old goat path winding through the rocks. Gil watched from the rear as Anya's hooves easily handled the stony ground. Despite his worries about shoeing the beasts, shifting weight worked best when navigating the terrain, and shoes would restrict that. Against his will, he found himself admiring the way mules took to the unwelcoming landscape. Anya did, at least. Fritz was a solid enough pack animal, although as slow as any he'd seen. The john seemed to do just fine and kept looking back at Meier with what looked like affection. He and Gil ignored each other as much as possible.

Orel led the way, whistling idly to himself. Meier, of course, said bugger all from the rear. That left Gil alone with his thoughts, which ricocheted wildly inside his skull. He missed the regimen of the stables, not to mention a decent, well-made cot. Wrapping and stowing a good tight bedroll didn't hold the same satisfaction.

And why were they chasing these cowards anyway? They didn't want to be soldiers, which meant they'd be useless as tits on a boar when the real fighting started. He thought about what Orel said, that loyalty to your fellow soldiers meant everything. Maybe. He'd still rather be back at Sidi Bel Abbès. He cared about his compatriots only as far as they could keep him alive.

In his marching trance, he daydreamed of Marseille and his days as *Le Lion*. What was old Vincente doing? How much of a mess had he left behind after that bloody incident at La Barasse? He even allowed himself a passing thought for Colette. Mostly, he'd blanked her from his memory, but several nights in a row she appeared in his dreams. Not the real her, the sweet girl nursing him after his incident. His imagination created far more erotic situations than ever really happened. She was always loving, but tentative and innocent, practically chaste. The girl was the stuff of romantic fantasies, not nighttime fever dreams. Nevertheless, he woke that morning uncomfortably hard and unable to do anything about it. He doubted Meier would say anything if he did. It took a lot to incite conversation with that man.

Gil focused, shutting out everything but the need to keep marching. *Hup-hup-hup-hup.*

"Hold it," Orel commanded. Gil froze. He watched as the officer picked up a piece of blue cloth, waving like a tiny pennant from the branch of a spiny bush. "Ha. I'm never wrong."

The Russian reached into his bag and pulled out a set of field glasses to scan the panorama.

"How far ahead are they, sir?" Gil shifted his feet impatiently. Every shadow on every rock was a turban or a shaggy-bearded face.

They were too exposed on the hillside, but he seemed the only one concerned. Orel carefully stowed his binoculars, letting out a satisfied grunt. Meier rubbed Fritz's nose and whispered something endearing in German, oblivious to the danger. Gil held his breath and lifted his rifle until the movement out of the corner of his eye turned out to be a hopping vulture with a snake in its sickle-shaped beak. He sighed, and his shoulders relaxed.

The echo of a gunshot somewhere in the hills ahead snapped him out of his reverie. He and Meier unslung their Lebels and checked their cartridges. Orel just whistled and tugged on Anya's reins, perfectly happy to march into whatever the hell was going on up there. Gil rolled his eyes, checked the horizon, and followed. He wasn't ashamed to crouch beside Fritz, leaving himself exposed on only one side.

A hundred yards later, they had to go through a narrow pass leading to a blind turn. Orel paused for a moment, recognizing the danger. Gil thought maybe the Colonel was going to show good sense and hold off, but a second shot and a high-pitched scream impelled him and Anya through the gap. The privates followed, with Gil cursing under his breath.

Whoever screamed spoke German. Over the sound of two more shots, someone yelled in French with a thick German accent, "Oh Christ, they got me. The motherless dogs—"

Another voice shouted, *"Dieter, geht es dir gut?"* Dieter didn't answer, and the second German repeated the question, an octave higher and much louder. Two more rifles barked out, and everything was quiet for a moment.

Orel crouched low and motioned Gil and Meier forward. He took a deep breath and risked a quick glance around the corner, then stiffened his back and walked on without waiting to see if they followed. For a second, Gil couldn't get his feet to move, but the sensation of Meier brushing past him snapped him back to reality.

After the blind corner, the trail plunged steeply into a stony basin. At the bottom, something in a dark blue uniform lay spread-eagled on the ground, face down and deathly still. So much for Dieter, Gil thought. The other deserter sat in the shadow of a rocky tor, hugging his knees with his head down.

Two figures in homespun tunics scrambled down the rocks, holding their rifles over their heads and shouting defiance. The dialect was incomprehensible, but Gil recognized a victory yell when he heard it.

"Heathen bastards," Orel shouted and fired at the nearest Berber. With a surprised shriek, the running figure changed direction and took shelter further up the hill. He turned to his companions. "I'll hold them off. You get that one." He pointed at the live soldier and handed Gil a set of heavy iron manacles.

Gil moved automatically. He went several yards before he thought to ask what the hell he was doing, and why was he risking himself for a worthless traitor? He had no love for the police, even less after half a decade in Marseille. Unlike most little boys, he'd never dreamed of being one. Still, orders were orders.

Orel leaned against an outcrop and fired off three shots in succession, two at the fleeing Berber and one on the other side of the rocky bowl where the second one hid. That brought an angry shout from a much older voice and a return of gunfire.

Duck walking down the gravel slope, Meier and Gil cursed Orel and the deserters while trying to avoid becoming targets themselves. They were a couple of hundred feet from where the nameless German crouched when Gil felt his footing slip. He skied down the hill, tucking into a roll and winding up in a heap beside the sobbing deserter.

The German stopped blubbering long enough to ask in French, "Who the hell are you?"

Gil crawled on hands and knees into what little shelter was left. "I'm here to rescue you. Show some gratitude, you jackass."

The firing had reached a stalemate. An occasional shot rang out, but mostly Orel, Meier and the two Berbers stared across the stony wadi, daring the others to show themselves like men. In the gully, the two legionnaires stared each other down. Finally, Gil grabbed the man's shirtfront but got his hand swatted.

"*Nein.* I'm not going back."

"Well, you can't bloody stay here, can you? Come on." Gil shut up when he saw a service revolver pointing at his face.

"I'm never going back. I'm going home. Screw the French. Screw the Legion. Doubly screw Morocco or wherever the hell we are."

Gil saw Meier had stopped halfway down the hill. The Alsatian would provide cover fire if needed, but he was alone with someone who had no intention of returning with him. "I'm Gil. Gil Vincente. Who are you?"

The stranger reached into his shirt and pulled out his metal *plaque d'identification*. He threw it on the ground and stomped it with his boot. "Fuck the Legion and fuck you. I'm just a German going home."

Gil tried grabbing at the man, but the German punched him square in the face. He groaned and cupped his hands over his nose, trying to clear his vision and stop the stars orbiting his head. "Christ, what did you do that for?"

The nameless German stood, ignoring the danger from the tribesmen. He yelled at Gil, "You're English, *ja*? Come with us. They're helping people like us go home."

Between the thick accent and still reeling from that punch to the face, Gil understood very little of what the man said. "Who's helping you?"

He never got his answer. A single shot came from far enough away that the back of the deserter's head exploded a split second before he heard the sound. A tribesman ululated in triumph as the body crumpled at Gil's feet.

Five shots in rapid succession from Orel and Meier sent the enemy skittering away, empty-handed but happy with the body count for one day. A deathly silence followed.

When it was clear they were gone for good, Orel joined Gil. Meier returned to watch the mules. The officer stomped over to Dieter first, patting him down and picking up the man's sidearm, a shopworn *Revolver de Ordonnance Modèle 1892.*

Then he dug into the dead man's pockets. First, he pulled out the man's identification book. Then, he took a single sheet of crumpled paper and examined it before wadding it up and shoving it into his own pocket. He pointed at the other body, exposed on the desert floor.

"Don't just stand there looking like an idiot. Get the other one's identification and weapons. Leave the bodies."

"Really?" Gil tried lugging the dead man's corpse, but it was too heavy. He tugged a second time. "We can't just leave them here."

Orel stood and wiped his brow. "You want to haul rotten meat across a desert? Help yourself. They were perfectly happy to leave everyone else. The Arabs did us a favor. We have proof they're dead. We did our job." Orel stared at Gil. "Thank you, private."

Gil dropped the body and wiped his hands on his pants, the blood and dust forming a grisly muck that left muddy tracks. With a heavy sigh, he pulled out the small identification booklet. "What kind of cretin deserts but keeps his military passport on him?"

Orel snorted. "The same kind of idiot who thought he could get away from me."

The man, whose *anonymat* was Alexander Flieder, had the same note in his pocket as his compatriot. Gill uncrumpled the paper. In both French and German, it read:

Men of the Legion,

Why die for France? The Kaiser and his government will help.

Anyone who wishes to return home. We will return you to your country of origin.

Come with us and live.

Gil asked, "What does this mean?"

Orel pulled the paper from his pocket and waved it at Gil. "Means we are in trouble, is what it means."

CHAPTER 22

"I'm going to miss you," Thibault said. The shovelful of mule crap landed inches from the old man's foot.

Gil grunted and launched another load, closer but not hitting the old stable master's boots. It kept him from getting too close. "*Bien sur*, where else will you find someone who cleans a stable like I do?"

"Heh heh. Not with your aim for sure. But I'm sorry they're sending you out. You're good with the mules. You treat them well, but don't care too much."

"So now I'm officer material?" The men laughed. Gil leaned on his shovel, taking a break while Thibault rolled and lit a poor excuse for a cigarette. Half of the tobacco wound up on his shirt. Both men pretended not to notice.

After a few moments of quiet, Thibault took a seat on Gauthier's carved stool. "The whole Twenty-Fourth is going to Béchar. Something is coming."

Gil grabbed handfuls of straw and threw them onto the stable floor. "I heard that. Don't know what they expect. There's nothing there but rocks and sand. A couple of toothless tribesmen. Hardly worth fighting for."

Someone thought it was. "Since when did that ever stop them? When do you leave?"

Two days. In two days, he would head out with dozens of others to join the madness back at Fort Béchar in the *Sud Orananais*. He'd just gotten used to life back in the barracks again; well-made beds, decent food, a daily routine with just enough variance to keep the soul from going numb, but no one shooting at you. It felt too good to last. Of course it was.

But with routine came other problems. Too much time alone with his thoughts, for starters. Like most nights since his return, his dreams of Colette were becoming problematic. He woke in the middle of the night, achingly hard. Sex with her was never great in reality. Certainly not frequent. She was more romance than ardor, and her list of taboos was impressive, not to mention frustrating. Still, she was a warm and bright spot in the darkness that was life on the streets of Marseille. It was the touch, any touch, he supposed. And she had nursed him after his pathetic attempt at self-destruction. Maybe it was gratitude he felt.

Still, in a barracks there were only so many ways to handle a growing problem. Gil groaned at his own pun. He could try to solve the matter under the blankets, but that risked exposure and mockery if caught. There were the latrines, but they were hardly conducive to erotic, let alone romantic, thoughts. Like all places full of lonely men, there were colleagues who would gladly give him relief. Everyone knew who was game, and who wasn't. That mattered, because approaching the wrong person could get you killed. Such behavior was frowned on, of course, but as long as everyone was discrete and there were no romantic entanglements leading to fights, it was like gambling. Officially taboo, but largely ignored unless it became a problem, then punishment was fast and severe.

It wasn't Gil's thing. He wasn't opposed to the idea on principle, but never wanted unnecessary attachments, and sharing a tent or bunkhouse with anyone who knew his secrets made him uneasy.

That left one option. He was never one to frequent whorehouses. It was too impersonal for the most intimate of acts and seldom satisfied the actual ache. But after being gone almost a month with no way to spend his money, he had the means. God knows he had the need. Maybe it was time to finally pay Rose a visit.

First things first. Gil was supposed to meet Dupre and the others at le Chat Noir later that evening, but he had plenty of time to go over his pack for the tenth time. He carefully removed each item and laid it on his perfectly made bed. The last thing he pulled out was the ornate knife he'd taken from the bandit on his first trip out. He held it in his hand, gratified by the balance and how it felt in his grip. Here was a good-luck charm, too good to lose. He placed it at the very bottom corner of his pack, then added each item of his uniform. Last was his toiletry kit.

Gil glimpsed himself in the mirror and disapproved of what he saw. His beard grew quickly, and the face looking back at him uncomfortably resembled his *Gilbert Le Lion* days. That wouldn't do. He looked shaggy but respectable, even if he smelled like mule crap. A visit to the barber before leaving and he'd be the soldier he wanted to be and not the loser he left behind in France. A quick rinse before heading to town would be the polite thing to do, given his evening plans.

Dupre, LaForce, and Gomez were already at the café waiting for him when he entered. There was no sign of Meier, who had been sent back with him. Someone thought he and Gil were a team now. Not likely. He'd been sure not to invite the man and didn't think anyone else would.

It had been a month since he had seen the others, so he stared in surprise at the table. "What the hell is that thing?" Dupre's face was covered with a full black beard, so thick and coarse it looked like he'd glued steel wool to his face.

Dupre laughed. "It's a real legionnaire's beard. Beautiful, isn't it?" He stroked his facial hair, dislodging a bread crumb the size of a *centime,* which fell to the table. Next to him, Jean LaForce had also attempted to grow a beard in imitation of his hero, but with far less successful results. Uneven patches of blond fuzz covered his cheeks, with a little thicker growth under his chin. Gomez had allowed his moustache to thicken nicely but was otherwise shorn, claiming his girl liked to see his face.

Gil nodded to Jean. "Looks good." The kid beamed back.

Dupre shook his head. "I've got more hair bet32wen my legs, but our little boy is growing into a man, huh?" The sparse beard couldn't hide the flush on the lad's cheeks. "What's with you? Why bother shaving? We're heading out to the middle of Christ knows where in two days."

Gil had his reasons. Routine. Maintaining a new life. Order. Nobody else knew or cared. "You don't hide a work of art like this behind a shower curtain."

The owner's wife came by with their drinks, her loose breasts swaying behind a thin cotton chemise. "What's so funny?"

Dupre slapped the table. "The Englishman thinks his naked face looks better than my beautiful hairiness."

She sniffed. "My old man's naked arse looks better than that furry monstrosity." Dupre stuck out his lip and feigned outrage until she grabbed his head and held it to her chest, making the breasts slap his cheeks. After a second, she released him and turned away to the next table.

"She loves it. They all do," said Dupre.

Gil only half listened. His eyes scanned the room for Rose, but the only woman in the place beside the landlady was a too-young Arab girl who was flirting shamelessly with all the older soldiers. Gil tsked through his teeth. That wouldn't do for so many reasons.

Was she still there? Maybe she found herself a husband—it wouldn't be the first time a woman like her found a lonely widower or farmer and retired. He couldn't imagine her just leaving a goldmine like Sidi Bel Abbès, although the lure of France or children may have been too much for her. More likely, she was just out for a smoke. Gil calmed his thinking and pretended to care about Gomez's latest story.

Maybe it wasn't his night.

Not wanting to waste his money on alcohol, and not wanting it to affect his performance if the opportunity presented itself, he thought to check outside where he'd seen Rose smoking before. It took some maneuvering to get through the crowd. With so many men marching out in two days, everyone was eager to say goodbye to each other and use up pay that would be useless on the march.

She wasn't there. Maybe just as well. He resisted bumming a smoke and stepped out to feel the cool, fresh evening air. A thin line of orange separated the ground from sky, and he leaned against the stone building, enjoying the scene. A warbler sang goodnight to the town, then fell silent as darkness took over and the gas lights sputtered to life.

Gil was about to head back to barracks when a female figure emerged from the side of the café. Rose wore a green dress, a little frayed at the hem, but it clung to her body and moved in a way that made him smile.

"Good evening," she said in response to his friendly nod. Rose stopped and pulled a cheroot from her handbag. She waited for Gil to light it, but he held his hands out to show he didn't have a light. With a crooked grin, she handed him a book of matches. He lit it for her, shielding the flame. She touched his hand and leaned forward.

Letting the smoke escape her nose in two streams, she picked tobacco from her teeth. "Just catching the air?"

Gil paused just a second before answering, "Actually, I was looking for you, if you can believe it."

"Don't tell me it's someday already." Her mouth smiled wider than her eyes did.

"It would appear so. Would you like to..." His voice trailed off, unsure how to finish the sentence that didn't sound ridiculous. This transaction was always ridiculous, one reason he seldom went to professionals. Your dignity was shot before you even began.

She patted his arm. "Go up to number three. I have to tell the old bat I'm here, then I'll meet you."

He felt his shoulders relax. That would spare him everyone watching them go upstairs together. "Sounds terrific." He hoped it sounded appropriately enthusiastic, but not too eager.

The mythical, magical Number Three was a room he'd been in many times; Newcastle, Capetown, Marseille, they all looked alike. A vanity with perfume bottles, a washbasin and a pitcher of water, a changing screen, a threadbare chair and a narrow bed took up every inch of space. He was relieved to see the bed was well made. There were clear advantages in being the first customer of the evening.

Unsure what else to do, he sat on the bed, facing the door. With each set of footsteps passing the door, he felt more and more like this was a stupid mistake.

He rose to his feet and tucked in his shirt, determined to call it off. He sat back down when the doorknob rattled and Rose stepped in.

"Still dressed?" she asked, removing her earrings as she walked to the vanity. She gave him an appraising glance. "You have something for me, I presume?"

Feeling like a stupid schoolboy, Gil handed her several franc notes. She stuffed it in the top of her dress and stepped behind the screen. "Well, get ready for me, dearie. I promise not to peek."

Gil quickly stripped to his undershirt and shorts, carefully folding his uniform over the chair. He felt more nervous than aroused, but knew from experience that would pass.

Rose emerged in a black basque that had seen better days. She wore fishnet stockings with jagged runs down the back of each leg. With no panties, her thick patch was visible in the dim light.

She sat on the bed and patted the spot next to her. "What did you have in mind? Anything special?"

Gil obeyed without looking at her. "Nothing special, just- you know."

Her hand rested on his thigh and slowly trailed up. "I do know. Rose knows all about it." She reached into his shorts and found his manhood. It just lay there, uncharmed by her smile.

"I- " Gil sputtered something indecipherable, but she held a finger to his lips.

"It's okay. When was the last time for you?"

"Months ago. In Marseille."

"You had a girl?" He nodded. She smiled, one hand on his leg, one rubbing his back. She leaned in and whispered in his ear, "She won't know.... Just relax."

God knows he tried. Rose shifted on the bed and patted the pillow. Gil laid back, looking at a crack that ran across the ceiling. "Here, now tell me. What was her name?"

Gil didn't know why he answered, "Colette. But..."

"Shhh. Did she touch you like this?" Her hand snaked inside his underwear, cool against the warm but unresponsive flesh.

"No," he said, his voice harsh. "She wouldn't, she was nothing like- "

"Me? Ah. So she was a good girl? Lucky you." Her fingernails scratched lightly all around his groin. Her blue, bloodshot eyes were locked on his. "But when you think about her, she's not a good girl, is she?" They both felt him twitch.

"In fact, you think about her being a very naughty girl. Don't you? Her hand was probably very little and soft, so ladylike. Not like Rose's. But then, she never made you feel like this, did she? Never liked the feel of a man in her hand like I do."

Gil groaned as he felt himself harden. Encouraged, Rose squeezed tighter, stroking now. Hot breath hissed in his ear. "You wish she did, though. You want your sweet little Colette to act like a naughty girl? Go ahead, picture it." She licked her lips, and her eyes really smiled at him as he grew harder. Her hand grew more insistent.

"Oh, my God." Gil couldn't help himself. A vision of Colette in Rose's place filled his mind. She wasn't the nearly chaste, sweet nurturer but a wanton, needy woman, taking delight in the feel of her man in her hand. Gil felt his body tense and shut his eyes harder.

Rose suddenly pulled her hand away, leaving him hard and aching. She turned and scooped something from a jar on the bedside table. Petroleum jelly. She returned her hand, now slick and cool.

The woman's voice was sibilant in his ear, the breath warm on his skin. He closed his eyes. "That's it. Give it to her. Give it to Colette. She wants it. I want it. Do it. For me. Do it for me, *Cherie.*"

His mind swam with images, some romantic and lovely, some unimaginably filthy and dark. Unable to help himself, Gil's muscles tightened.

Rose chuckled and kept stroking, laughing with pride. "That's it. Let it go." With a growl like a bear, he gritted his teeth, threw his head back against the pillows, and climaxed. She stroked and squeezed until he pushed her hand away, far too sensitive to take any more.

Rose stood and used a handkerchief to clean her hands. "Feel better? Oh, maybe not what you were expecting, but sometimes the unexpected is good, *non?*"

A little unsure what happened, Gil sat up on one elbow. "No, it was... good. Thank you. And a little... unexpected."

Rose was already slipping her dress on. "Are you leaving with that lot on Thursday?"

Gil nodded. "Yeah. Morocco. Well, Fort Béchar. Almost Morocco."

Rose slipped her earrings into her lobes. "I don't suppose you'll visit me before you leave? No, never mind. But I expect you to come to me when you get back. We'll celebrate. What do you say?"

Gil stood and reached for his clothes. "Yes, that sounds good. I mean, thank you. It was... nice."

Rose gave a wicked smile. "But not too nice. Apparently, that's not your type." She kissed him on the cheek and held the door open.

With burning cheeks, he stepped through the door and turned as if to say something. Whatever it was, it stuck in his throat. Quietly, Gil slipped down the back stairs so he wouldn't have to go through the crowded bar.

CHAPTER 23

Whoever said they were headed to Morocco to put down a few renegade tribesmen, or yet another religious uprising, was a goddamned liar. Hundreds of troops, some from Sidi, some from other forts and encampments across the civilized parts of Algeria, set out at dawn. They were an invasion force.

Thibault handed Gil his flask, already half-drained. "For luck, *mon ami*. Most of these poor buggers will never come back."

"You're a cheery bastard this morning. They're good men, good enough anyway. What I've seen of the local tribes doesn't exactly scare me."

Since Gil hadn't taken a drink, the old stable master grabbed it back and took another swig. "Soldiers are replaceable. I was talking about the mules. Heh-heh."

Hooves stomped the ground. Long-eared heads tossed wildly, and braying protests filled the dawn air. The animals seemed to have a better sense of what they were walking into than the men. Reaching to his left, Gil patted Fritz's nose. Meier stood on the other side, patting the black animal's withers and tail. Somehow, the taciturn Alsatian found him and got assigned as his marching partner.

Some legionnaires smoked and joked nervously with each other and shifted from foot to foot, awaiting the order to march. Less than half of them, although too many for Gil's liking, stared straight ahead, eyes dead, biting their lips, not saying a thing.

That wasn't quite true, he realized. An unexpected number muttered prayers, lying to themselves that someone up there would keep them safe. Gil ignored the fatalists. If you imagined the worst, you'd not be disappointed. He plastered a determined look on his face and awaited the order to march. It's what legionnaires did.

Somewhere among the hundreds of men were Dupre and LaForce. The boy had bolted himself to the big oaf who loved playing the role of big brother. Gil hoped he'd find them when they stopped for the night. Meier was inoffensive, but not brilliant company. Usually, he wished his bunkmates would shut up, but his current partner saved all his best conversations for Fritz.

There were too many of them to muster in the parade ground, so they gathered on the flat plain in back of the fort. Hundreds of men, mules and horses stomped the ground and kicked up clouds of dust, anticipating or dreading the command to march.

A buzz like a hundred beehives caught Gil's attention. Up ahead, through the gates, he saw the chaos become order as men fell in line. Huge caissons carrying the artillery took their positions.

Thibault's eyes were watery, and he wondered if it was more than the drink. "*Bien.* You're off. Stay safe and take care of them."

Gil grinned and shouldered his pack. "I know. You mean the mules."

Thibault shrugged. "And yourself, you grumpy tightass."

Meier whistled and said something in German. Fritz shook his shaggy mane, twitched his ears and stepped forward.

Gil looked at his partner over the mounds of gear on the mule's back. He felt the tiniest pang of jealousy. "You talk to him in German? He's a French mule, you know."

Meier scratched at the big velvety ears. "I'm the only one that talks to him."

"You talk to him more than you talk to me."

Meier smirked. "He tells better jokes." As if on cue, Fritz lifted his wispy tail and dropped three soft, wet turd balls on Gil's boot. "See?"

Gil cursed loudly and knelt to clean his boot, only to realize he didn't have a cloth or anything handy. There was no way he was going to use his hand. Frozen in place, panicky eyes searched everywhere for something to use until he heard a loud cough.

Meier handed him an old shoe rag. "Here." Gil took it gratefully and removed every smear and flake of the mess. Meier leaned forward and whispered in the mule's ear, "Good boy." Gil tossed the scrap of cloth as far from him as he could, as if it were a grenade with a hair trigger.

He groaned as from the front of the long, snaking line the familiar refrain began:

Our ancestors knew how to die
For the glory of the Legion.
We will all know how to perish
Following tradition.
During our far-off campaigns,
Facing fever and fire,

To his amazement, Meier piped up, singing loud and strong in a surprisingly lovely tenor. Who knew he could sing? Fritz honked loudly, joining in. At Meier's urging, Gil finally added his voice, imperceptible at first and then louder.

The line in front thinned out, and the soldiers still inside the fort formed ranks and set out the gates. The Twenty-Fourth Mobile began its march to war. Gil was in perfect form, one arm shouldering his Lebel, the other swinging confidently. That stupid song seemed to help. He felt good. Alive.

Like a soldier.

Their first overnight was at a poor excuse for an oasis, but on a flat plain with plenty of room for the swelling army and no worries about ambushes or attacks. Anyone coming would be visible miles away. The men quickly unpacked the tents off their mules, set up home for the night, and then gathered around a series of campfires.

The mood was relaxed. Men smoked and laughed, still glowing with the rush that accompanies the beginning of a campaign. It would wear off soon enough. They should enjoy it while they could.

Gil found himself smiling. He'd slept well last night. Probably would again tonight. After his evening with Rose, Colette's nocturnal visits were sweet and chaste again. She was a comfort rather than a torment. And here he was, being a soldier. Everything was right in his world.

"There you are, you miserable bastard." Gil heard a booming laugh and looked up to see Dupre stomping towards him, arms wide open. His gigantic beard was so black against the darkness he looked faceless. Behind him trailed LaForce, beaming as well.

Gil groaned and rose to his feet, meekly accepting his friend's bear hug. Resistance was futile, and it would be over faster if he just gave in. The burst of joyous silliness was a welcome respite from Meier's practically mute company.

"I knew you'd be here somewhere. Someone has to tend to our noble mounts while we actual soldiers do the fighting, huh?" Dupre was in high spirits.

"Well, you know how it is. When you get yourself killed, someone has to tote your carcass home." Dupre threw his head back and laughed. LaForce forced himself to laugh along.

"Oh, Meier. This hairy whoreson is Gus Dupre." Meier stood and the two men nodded companionably across the fire. "The skinny one there is another bloody Alsatian. Jean LaForce. Johnny Strong, we call him."

LaForce took a step forward, then stopped. Meier had extended his hand, but quickly pulled it back. The two young men stiffened and crossed their arms, glaring at each other through the fire's smoke.

Meier spoke out of the corner of his mouth, his eyes never leaving LaForce's. "He's a friend of yours?"

Dupre's smile fell, and he asked, "You two know each other?" Despite the roaring fire, the mood was icy as the countrymen stared each other down. Neither spoke for an eternity.

Dupre was not to be denied. "Is there a problem here?"

Meier dropped his tin mug to the ground. "Yes, there is. This little maggot knows what it is." Dupre and Gil exchanged shocked looks.

LaForce brought himself to his full height and lifted his chin defiantly. He turned his back on the men, intending to leave. Meier wasn't having it. "Don't you walk away from me, Manot."

Dupre asked, "Who the hell's Manot?" Gil shook his head at the big man. Now was not the time. The air smelled of smoke and latent violence.

"I said don't walk away from me. You killed him, you son of a bitch."

LaForce glared back, his lip quivering, eyes shining in the firelight. His hands clenched into fists, and he pounded them against his thighs again and again.

Dupre leaned towards Gil and whispered, "Who did he kill?"

Meier provided the answer. "My uncle."

"A pig who beats on women," said LaForce through clenched teeth.

"Maybe the fat whore had it coming."

The words had barely left Meier's mouth when LaForce let out a war cry, and leapt across the campfire in a headlong attack. Meier put his hands up in time to grab the younger man and spin him away into the darkness. Then he leapt on top of him, fists pounding like piledrivers. LaForce tried to protect himself, rolling into as tight a ball as he could.

By now, the chaos had attracted a crowd of legionnaires, delighted to get a little free entertainment. Lard-Ass had a happy grin on his face. "Kick his ass!"

"What did he do?" asked a corporal.

"Who cares?" the fat soldier chuckled.

A sharp whistle cut through the night. Sergeant Becker blew it three times and yelled, "What the Christ is going on here?" The crowd parted to afford him a good look. By now, LaForce had managed to get to his feet and was throwing punches at Meier with lethal intentions.

The Sergeant blew his whistle again. "Knock it off. Save it for the Arabs." Neither combatant was willing to stop. A nod from the sergeant and four legionnaires stepped in between the combatants, separating the men.

"You should both be in the stockade for this, but we need you for cannon fodder." The sergeant pointed at LaForce, who'd taken most of the damage. "Who does this one belong to?"

Dupre raised his hand. "I have him, sir. We're way back there," he said, pointing behind them. At a nod from the officer, he grabbed the young man's elbow and yanked him away to groans of disappointment from the other men.

"This isn't over," shouted Meier, his face red, the beginnings of a shiner visible in the firelight.

Becker got in his face. "The hell it's not! I don't want to hear any more about it. Every man here is your comrade. Get it through your thick skulls. You depend on each other to stay alive."

Meier stamped his foot, ignoring the difference in rank. "The hell I will. He's a filthy murderer."

The sergeant sniffed. "Half the men here are murderers. Hell, the chaplain's killed two men that I know of. This is the last of it. Anybody kills anyone, I'll do it. Understand?" Both combatants muttered their assent. It didn't satisfy the big soldier. "Excuse me?"

"Yes, sir," they both answered with a salute. Each stared daggers at the other.

"Get them out of my sight," he barked. Dupre led LaForce away and Gil stepped in front of Meier, cutting off any attempt to follow.

Gil put his hands on Meier's shoulders and said, "Enough. Let's go."

Meier nodded, but glared at LaForce's retreating back.

"Your friend is a dead man," seethed Meier.

Gil looked at Meier. "We all are. We just don't know it yet. This is the Legion, right?" It was a half-hearted attempt to break the mood, but all he could think of was a night weeks ago. When a drunken LaForce told him that the bandit wasn't the first man he'd killed. At the time, he'd laughed it off.

No one was laughing now.

CHAPTER 24

"He sliced my uncle up like a hog."

After weeks of having to drag even a full sentence out of Meier, Gil found he couldn't shut him up now. Morning was coming, and with it, another endless day of marching. "And I can't believe you're friends with the little schwanzlutscher."

Gil rolled over and turned his back to his tent-mate. "Christ, get some sleep. And he's not my friend—exactly. We enlisted at the same time, is all. You know how it is."

He pictured LaForce's—no; he was still Jacques Manot then—cherubic face that morning in the recruiting office. Innocent, frightened. Even with a month's worth of beard, the kid looked more like a bank clerk or school-teacher than a killer.

Then he remembered the look on the bandit's face and the chilling banshee cry when LaForce's bayonet ripped through his throat. Certainly, the kid was a killer. But a murderer? Every soldier understood the difference. He ignored his partner's rant as best he could and drifted into a fitful sleep that offered no proper rest.

Far too early reveille ripped through the dawn's light. Gil groaned and rolled over to see Meier flat on his back, snoring. Burning with resentment, he buttoned his pants and pulled on his shirt. Then he indulged himself and kicked Meier's foot not too gently. "Get your ass up."

Without waiting for an answer, he stooped low, stepped out of the tent, then stood and grabbed his back to stretch. The scene in front of him was like an anthill kicked by a schoolboy. Men shouted and darted everywhere, mules brayed, and the clamoring chaos of camp breaking was deafening.

Thankfully, he didn't see LaForce or Dupre. Gil had no need or desire to find himself in the middle of a brewing feud. He walked to the smoking embers of a campfire and got a tin mug of the brown sludge that passed for coffee. The scalding metal burned his hands, but the need for caffeine outweighed the discomfort. When the fog behind his eyes finally lifted, he set out for the makeshift pen where Fritz waited.

The mule wasn't happy to see its least-favorite master, but after one good tug on the rope, it consented to be led back to the tent for loading. Gil shh-shhed him and stroked his nose. If not with affection, at least in an effort at calling a truce.

"What in Christ's name was all that last night?" A familiar voice reached Gil from behind. Dupre's huge hand caught his shoulder and spun him around.

Gil pushed the hand away. "I don't know, Gus, but it's got nothing to do with you or me. It's their fight."

Before he could answer, they heard a third voice. "What are you doing here? Come to fight your boyfriend's battles?" Gus groaned as Meier stomped up and got in Dupre's face. His chin barely reached the bottom of the bigger man's beard, but his eyes glared with too much hatred for so early in the day.

Dupre bristled and shoved Meier back a step. Not too hard, but the message was clear. "Back off, or I'll kick your arse into tomorrow."

Gil wanted nothing more than to walk away and get Fritz properly loaded, but both men turned to him as if expecting him to take their side. Before he was forced to say or do anything, Sergeant Becker stormed up to them and yelled, "What the hell do you think you're doing? Get your gear loaded and quit gabbing like old women."

Gil stepped back and snapped to attention, complete with a salute. Dupre did the same, if more lackadaisical about it. Meier's good sense abandoned him. "Sergeant—"

"Did I ask you to speak? I gave you an order, private."

Meier's good sense returned, and he saluted, muttering something under his breath. Becker's best glare strangled the complaint in its crib. "Sir."

Becker had already moved on to the next group of incompetents before the word was out of Meier's mouth. Gil took his arm and led him away. "Let's go. We have work to do."

Dupre shouted, "We need to talk about this."

"The hell we do," Gil responded.

It took less than a minute to break down the tent. The poles and canvas were perfectly rolled and piled on Fritz's stoic back. In his anger, Meier tossed his saddlebags on, dislodging Gil's. Everything was askew, forming a misshapen lump. Fritz objected to having the burden slammed onto his back and kicked back, barely missing Gil's crotch.

He shouted at the mule, "What the hell did I do?"

He watched as Meier, fuming silently, shoved anything loose in between cracks and holes in the cargo. His cheeks burned, his hands sweated, and at last he couldn't take it a second more.

"Stop, goddammit. What are you doing? You can't pack it like that!" Gil knew he was shouting, but couldn't help himself. In a fury, he unstrapped a leather belt and watched as half Fritz's load slipped to the ground, then grabbed the rest and began pulling it off, dropping it into the dirt. He stripped Fritz to the blanket, throwing gear with loud grunts and curses.

Meier's mouth gaped open. "What are you doing? I just loaded—"

"You were doing a crappy job of it. These things have to be done properly."

"It was fine," Meier sulked.

Gil felt his palms dampen. "It was bloody awful. You need to take care of these things, or you'll damage your gear. Not to mention poor Fritz here. You have to have order. See? Order."

He placed the saddlebags back and adjusted them carefully. Then the ammo. Piece by piece, he built a masterpiece of organization and straight lines. Fritz accepted the banging and pulling on his back with equanimity.

Meier just gawked. "You're a madman."

Gil inspected and reinspected his work. "A place for everything, everything in its place." He repeated it over and over before realizing he was speaking in English.

"Vincente. Meier. What's the holdup?" Sergeant Becker shouted. Gil was too busy loosening and re-tightening the breast strap and rear buckles to respond.

Finally, Meier piped up. "Almost done, sergeant."

"Get a move on. Whatever lover's quarrel you two have going on, we don't have time for it today. Last idiots in line get guard duty."

With that threat hanging in the air, Meier reached for the last strap, but Gil slapped his hands away. "Don't. I'll do it. It has to be right."

"Suit yourself, you mad turd. But if I wind up on guard duty because of you, you'll regret it."

In French he said, "Come on you." He tugged on Fritz's reins and nearly fell on his ass when the big mule didn't move. Gil stood up and clenched his fist, glaring at the beast. "I said come on." He yanked on the reins again. The john stood still, then took a few grudging steps forward.

Meier ran his hand over Fritz's mane. "Good boy. Ignore the crazy man."

"Kiss my arse," Gil said in English.

CHAPTER 25

They wound up on watch anyway. The overnight bivouac was on a flat plain close to water, or at least a shallow brackish pool. Five campfires provided enough heat for coffee. One of the fires smelled of roasted meat. Some lucky bastard shot an antelope on the march and was able to share the stringy, gamey spoils with a few of his mates.

Gil and Meier weren't so lucky. They were walking their assigned part of the perimeter, fueled by coffee, stale bread, and dry, tasteless sausage. The rest of their energy came from simmering resentment. Meier was still furious about the scene with the stubborn animal, and that Gil didn't seem ready to just slit LaForce's throat there and then. Gil couldn't understand why he couldn't get through to his campmate that he wanted no part of a feud, and reloading the mule wasn't personal. Order was order, and nothing mattered more.

Becker clearly realized that keeping them separated might be the best plan and sent them to patrol opposite ends of the camp. That was fine with Gil. He walked his patrol in blessed silence. Every few minutes, he stopped to look up at the ceiling of white pinpricks. A shooting star traced a faint line across the horizon. A chilly breeze found its way inside his coat, and he buttoned it to the neck. His stubbly cheeks stung pleasantly. He allowed himself to crack his first smile in days.

An hour into his watch, he heard gravel crunch to his right. His breath caught, and he raised his weapon. Squinting down the barrel, he swung left then right but couldn't spot any movement. He lowered his rifle, shook his head to clear it, and raised it again. "Halt. *Qui va là-bas?*"

A voice hissed out, "It's me." That was no answer. Gil pointed his Lebel at the source of the sound.

"Identify yourself." He raised the tin whistle, ready to put it between his lips.

A skinny figure stepped close enough for him to recognize. The shape raised its hands. "Don't shoot."

"Christ, LaForce. What are you doing out here?"

"I needed to talk to you."

Gil's shoulders sagged. "You're lucky I'm not Meier."

"Schmidt, you mean. Daniel Schmidt." LaForce put a thin, messy, hand-rolled cigarette to his lips and struck a match.

"Jesus, cover that match. You want to get shot?" He mimed cupping his hands together. The kid had no clue what he was doing. Again. "Since when do you smoke?"

"Dupre shared some of his tobacco with me." He held the cigarette out to Gil, who shook it off. Smoking was an expensive, not to mention messy, habit. He'd quit before and was determined it would stick this time.

Grateful that the boy had detached himself, Gil couldn't help wondering if clinging to Gus Dupre like a barnacle on a whale's arse was a good thing for anyone. Then he wondered why he gave a crap.

"What are you doing out here?" Gil looked around to make sure nobody, especially Meier, saw them speaking. He was on duty, after all.

"What he said..." Gil didn't need to ask who he meant. "It's not true. Not exactly."

"Did you kill him? His uncle?"

LaForce threw his cigarette to the ground, the red cherry looking like a shooting star as it crashed to earth. "He was hurting my mother. They were...together. He would beat up on us. Her mostly. Me when I was around. Finally..."

Gil had the picture. The story had been played out a million times, so common it was both tragic and mundane. Even his own ass of a father raised fists to his mother when the drink took hold, and they'd been fond of each other. He finally backed down when young Gilbert stood up to him. What if he hadn't?

"It was self-defense. I swear."

Butchered like a hog, Meier had said.

"I don't care, I really don't," Gil said. "We've all done... things. Nobody is here because they're some kind of saint. All that matters is you're a soldier now. You're not that scared kid. You're Johnny goddamn Strong. Just stay out of Meier's way."

In the dark, it was hard to tell, but it looked like the kid was pouting. Jean LaForce kicked a stone. "What if he won't let it go?"

He didn't need all the drama and distraction. Gil turned away to look up at the moon hanging in the sky. There were no answers written there, but it helped calm him. He avoided looking at Jean. "The real fighting will start soon enough. They'll break the Twenty-Fourth into platoons, and you'll never have to see him again. Maybe he'll get shot. Maybe you will. If I'm lucky, it will be me, and I won't have to deal with either of you anymore."

Off in the distance, he saw two soldiers approaching to relieve him. "You'd best get out of here."

LaForce nodded. "Keep him away from me?"

Gil nodded and pointed back to the camp. "Yeah. Best I can."

LaForce was gone in a moment. Once he was relieved, Gil headed back to his bedroll. Meier intercepted him, and he groaned inwardly but gave a friendly head bob.

"Who were you talking to? Back there? I saw you with someone."

"An idiot out for a piss. He'd rather get shot than use the latrine like everyone else. It's quiet out there."

"Keep that kid away from me. Manot. LaForce. Whatever the little bastard calls himself now."

Gil stopped, locking eyes with his mule-mate. "I'll tell you what I told him. I'm not in the middle of anything. You two have a problem? Kill each other or don't, just don't drag me into it. My advice? Don't do anything. They'll split us up soon enough, and you'll never have to see him again."

"But he killed my uncle."

"So? Sounds like a real piece of shit to me, not that I knew the man."

Meier clenched his fist and took a step forward, but the warning flare in Gil's eyes stopped him cold. "He deserves to die."

"Deserve's got nothing to do with it. Happens to everyone. It's just a matter of when." He slapped Meier on the arm. "Come on, I need some shuteye. Morning is going to come too bloody early."

Their heavy boots trudged through the sand and gravel, past dozens of lean-to tents and dying campfires. "How much farther do you think?" asked Meier.

Gil yawned without covering his mouth. "Day after tomorrow, maybe? Mehnaba's closer than Fort Béchar, so... yeah. Day after."

"Keep him away from me til then."

"If you promise to shut up about him," said Gil.

<h1 style="text-align:center">CHAPTER 26</h1>

The trek became unbearable overnight.

Without warning, the days grew hotter. Yesterday, they marched and sang with a warm but steady breeze on their backs. Now, the wind had returned to its home on the Mediterranean, leaving dead air, baked thick by the desert sun. The Atlas Mountains thwarted any relief from the Atlantic winds. The day's march was like passing an open bread oven for hours at a time.

Besides the heat, the rising terrain complicated the march. It restricted the movement of men, mules and machine guns to a single narrow track, a glorified goat path barely distinguished from the scrub brush and loose stones. Rather than establish a solid rhythm to put one's mind elsewhere, the troop would slow to a crawl, pause, then they'd hurry to catch up. This was awful enough in daylight. The heat would soon require a switch to night marches, which brought their own brand of misery.

Gil and Meier had a tacit agreement to ignore each other as best they could. Meier murmured endearments to Fritz while Gil took on sole responsibility for loading the animal, who seemed to side with the Alsatian. Not that their feelings mattered a damn. Order mattered. If you want something done right, do it yourself. The effort left him satisfied with the results, but sweaty and ornery before they even took a step.

Wild speculation whispered down the line that there was a fight coming. Rumors were like that: Captain Vautier told someone who told the gunners who might have heard it from the lieutenant's valet. Whatever the source, they all said more or less the same thing. The meddlesome fake Mahdi had been dismissed as an annoyance, a flea on a camel's hairy brown ass. Instead, he secured surreptitious help from the Moroccan king and the local German consul. To absolutely no one's surprise but their own, the politicians and their pet strategists misjudged the level of resistance to the new French landlords.

By the time the sun was directly overhead, men began wilting. A few fell out of formation, faces scorched red, tongues thick with thirst. The pebble trick was insufficient under these conditions. Sergeants bellowed, berated and sometimes beat or kicked those who claimed they could go no further. Sun-drunk officers pretended not to notice the breach in military discipline. Captain Vautier, in particular, was in a foul mood and wouldn't tolerate any slacking.

The local *goumiers* watched and snickered from camelback or under the protection of lightweight cotton robes. They were support workers recruited, bribed, or threatened to join the French from the local, more compliant tribes. Whenever another legionnaire hit the ground, one of them would snort, then straighten their face and slowly approach with a gourd of water, offering just enough to get the slacker upright again.

In fits and starts, the men managed about fifteen miles before the line staggered to a complete stop. With no natural shade, men squatted in the shadow their mules provided, sometimes shoving and nearly coming to blows as they fought over what little shade they found.

Questions ran like dominoes up the line, and rumors drifted back.

"What's the problem?"

"Is the road blocked?"

"I heard someone's dead. Is it snipers?"

Gil did his best to ignore the nonsense. It was best never to respond to a rumor until you knew exactly what you were dealing with, no matter how tempting. It was too easy to take action, any action. More often or not, that got you in trouble. Measure twice, cut once.

Feeling slightly superior to those frantically making up answers, he closed his eyes and sat on a rock. He covered his face with his sash and breathed steadily. His thoughts drifted far enough into the desert. It took a while for the voice to reach his mind.

"Vincente. Gil Vincente. Where is he?"

At first, he tried pretending he couldn't hear. Unfortunately, Meier's ears worked just fine. "Here, Sergeant. He's here."

"Arsehole," Gil thought, slowly rising to his feet.

Becker was soaked with sweat, and the skin on his nose was already flaking and peeling. "Vincente!"

In a cracked, dry voice he said, "*Ici, Sergent.*"

"Grab your gear. Come with me." The sergeant mercifully pretended not to hear Gil's profane response.

Meier piped up, "Me too?" He was already gathering up Fritz's reins. Whatever the problem was, it had to be better than roasting in his own juices, bored out of his skull.

Becker shook his head. "Come if you want. We need Vincente. There's a mule causing trouble."

Gil didn't understand why, of the hundreds of men, they needed him, but he obeyed. It was what soldiers did, no matter how ridiculous the order.

"Vincente. Can I come?" Meier asked.

"If you think you can be useful." Gil took a swig from his canteen, reattached it to his pack, and followed Becker, who was already several steps ahead. Meier clicked his tongue and led Fritz past the bewildered soldiers, leaving whispers and even more rumors in their wake.

It took a quarter mile squeezing past soldiers, mules and a two-mule team hauling a seventy-five-millimeter *Canon de Montagne*, a mountain gun that would be devastating if they could get it to its destination in one piece. And assuming the battle wasn't over by the time it finally arrived.

Up ahead, the men clumped together, not allowing Gil to see anything. Over the buzzing, shouting and madness came the braying of a clearly annoyed johnny mule.

"Clear the way, you animals." Becker shouted as he, Gil, and Meier neared the scene of the commotion. Hearing his fellow pack mule in trouble, Fritz dug his hooves into the dusty sand. Meier tugged on the reins impatiently, then motioned for Gil to go ahead and patted the mule's mane while singing under his breath.

Stepping around a wagon, he saw the problem. A dun-colored mule sprawled on the ground, panting and snorting. It lay on its side, occasionally kicking a hind leg out at anyone foolish enough to be within reach. Two Maxim machine guns and a case of ammo were strapped to its back. The precious equipment was covered in dust, and the gun on the ground side was getting badly abused by the dirt and stones.

A pair of chagrined legionnaires looked up with wide eyes as Becker returned with Gil, who they assumed to be their savior. The crowd parted to allow him through, then closed tight behind him. No one wanted to miss the show.

The taller of the men saluted Becker, then spoke to Gil in a thick Belgian Flemish accent. "I don't know what happened. She was doing fine, and then she just laid down and refused to go any further." He grabbed the reins and yanked, causing the bit to tear at the corners of the mule's mouth. She protested loudly and tossed her head, pulling the reins from the Belgian's grasp. He landed in the dirt. Cursing and pointing.

"Just like that!" the soldier blew on his hands, burned by the leather straps being pulled across his palm.

Gil knelt down, out of arm's reach but focused intently on the animal. It was panting, but didn't seem otherwise hurt. There was no obvious blood, other than in the soft flesh of its mouth where the bit dug deep.

He walked a little closer on his knees and extended a shaking hand. "Hey girl, what's going on? We're not going to hurt each other, right?" His palm ran over her sweaty withers, then over the stomach. The mule looked at him with its big brown eyes. He continued his examination as best he could, staying out of range of those back legs or her bared teeth. His hands passed over ribs like a xylophone. The animal was far too skinny. That might be overwork, hunger, or both. Besides that, he found nothing wrong.

Gil heard the clip-clop of of horse hooves on stone and then a deep voice shouted, "What's the holdup? Get these men moving, Sergeant." Captain Vautier had black eyebrows like two pot brushes on a pale face. He rode a sweat-foamed black horse. The gelding brushed soldiers aside so Vautier could get a look at the obstacle to his precious plans.

"Mule down, sir," Becker explained. "We're working on it."

"What's wrong with it?" That question was aimed directly at Gil.

"I... I'm not sure yet. I just—" He squirmed at the unwanted attention.

The captain sniffed. "Is it wounded or just bloody useless?" The Belgian and his partner, who might have been his brother from the identical beard and blue eyes, were too terrified to answer.

Gil continued his inspection and found no reason for the mule to quit, other than it was hot. The machine guns were heavy—although less than the packs they all carried when they began the journey—and it was a damned mule.

"If it won't get up, it's no use to us and it's holding everyone up." The officer pulled out his pistol. A collective gasp went up from the assembly when they heard the hammer cock.

Gil held up his hands. "Wait! Sir, I mean, let me get these straps off her. I think she just needs to be reloaded, and she'll be fine."

"If it's not, you know what you have to do. We can't have any more delays." The captain released the hammer on the pistol.

Gil reached for the buckles. Damn the man. There was no need to kill a helpless animal, no matter how annoying it might be. He snapped at the Belgian, "Make yourself useful. Help me get these guns off her." The mule brayed once, then lay still for a few seconds of fumbling and a lot of cursing.

As soon as the guns fell to the ground and she was unencumbered, the molly snorted once and scrambled to her feet, looking at Gil as if wondering what all the fuss had been about. The congregation applauded, whistled and whooped as Gil stood. He shook the ache from his knees and pointed to the abashed Belgians.

"Get her packed. And make sure the load is evenly distributed. I think she was trying to tell you something," Gil said.

"Is that all?" demanded the officer.

"I think so. *Capitaine.*" He gave a filthy-palmed salute and tried not to show his disdain for the pompous ass.

The officer sniffed loudly, wheeled his mount around, nearly knocking over a couple of privates, and rode off without another word.

The offending mule stood quietly as she was reloaded with the guns and ammo. They handed extra cargo off to other teams of mules and riders. With a lighter, and properly distributed, load she dipped her head and started walking, following the trail. She looked back as if wondering what was keeping everyone else.

Sergeant Becker clapped Gil on the back. "Good work. Stay close. The animals hauling the wagons are acting up as well. We may need your expertise."

Heat sapped the last of the diplomacy from Gil's soul, and he snapped, "It's just common bloody sense. If those whoresons knew how to load her properly, this wouldn't have happened."

The Belgian, a well-meaning but incompetent former baker, bobbed his head in gratitude and offered his canteen to Gil. "Name's Baldewijns. Thanks."

Taking a swig and letting some run down his chin into his shirt, Gil handed it back. "Just don't let it happen again. It's not that goddamn difficult to pack a mule properly. A little order is all you need." His voice trailed off as he kept speaking. "Details. Details matter. Details."

Becker nodded and cupped his hand to his mouth. "Forward. March."

CHAPTER 27

C learly, someone with epaulets made the decision. With only two days to go, "they" determined it would be easier to continue the day marches. Probably Lieutenant Coste with the handlebar moustaches, or Vautier with the hair-trigger temper and the out-of-control eyebrows. It sure as hell wasn't one of the legionnaires in the long, ragged line trudging through the *Sud Oran* making that call.

Experienced troopers knew night marches sounded easier but held hazards all their own. Not seeing where you're going was only one issue. Travel was compounded by exhaustion after a few miles of walking. Men and mules both became susceptible to accidents with only a quarter moon for light. The only real advantage was that it was cooler. Gil thought that was reason enough to try, but as usual, kept his mouth shut. He maintained silence except for the whispered *hup hup hup hup* that drove him on.

The profound heat left little time for conversation. So far, he'd not seen Dupre or LaForce, and what little conversation Meier engaged in was mostly with his new best friends, the Belgian Baldewijns brothers. Since their mule went down, Ollie and Johan tried befriending Gil, who just glared at them most of the time, and they backed off. Meier, though, was a different story.

"Your friend Meier, he's a hoot." Ollie, the one who'd been responsible for their mule, told Gil the night before. "So funny." His brother agreed.

If one added up all the words he and Meier had spoken in weeks, especially since the incident with LaForce, it wouldn't add up to a short riddle, let alone a joke. Still, they amused each other and left him alone. Perfect.

If Lieutenant Maurice Coste had his way, and he usually did, they would arrive at the oasis at Talzala sometime tomorrow. If they survived. One out of twenty soldiers suffered some sort of heatstroke or dehydration. Water and a few hours of riding mule-back, often at the expense of their partners, meant they left no one behind. The *gourmiers* and *Zouave* troops that joined them over the last couple of days were either more used to, or were naturally resistant to, the cruel sun and heat. They tried to look sympathetic perched on their camels while wearing lightweight uniforms.

On what should be the last morning, Gil had just finished loading Fritz for the second time. The first time, he couldn't quite get the weight evenly distributed. It annoyed the hell out of both him and the mule. Meier ran one last check for anything left behind when a voice several tents down shouted for help.

"Help. Ollie's been stung by a scorpion."

Meier hustled and Gil walked behind him, in less of a hurry. Sure enough, Ollie Baldewijns was bare to the waist, clutching his elbow. A bright red lump, the size of half a cricket ball, looked like it was trying to burst through the skin. While Ollie moaned and cursed, his brother looked around, frantic.

"Do something."

"What? What am I supposed to do?" He was sickly white and panicky. He wanted to help his brother, but Gil supposed scorpions were no more common in Belgium than they were in the North of England.

Half a dozen men stared, equally helpless. On the edge of the watchers, two local Arab men were deep in conversation, looking at the commotion and shaking their heads.

"Hey," Meier shouted. "You- is there some, Christ, I don't know... local cure, you know, for this?"

The ugliest and oldest of the men shrugged, not understanding, or at least pretending not to. The younger one patted him on the arm and took a step forward, offering a salaam. In terrible French he said, "My uncle wants to know what you say to him."

Meier ran up to him. He began miming the ball on Ollie's arm and pointing at him. "Is there anything you can do? Some voodoo or magic or something? You people must know how to deal with this."

The younger man looked thoughtful. "I don't know. It may be too late already."

Meier pulled out his knife and pretended to stab with it. "Do we need to lance it?" The local didn't recognize the word, and Meier rolled his eyes in frustration and mimed more frantically. "Cut it out. Do we need to cut him?"

"Oh Jesus, Jo, don't let him cut my arm off!" Ollie screamed, his eyes growing even wider.

Gil and Johan tried convincing Ollie Baldewijns that amputation was a last resort, and surely it wouldn't come to that. The Belgian thrashed and cried, not believing them at all and rubbing at the swollen flesh.

The older man whispered something to his nephew. They turned away from the legionnaires, deep in conversation. Finally, the younger one turned back.

"Is something you can try, but..."

"Anything," Johan said. "What do I need to do?"

He looked uncomfortable. At Johan and Meier's urging, he finally said, "you must, I don't know the word, *altabawul*, on it."

"What the hell is alta... whatever he said?" Meier asked Gil, who simply shrugged. In frustration, the man held his hands at his waist and mimed urinating. They didn't seem to understand him, so he mimicked peeing again, more emphatically.

"He says we need to pee on it." Meier said, finally grasping the pantomime.

Johan stared uncomprehendingly for a moment, then his eyes squinted. "Like with a jellyfish sting?" The men had never heard of a jellyfish, but nodded enthusiastically.

Ollie had tears streaming down his face. "Do it. Whatever they said, do it. Oh Christ, it burns so bad. I'm going to die, aren't I?"

Johan stood up. "Ollie, I—"

"Do it. Whatever you have to do!" Ollie held his arm out and closed his eyes, looking away. Loving his brother more than his dignity, Johan Baldewijns unbuttoned his pants. He pulled out his manhood and aimed it at his brother.

Whether it was dehydration or the stares of half a dozen other men, nothing happened. Johan closed his eyes, but couldn't produce anything except a helpless moan.

"Goddamn it. Piss on me!" Ollie shouted. Gil looked away in time to see Sergeant Becker storming up.

"What's the holdup? You men should be in line." He stopped when he saw Johan Baldewijns with his penis in his fist, standing over his brother. "What the hell are you doing?"

Meier stepped up. "Ollie got stung by a scorpion, sir. Johan's trying to… to urinate on him."

"Why?"

"They said it was the only way to save his arm," Meier offered weakly.

Becker snorted. "Nobody loses an arm over a scorpion sting. In two or three hours, it will just be a bad rash."

Meier had no response other than to protest. "But they said—"

Becker bit his lip. "Who said?"

Meier pointed to the robed men just in time to see them far away, high-tailing it towards their camels. They looked back, nearly falling over each other in laughter.

Johan let his penis out of his grasp long enough to grab his sidearm. He pointed it at the disappearing goumiers. "You filthy buggers. You think this is funny?"

If he didn't, the men watching did. Johan spun towards them, his pistol still raised and waving wildly, his face red, eyes wide, and lips quivering.

Becker barked at the humiliated man. "Put that away, Private, before someone gets hurt." Johan paused, then obeyed. "And that too," the sergeant added. He pointed to the Belgian's crotch.

The audience howled as Johan holstered his weapon and buttoned his pants. Ollie, who was so absorbed in his misery he didn't really grasp the situation, looked at his brother. "Does this mean I'm going to live?"

"If I don't kill you first, you idiot."

The sergeant bellowed, "In line. Now. If we're not in Talzala by nightfall, bugs will be the least of your problems. Move it!" He turned away before anyone saw the smirk under his hairy lip.

Gil shook Meier by the arm and took Fritz's reins. "Come on." Meier nodded, but spared a look back at his buddies.

Gil shook his head. "Seems so." Then he couldn't help himself. The foolish lyrics to Le Boudin seemed appropriate, and he found himself singing the bloody Sausage Song at the top of his lungs.

"Hey, here's blood sausage, here's blood sausage, here's blood sausage,
For the Alsatians, the Swiss, and the Lorrains,
For the Belgians, there is none left.
For the Belgians, there is none left.
They are lazy."

Gil threw his head back and laughed. Meier sang harmony in his pleasant tenor. He seemed content enough, although the sunburn on his face looked painful. Fritz honked along, leaving the Baldewijns brothers to pull themselves together.

Chapter 28

Gil was almost blind from exhaustion and the thick layer of dust that covered his face. For miles now-who knew how many- he and Meier took turns riding Fritz. They each got an hour reprieve from marching when the sergeant's whistle blew and shouts of "*changez*" filled the air.

At sundown they were so close a few soldiers claimed they could smell the water from the oasis. That was ridiculous, as much of a mirage as thinking they could see it, but it meant no more camping. They finished the last steps in the chilly dark.

Blessedly, he was in the group that was stopping in Menhaba. Most of the men were marching on to Talzala, since Fort Béchar was full to bursting. The men who'd arrived earlier stood watch, and the local *spahis* and *goumiers* assisted with supplies.

The next morning, Gil woke early. Meier was snoring so loud he was sure it would attract the enemy, but he wasn't talking or being underfoot, so he let his tent-mate sleep. On hands and knees, he crawled from the canvas covering and looked around him. HIs first look at the oasis at their temporary home was a pleasant surprise. They and the rest of the Twenty-Fourth Mounted found themselves on a pleasant plain with scattered palm trees and a deep stream and wide, calm pool.

Water.

Gil looked at his hands, stained gray by road dust and sand. The scars on his wrists stood out bright pink. No amount of filth ever seemed to conceal them. He ran a hand over his face and felt more than stubble, the beginnings of a full-blown beard. Retrieving a small shaving mirror from his pack, he studied his reflection. Gilbert le Lion de Marseille stared back at him, hairy and feral.

That wouldn't do. He needed to be Gil Vincente, even out in the wilderness. Maybe especially there. A shave and a haircut would get him back to his old self.

Careful not to pollute the water source, he scooped a metal bucket of water and found a comfortable rock. With his back to the sun, he set to putting the road dirt back on the ground where it belonged. Using a bar of lye soap that may as well have been a rasp, he finally revealed the skin underneath, and the cleaner his hands, the paler the scars looked against them.

Finally, he took his razor and honed it against a rock until it was as sharp as could be. The soap was useless as a lubricant, but Gil rubbed it on his cheeks, unable to make a decent lather. He took a deep breath, placed the blade against his cheek, and scraped a small patch clean. Cleaner, at least.

"You could just grow a beard like a real man." Gus Dupre laughed and slapped him on the back. The move would have been more appreciated if there wasn't a razor to his throat, but Gil smiled.

Dupre's beard had grown even thicker on the march, nearly concealing him from upper lip to Adam's apple. Gil shuddered to think about what might be living in there. "We're not all blessed with perfection like you."

"True. God loves me best. Still, why bother shaving out here in the middle of nowhere?"

Gil carried on the conversation while trying not to slice open his jugular. "I don't like myself hairy, is all." He didn't add that it made him look like a lion. The Lion.

He concentrated, scraping his face as clean as possible while leaving his nose and lips intact. Orange dawn reflected as he checked himself in the mirror. Small flecks of blood dotted his face and attracted biting flies, but it was better than nothing. He ran a hand through his blond hair, wishing he could keep it out of his face.

"Here. Give me the razor." Dupre held his hand out. "I'll give you a trim."

He doubted the wisdom of giving the big oaf something so sharp, but the need for a haircut overrode his trepidation. As in every army since Rome, legionnaires knew how to use a straight razor to keep each other's hair short. The result was ragged but helped with the heat. Not to mention the fleas and lice.

Gus talked as he cut away hair, despite Gil hoping he'd concentrate at least a little. "The Moustache says we're attacking in four days." General Lyautey had taken control of Béchar and the entire operation along the Sud Oranais-Moroccan frontier. The incursion into the Atlas Mountains was meeting massive resistance, which it seemed the officer took personally.

"Easy, there. I like my ears." Gil closed his eyes and held as still as possible.

"Coward." Gus prattled on. "They're camped about nine or ten miles out. The usual bunch of ignorant riffraff. It'll be easy work. At least that's what he told Lieutenant Coste. There, you're done."

He handed the razor to Gil and took his place on the rock throne. Gil thought about sharpening the razor but didn't think his friend would even notice the difference, so began hacking away at the greasy knots on Dupre's head.

Easy work. Right. Every battle was supposed to be simple. He thought of the high hopes for routing Boers and Zulus. Reality had a way of playing havoc with such pronouncements.

Gil squished a critter between his fingertips and measured a length of hair between two fingers. Then he sliced it as straight as he could. "There you go. Back to perfection."

"There you are," LaForce said. After a quick embrace, Gil looked at him. Hard to believe this was the same skinny kid he'd met in Marseille. He'd filled out, for one thing. Marching and drilling added muscle to his thin frame. Only that poor excuse for a beard, more a patchy collection of long blond horse hair, kept him from looking like a full-grown man.

"Let's get that beard off you," Gil said. He picked up the whetstone and began honing the straight razor.

"No. I like it," said LaForce.

Dupre stroked his own beard. "I like it. It's getting there. Keep it."

Gil snorted.

Dupre spit on the ground. "I know that whore thought it was cute. What's her name, Vincente? Rose?" LaForce laughed.

Gil flinched. He hadn't told anyone about his visit to Room Three. In truth, part of him hoped nobody, especially those two, knew about it.

"Can't blame you, although that pretty young Arab girl is more my style. She likes her men big and furry." Dupre turned to the side, as if posing for a picture, hand stroking his monstrous face cover.

"Rose likes my beard," LaForce stroked his chin proudly.

Like she enjoyed those marks on her neck, Gil thought. "At least let me cut that mop before birds nest in it." The boy obeyed and nudged Dupre off the rock.

As Gil sliced and hacked at LaForce's curling locks, the camp came to life. More men came down to the pool, some to refill canteens, some to clean themselves as best they could. Nervously, he kept an eye out for Meier, who was probably making sure Fritz was being taken care of. So far, he'd been able to keep the enemies separated. Maybe his luck would hold.

Local porters and peddlers wandered through the camp. Some sold dried fruit and meat; others sold equipment and uniform parts without mentioning where they came from. Boots in particular were in high demand after a long desert hike. The original owners certainly couldn't complain.

Gil wrinkled his forehead as he watched the white burnooses drift among the tents and groups of soldiers. "They just let them come and go like that?" He felt a shiver run up spine. In the Queen's army, he learned some painful lessons about trusting the locals.

LaForce nodded and spoke through a mouthful of dried meat. "The village is just on the other side of that hill. They're scared to death of the Mahdi because they play nicely with us. They need us. Til we chase the buggers out of here, anyway. Meanwhile, we have food, supplies—"

"And women," he and Dupre said at the same time. They guffawed together while Gil pasted on a smile and pretended to chuckle along. He couldn't share

Dupre's, and now the boy's, taste for the exotic. He could only imagine what the women in that village looked like under those scarves and robes.

Now that the sun was up, it was easier to take a hard look at the camp. The heavy artillery was placed to the north, facing the mountains and the most likely site of an attack. To the west and northwest, the Twenty-Third was firmly dug in. Native Algerians and the zouaves guarded the eastern approaches, leaving the Twenty-Fourth looking south onto the flat, wide but rocky plain. They were open to attack, but you could see the enemy approaching a mile or more away.

Almost as many more men were not too far away at Talzala, and command was at Fort Béchar. They'd rendezvous when it was time for the attack.

Sergeant Becker's voice reached them from somewhere off to the West. They stood and saw him, along with Captain Vautier and a young lieutenant who had to be Moste.

He was thin, a year or two younger than Gil, with a handlebar moustache as glorious as the stories claimed and a permanent knowing smirk that instantly marked him as the son of an officer. The boy was here by right and the grace of God, rather than merit. That kind could get you killed.

The three soldiers watched as the officers did a lot of pointing and arguing among themselves. Finally, Becker saluted smartly and yelled out to the team as the lieutenant and captain strode off to the relative comfort of the command tent.

"Alright! You're not here on vacation, *mes braves*." He bellowed. "Let's get going. We need a rock wall the length of the camp and high enough to hide behind."

A well-practiced stare cut any groans off. While the thought of hauling and piling rocks in the scorching sun wasn't pleasant, neither was being exposed to a potential attack, and when they weren't marching, legionnaires worked.

"We'd best get back to our side of the tracks," Dupre said. He and LaForce embraced Gil once more and headed out. Gil gathered his gear and trudged back to his tent, all traces of the Lion invisible to the world once more.

Twenty minutes later, he was stripped to the waist. Only his kepi kept the sun from his neck. Some of the men, the ones used to the desert, used their shirts as turbans or found other ways to hide from the sun, despite the sweat soaking through their clothes. Others, like Meier, wore as little clothing as possible.

Meier had a tentative grip on a stone while Gil held the other ed. Meier grunted, "Alright, heave!" Together they hoisted the rock, so it settled in the crack between two larger stones. He pulled his fingers away before they got crushed.

Gil grunted, "Jesus, watch what you're doing!"

Meier mumbled an apology. He was too hot and uncomfortable to protest Gil's tone. His skin was already bright pink, halfway to sunstroke, and the day had just begun. Of every hundred men on the march, two were felled by disease or infection, one by accident, and the sun and heat claimed at least half a dozen more. They seldom died, but were rendered useless when they were needed most. Nobody seemed to question if Northern Europeans had any business in this climate. Easier for some to pay the price for the rest.

For an Englishman, Gil tolerated the weather better than expected. Maybe those years at the south end of the continent inured him to sunstroke and dehydration. It was easy to apply his *hup hup hup hup* to stacking rocks. Put your mind elsewhere and lift with your knees.

Soon enough, his partner was relieved by Johan Baldewijns, whose brother Ollie was still claiming the ill effects of the scorpion's sting.

Gil couldn't resist. "If I get hurt, don't piss on me, okay?"

Johan grunted and placed another stone in the wall. "Next time I'm going to save time and just amputate."

Gil gritted his teeth and dug his raw fingers into the sand to grip another rock. "Good idea. Help me with this, will you?" Johan obliged without protest.

Working in forty-five minute shifts, they nearly had the wall done by the end of the day. It offended Gil's sense of order and alignment, but it was tall enough to hide behind, and the stone would stop a bullet. It would have to do.

When the night blessedly arrived, it was all Gil could do to crawl into the tent he and Meier shared. His arms and back ached, and his skin radiated heat. Meiers tossed, moaning in agony from the horrific sunburn that was already peeling.

Heeding Becker's order, they tied their Lebels to their wrists in case of attack. It seemed an unnecessary precaution. They outnumbered the Arabs, and they planned their own attack for four days from now.

Only three nights of sleep before the real fighting started. May as well catch up on his shuteye.

Gil fell asleep right away. His dreams featured scorpions, Rose, and Fritz. Gauthier's bloated, swinging corpse paid a brief visit to stare at him in accusing silence.

It was the best night's sleep in weeks.

Chapter 29

The first few gunshots he heard, Gil chalked up to a dream. Then he sat bolt upright and grabbed the Lebel tied to his wrist. His body remembered what to do before his brain fully awakened. He was up and chambering the first bullet before he left the tent, with Meier stumbling behind him.

The camp was under attack.

It was still dark except for the flash of gun muzzles firing sporadically. After a few minutes, the booming eighty-millimeter guns on the hill joined the chorus of chaos, and shells sailed overhead to kick up geysers of rock and sand out on the plain. The confused shouts of men just roused from sleep joined the murderous war cries of the Berber warriors.

Somewhere in the back of his mind, Gil wondered how so many of the bastards were inside the camp when they'd spent the day constructing walls. Patrols were set at three hundred yards out. A bullet struck the ground at his feet and ended any idle speculation.

He raised his rifle and pointed rather than aimed his gun at the first moving object he saw. A short, bearded man in a brown burnoose spun wildly and hit the ground, immobile. Meier and Gil stood shoulder to shoulder, each moving their heads ninety degrees.

His tent-mate's face was bright red. Skin peeled off his narrow nose, and his eyes were puffy and crimson, swollen to the point Gil wondered how he could see.

"Where's Becker?" Meier asked. Even this close, the cacophony of bugles, gunfire, and the screams of the wounded nearly drowned his voice out. Gil frantically searched for the biggest gathering of heads in kepis. That's where you'd find someone in command. Someone to help impose order. Painful experience taught him that the attacker had the advantage as long as the defenders couldn't form a square or organize resistance. They were just so many ducks waiting to be picked off the pond.

To the west, he saw a cluster of soldiers. From the center of the mob, a sword waved and pointed wildly in the air. An officer. Gil slapped Meier on the shoulder, ducked low, and sprinted in that direction. He was so focused on reaching the safety of numbers, he didn't see the oncoming figure until it knocked him to the ground.

Chest heaving and his lungs unable to catch air, he gasped and flopped on the ground. A beardless man, more of a boy, stabbed at his flailing body. A last-second twist of his head meant the lad's dagger struck sand rather than his throat. One blessed lungful of air gave him enough to roll over and grab his gun. The young Berber snatched at the barrel and tried wrestling it from Gil's hand.

Desperate, Gil yanked on the rifle, bringing it close to his face, then sank his teeth into the other man's hand. The attacker yelped and pulled his hand off the gun's barrel. Too close to get a shot off, or even stab properly, he slashed his bayonet across the young man's face.

The Berber rolled onto his back, clutching his bloody cheek and shrieking. Gil rolled onto his knees, raised his rifle and drove Rosalie through the man's throat. He lay pinned to the ground, still thrashing but surely dead. Using his gun for leverage, he rose to his feet. With a grunt, he pulled the bloody metal from the dead man's throat. A crimson fountain spurted onto his pants and boots.

There was no time to celebrate or even think. A bullet ripped through the canvas of a tent not a foot away. He whirled and fired, missing the onrushing figure, but making it freeze in its tracks. The moment the man stood up, Meier's shot caught him dead in the belly. With a grunt, the man grabbed his guts and fell forward.

Gil nodded his thanks to Meier but stood frozen in place, as if cast in stone. Gil wondered if it was the first time Meier had ever killed a man, but there was no time to be gentle. When it was clear they were safe, he grabbed Meier's sleeve and led him towards a cluster of men who'd formed a rough but effective square.

They waved the two men over, three sides firing, one holding fire just long enough for Gil and Meier to dive between the legs of the legionnaires in front and land at the boots of Sergeant Becker.

"*Bien.* On your feet, *mes braves.*" Gil nodded and slid a cartridge into his Lebel. A second later, Meier got to his feet and did the same. They took their places in the second line of the square. In front and on all four sides, the first line knelt, firing, reloading and firing again until they were out of ammunition, then the second line, Gil included, took their spot.

Exposed as he was, he felt safe in the square. There was order. Logically, it was no defense against bullets, but it prevented chaos and madness. That was infinitely worse in his mind.

Gil nearly dropped his rifle when he saw a dozen men on camels charge the camp. The huge, ugly beasts never slowed down as the riders bounced up and down in the wooden saddles on their backs and ran down the men's tents. Wood poles, canvas, and bedrolls scattered in their wake. From that height, it was simple for the tribesmen to spot their victims. Any soldier left in the open was easy pickings.

One man in a dusty white robe and blue burnoose used an ancient lever-action rifle to potshot running soldiers. Gil watched as one, then a second man, went face-down in the dirt. The shooter had an American weapon. Maybe a Winchester? Part of him was looking for cover as he wondered where they had gotten such weapons from.

"Filthy bugger," he muttered, lifting his Lebel. While not a great shot, he could hardly miss the target high in the air like that. He held his breath, fired, and the camel's rider grunted, looked at Gil with surprise, and tumbled to the ground. The camel ran off, snorting, roaring and kicking up sand without a thought for its former rider, back to the quieter plain beyond the brick wall.

"Vincente! You and these others. Get to that wall. Stop them from coming in." Then Becker saw Meier's puffy, sun-baked face. "*Merde,* take this one with you. He'll be safer behind the wall."

Gil cursed under his breath. He knew the importance of setting up fire out there. After all, he'd built the damned wall. He also knew that it was no help at all when the enemy had already infiltrated the camp. On the right side of a wall, you were protected. On the wrong side, you had your back to stone with nowhere to run. It was a setting for a firing squad.

They would be at that barricade for a while. Ten men joined Meier and Gil. Two of them carried a box half-full of cartridges between them. "Get a move on. We built that goddamn wall for a reason. *Vite.*"

Gil studied the people with him. They looked competent enough, except for the deep-fried Meier. He could do this. He took a breath, dipped low, and sprinted for the relative safety of the stone wall. A grizzled veteran with an ancient Lebel in his grip led the way.

"Come on, that's it. Move your asses."

At his urging, the men picked up speed. They were almost to the wall when one of those carrying the ammunition box dropped face first into the stony dirt. Gil didn't stop to think. He grabbed the free end of the crate.

"Leave him," Gil shouted to the stunned soldier on the other end. "Get to the wall."

The stocky legionnaire grabbed the handle, spared one last look for his fallen partner, then nodded to Gil. They ran as fast as they could until they reached the stones. They squatted with their back to the wall, making sure nobody was coming behind them. The wooden box lay on the ground between them. "Take what you need, but don't be an asshole. These have to last," the veteran shouted.

Gil took two magazines and put them in his pants pocket. Then he allowed himself a peek over the wall. A bullet caught the neck flap of his kepi, tearing it from his head. He ducked low again.

Meiers shouted, "I can't see a damned thing. How many are there?"

Gil stuck his head over again and quickly withdrew it before answering. "Too damned many." The enemy kept coming; a sea of screaming men on camels and horses and on foot waving curved scimitars and castoff rifles.

"I... I can't see for shit," Meiers said. The fear choked him and he shook as he spoke.

Gil cursed his luck at being shackled to such a useless partner. "You'll be fine. Count to three, point over the wall and fire. There are so many you'll hit something. Ready? One. Two..."

On "three," he and Meier stood and fired without particularly taking aim. The other men behind the wall did the same. Miraculously, two of the attackers fell on the first salvo. The rest kept surging forward.

There was no sergeant or anyone of rank to tell them what to do. The old man barked the orders, and the others obeyed without question. Better to listen to someone who'd done this and survived than some officer, anyway.

Gil and Meier stood again, firing off four shots. With eight bullets to a cartridge, they could go two rounds without reloading. Half the men stood and fired, while the others reloaded or waited.

After a few minutes of this, the enemy fire slowed. Gil risked a look over the wall. The flood of attackers had slowed, although some of the crazy bastards were still coming. The sound of battle seemed to have shifted, now coming from the west. Booming guns drowned out everything else.

Dust and fleeing Berbers told him what he needed to know. Help was coming from Talzala. The question was, did they arrive in time?

CHAPTER 30

T he arrival of reinforcements sent the Moroccans running, but only long enough to regroup. Within the hour, hundreds of them had taken up residence on the hill to the southeast. This gave them the high ground over the plain. Gil and the others watched as one robed figure after another clambered like goats up the hill and took their positions.

"Vincente! Meier!" Sergeant Becker's voice was raspy from screaming into clouds of kicked-up dust all morning.

"Oui, Sergeant!" the two men responded immediately.

"Come with me. Now."

Gil picked up what gear he had with him. Meier hesitated. His eyes were swollen shut, and the crimson sun-burnt skin was barely discernible behind a layer of sweat and dust. "Where are we going?"

Becker barked, "Where I tell you to go, Private. Move your ass."

The Alsatian sagged and grabbed at his kit, missed, then bent and grabbed it again, throwing it over his shoulder with a groan that came from his toes. Becker was more reasonable and infinitely less profane than most sergeants in any army, French or British. Gil was every bit as curious as his partner, but now was no time to question orders.

They followed their commanding officer through the camp in silence. They seemed to be the only ones. Men hustled, carrying gear and weapons to new positions, shouting and grunting with the effort. Sergeants and officers pointed with their sabers and directed the defense. Everyone knew the next wave was coming sooner rather than later.

Wherever they were headed, they passed through the remnants of the peaceful campsite they'd left that morning. A square half-acre of stony ground was littered with tent poles, canvas, and gear. Gil's heart sank at the thought of his impeccably rolled bed. His pack had been so perfectly arranged. There had been order.

Now, it was chaos and destruction.

"Vincente, get a move on." Gil didn't even realize he'd stopped.

His kit. His gear. His life. He heard himself sound pathetic. "Sir, when can we—"

"When I say so, Private. Move on. Don't keep the Captain waiting. He hates that."

The Captain?

The sound of panicky animals was the first clue as to their destination. Mules, horses, and a few camels trotted nervously in an ancient stone corral. Their complaints filled the air, drowning out Gil's whispered vulgarity.

Between them and the livestock, Captain Vautier and his monstrous eyebrows sat astride his black horse. The frightened animal's nostrils flared, and it danced a jig, desperate to be away from the other, lesser, animals. Probably from its rider, too. Despite its gigantic frame and beautiful black coat, it was clear to Gil it hadn't been properly curried in a while.

"About goddamn time, Sergeant." Vautier barely acknowledged their salutes. With a groan, he dismounted, wincing as his thick boots hit the ground in a cloud of dust. "I see you brought our mule experts."

Gil kept a straight face. It took everything he had to keep staring straight ahead and resist looking back at the shambles of the campsite. He wanted to run. To scream. To find his belongings and restore order.

Instead, he stood at attention, gritting his teeth. Vautier took two steps closer. The man had eyes like ball bearings, steel-gray and soulless. "You seem to like these useless, ugly creatures. Well, you can protect them."

"Sir?"

"The bastards will be back. Probably in hours. There are only two things in this camp worth protecting; our ammunition and our transport."

More than anything, Gil wanted to reorganize his life, but that would have to wait. Barring that, he wanted to be in the mix of things. Fighting the enemy. He'd had enough of babysitting animals in South Africa. He was a by-God soldier, not a farmhand. Certainly not a prison guard. Never again. Then he looked at Meier, who stood at ease, but a strong breeze might knock him over. Damn the man. He needed water, shade, and sleep. He'd have to settle for water.

"Yes. Sir." He remembered to salute this time.

Vautier nodded. "You'll be under the command of Lieutenant Coste."

The young prick with the giant handlebar moustache crisply saluted. His uniform was spotless, except where the moustache wax dripped out of his facial hair onto the front of his uniform. Christ alone knew where he'd spent the last few hours, but it wasn't in the same battle as the rest of them.

Vautier had no more use for underlings than he had for recalcitrant mules. He turned to the younger officer and snapped, "What's the plan?"

Coste stood at parade rest. "Sir! If they come-"

"When," Vautier stroked his horse's nose, half listening. "There's no 'if.' They're coming."

"Pardon, sir. When they come, it'll be from the south or southeast. Hopefully, they won't get this far. If they do, we'll set up a couple of Maxims and about twenty men to protect the stock. They'll be under Sergeant Becker here."

"And you." Vautier put a foot into the stirrup and looked back at Lieutenant Coste. "You're not going anywhere."

Gil watched a flood of protests cross the young man's face. His lips twitched but didn't say a word in response. Alright then, the kid might be useless, but he wasn't stupid.

Vautier pulled himself up into the saddle. "Not one animal gets taken or killed. Understand?"

Gil watched, amused, as the once- cocky young officer bit his lower lip and saluted. "Yes, sir."

Vautier said, "You're in excellent hands with Becker." Then he rode off in a cloud of dust without another word.

The lieutenant stood dumbly for a moment. He squirmed under the men's gaze. Taking command, he shouted, "What are you waiting for? Get yourselves armed and ready. Grab a bite if you have anything." Then his bloodshot eyes fell on Meier. "Is he going to be alright?"

Gil grabbed his partner's shoulder, as much to keep him upright as to display any affection. "Yes, sir. Just a little too much sun. He'll be fine."

"He'd better be. See that the horses have water. If you have time, grab something to eat. It's going to be a long day." Then the Lieutenant Coste looked around, unsure what to do next.

Becker stepped in. "Get Meier in the shade. Buckets are back behind that wall. Let's go, *mes braves*. You think you're on holiday at the beach? *Vitement.*"

Gil helped a quickly fading Meier into the lee of the corral wall, taking advantage of what little shade existed. He grabbed the man's canteen and poured water into his mouth. As much landed on his parched, blistered lips as got into his throat. Then he turned Meier's kepi sideways, so the flap covered the part of his face exposed to the sun. "That should hold you."

A familiar booming voice came from behind him. "Where do you want these?" It was Gus Dupre, holding a wheelbarrow containing two Maxim machine guns. Behind him was LaForce, dragging a wooden crate of ammunition.

Gil was glad to see his friends, but cast a wary eye from Meier to LaForce and back. The last thing he needed was drama between them. "What are you doing here? You're not gunners."

Dupre bent, groaned, and hoisted one gun onto the corral's stone wall. "We are now."

"Do you even know what you're doing?"

LaForce piped up, an excited, childish grin on a face that could still use shaving. "Point at the enemy. Squeeze the trigger, right? I mean, it's not highly trained work like watering mules." If the lad saw Meier, he didn't acknowledge him. He concentrated on setting up the machine gun.

"Vincente, water. Now." Becker interrupted their reunion. "You four, go with him. And don't spill any on the way," he said, pointing to some legionnaires who looked relatively fresh and useful. They must have been back here when the fighting started, which, to Gil's mind, wasn't the worst place to be.

A decrepit water-wagon yoked behind two bored- looking, mangy mules was a few yards away. Gil grumbled and waved to the four others who'd been volunteered. "Okay, let's go." He turned back to Dupre and LaForce. "Make sure you point those in the right direction, huh? How they gave this job to you two idiots I'll never figure out."

Dupre shrugged. "The last owners weren't using them anymore."

On that cheery note, Gil took the reins and clambered up onto the wagon. He looked up at the gathering army on the southeastern hill, then at the sun. It was still high in the sky. The attack wouldn't come until later in the afternoon. There was plenty of time. Might even grab a bite. Then he remembered his kit was scattered somewhere in the middle of the battlefield. Lunch would be good, but knowing his gear was safe and stowed properly was more of a priority.

The squeaky wheels of the water wagon were louder than the growling in his stomach, but not by much. Three other soldiers sat with their legs hanging off of the wagon as it bounced its way to where the stream met the pond. The water would be cleaner and easy to access there.

It wasn't much of a wagon, just a simple bed of wooden planks, slapped together and held by rusty nails that rattled as it bounced over the trail. The galvanized metal barrel sat inside a wooden box. No doubt, the water would taste like zinc and rust, and sure as hell wouldn't be cold, but would be wet and accessible. The men could fill their canteens, at least. As soon as the mules got theirs, of course. Vautier had made the priorities crystal clear.

After some initial conversation, and more than a little grousing, they got to work. The three strangers set up a bucket brigade, ending with Gil. He stood on the platform and poured water through the open top of the barrel. The fuller it got, the more the wheels buckled inward, making Gil wonder if they would make the return trip. It was slow work, but all of them took full advantage of the water and allowed it to spill over them. That took the sting out of the afternoon heat.

"That should do it," Gil said as he dumped the last bucket.

"About damned time. I'm starving." A large soldier flopped onto his back, panting and staring up into the sun.

In German, one of his compatriots said something that made them all laugh. Gil forced himself to chuckle, even though he didn't have a clue what they said. The joker turned to him and said in French, "Sorry. We just said missing a meal or two wouldn't do much damage."

Gil smiled his gratitude for the translation. "Thanks. I'm with him, though. Let's get back and get some food in us before they come back."

That's when the first gun boomed in the southeast.

CHAPTER 31

"God damn it," Gil yelled. "Get on!" His three water fetchers leapt onto the cracked wooden deck of the wagon, flat on their stomachs, clinging to the edge. Gil snapped the reins and shouted, "Gee. Come on!"

The animals weren't eager to comply. They stomped their feet and tried breaking from their yoke. Gil gripped the leather straps tightly, despite the burning across his palms. After a few seconds, the animals realized there was no choice. They set off at a reluctant trot southeast.

Thick clouds of dust on the hillside billowed where the Legion's eighty-millimeter guns rained hell onto the Mahdi's followers. Most of the shooting and screaming, though, came from the southeast.

Screaming and cursing, he urged the reluctant mules on across the camp to the corral. This time, at least so far, the attackers were outside the armed perimeter instead of inside the camp. At least so far. From the pillars of dust reaching skyward, it looked like the regiment might be outnumbered.

Half-blinded by the sun and blowing sand, Gil and the wagon approached the ancient enclosure. LaForce and Dupre stood behind their Maxims, waving the muzzles back and forth but not finding anything to shoot at. Yet.

Half the men who'd been there earlier were gone. Likely sent to the front line. He was a little surprised to see Meier was gone, sunburnt and ill as he was. Then he looked at Jean LaForce's determined face. Just as well he was gone. Those two had enemies to fight besides each other.

Sergeant Becker shouted orders and pushed men when they didn't move fast enough. Lieutenant Coste echoed everything the older man said in a stuttering, faltering voice. Becker turned to the men on the wagon. He was about to say something when Coste interrupted him.

"Get these mules watered while you can. The bastards haven't broken through, and probably won't. The guns are pounding the hell out of them." Issuing the orders put some extra starch in the officer's backbone, even though Gil saw him check his peripheral vision. The young man's face relaxed when he caught the sergeant's approving nod.

"Vincente!" Gil looked up to see Becker storming towards him. "Nothing happens to these animals, understand?"

Gil grunted as he opened the spout, allowing water to pour into buckets. "*Oui, sergent.*" There was no salute, but Becker didn't stick around to notice. The men ran to each mule, offering a bucket of water. The animals shoved their noses deep, drinking as loudly as they could. Complaining when the pails got snatched away, refilled and offered to the next beast.

The scene struck him as surreal. While he an a few other soldiers played farmhand, less than half a mile away, cannons boomed, guns blasted, and men screamed their last words in both French and Berber.

LaForce shouted over his shoulder. "With luck, maybe they'll hold them off."

Gil filled another bucket from the wagon keg. "Yeah? How's your luck been so far?"

Dupre butted in. "Not bad. We're here and they're out there. Right, Kid?" He slapped LaForce on the back.

Gil tried making sense of the madness. Envisioning the battle and what came next took his mind off his belongings, probably scattered to the wind. The more he worried about that, the twitchier he got. Three deep breaths brought him back to the present. One crisis at a time.

It could be worse. The corral was far enough back to be out of immediate danger, though if the lines broke, they'd be next. The big guns looked like they were doing a decent job of pounding the hillside, scattering some of the enemy and keeping those tribesmen higher up pinned where they couldn't cause any real trouble.

A lone figure, young and skinny, stumble-ran towards them from the west. His arms windmilled and Gil heard him gasping from yards away. As he drew nearer, he choked out, "Captain Vautier. Captain."

Gil and one of the water-carriers ran out to him. They threw one arm over each of their shoulders and half-led, half-dragged him behind the corral's wall. His breathing was ragged, and he barely formed words due to the dust and dryness in his mouth.

Gil opened his canteen and poured water over the lad's lips. That allowed him one good gulp of water. Half of it dribbled onto his chin. "Captain... Vautier. I need to-"

Lieutenant Coste strode up, then bent one knee to look the courier in the face. "He's not here. I'm Lieutenant Coste. I'm in command. What is it?"

Gil watched Becker wince at the lieutenant's declaration, but was otherwise stoic. Others formed a semicircle around him, eager to hear what he had to say, although the older hands had no trouble guessing by his haste and how big his eyes were.

The lad attempted a salute that died halfway to his forehead. "Lieutenant, We can't hold them. They're breaking through from the palm grove. We didn't even know they were there."

Sergeant Becker's eyes locked on the boy's. He took the young man's chin in his hand. "Breathe and think. How long do we have?"

A shake of his head told the rest of them what they needed to know. Becker turned to the lieutenant.

"With permission, I'll get us set up to defend the corral. Three deep in a square. The Maxims will lay down covering fire."

"Yes, fine. Excellent." Coste sucked on one end of his once-glorious moustache. In a deep voice, he shouted, "*Attention, mes braves*. We protect the animals and each other. Nobody gets through." The rapidly shifting eyes slightly undercut his bravado, but it was a virtuoso performance. There might be hope for the green young officer yet, Gil thought.

LaForce and Dupre let out a whoop and adjusted their guns to the expected angle of attack. Legionnaires dropped ammunition belts at their feet where they could make a quick change if necessary.

No. When necessary.

The roaring cloud of dust and gunfire drew nearer. Gil glanced at the mules, stomping their feet and braying loudly. Those that were staked down tugged frantically at their tethers. The rest ran in tight, worried circles. The low stone walls of the corral wouldn't hold these animals long if they decided to make a break for it.

Jumping onto the wall, he spread his hands out wide, motioning for calm and shushing them as best he could. One got a gentle stroke on its nose, another got its ears scratched. He worked through the pack of pack animals. "Come on, it's okay. Don't worry; nothing's going to happen. Good girl."

The mules didn't believe him any more than he believed himself, but it made both parties feel better, and the tension in the corral eased a bit.

Becker pointed to Gil. "Stay in the rear of the square. Those animals are your responsibility, understand?"

"*Oui, sergent,*" Gil snapped back. The "screw you" and "why me" were unspoken.

The enemy was close enough that the men could make out individual voices. The first shots pierced the afternoon air. They went wild, meant more to intimidate and soften the French line rather than to kill. That would come soon enough.

The first wave of barbarians stormed into range. Most waved swords in the air, yelling death threats in the name of Allah. They knew they were likely dead men, simply clearing the path of the cavalry on camels and horseback. That didn't make them less determined to take as many *farengi* with them to Paradise as possible.

Becker's voice cut through the madness. "*En jou, feu!*" Take aim and fire. Right. Gil knew from shameful personal experience the men would fire, but few would aim worth a damn. Training tended to go out the window when faced with hundreds of oncoming bloodthirsty enemy troops. All those bodies made it hard to focus on which one you needed to kill first. Instead, most of the bullets sailed into the oncoming wave, lucky to hit anything at all. The men in the square fired, ducked, reloaded as those behind them took their shot, stood and fired again.

Machine guns atoned for the lack of accuracy. Gil heard LaForce scream with exhilaration as he released rapid bursts of fire into the wave and men in robes fell to the ground, kicking and crying out to their mothers. The young man had a manic grin on his scraggly face as he waved the nose of his Maxim twenty degrees one way, then back. "Woohoo! Take that, camel lovers. Gus, did you see that? Ha!"

Dupre took up the fire as LaForce reloaded. He had a much grimmer look on his face, equally deadly but enjoying himself less.

Gil got his own shots off, but slowly and more methodically. He'd rather make his ammo count than litter the ground. He watched down his rifle barrel as one of the sabre-waving tribesmen veered off, heading for the mules. Gil ended that plan with a single shot, but half a dozen more men in robes headed for the mules. Two of them hit the ground in front of the stone wall. The others scampered over the wall, only to be met by bayonets. All six fell, bloody and screaming.

But there were so many more.

Gil clapped three men on the shoulder and waved them over to a position behind the corral. If the bastards wanted the animals, that was the most likely path. Becker nodded in approval and shouted to the rest of the men. "Follow Vincente."

The lieutenant stood with the men in the square, using his sidearm to good effect. One of the enemy, recognizing an officer and an easy target, charged the young man. Coste fired, then braced himself as the Berber caught him by the waist, driving him to the ground. At such close quarters, guns made little sense. The attacker raised his dagger, prepared to drive it into Coste's throat.

As he rose, Gil took aim at the attacker's chest. The man fell on top of the lieutenant, dead. Coste let out a yelp and scrambled out from under the dead Berber.

"Are you alright, sir?" asked Becker. The officer responded with a stunned nod. His mouth gaped open. The sergeant took him by the arm and hustled him into the shelter of the wall.

As expected, the first wave of suicidal enemies had just been dispatched to heaven and their virgins when the second wave struck. These were experienced fighters, used to killing Frenchmen. Their camels not only gave them a height advantage, but the huge animals left a swath of destruction wherever they went. Legionnaires scattered for their lives.

Gil was sure one had taken aim at him, and he was a dead man. Instead, a mule screamed bloody murder and fell to the ground. He stared with his voice trapped in his throat. What kind of savages killed innocent animals? He fired off two quick rounds, dropping the man to the dirt.

That didn't solve the problem. Riderless, the camel and several of its unencumbered fellows rampaged wildly through the camp, scattering men from their positions. Several got into the corral and began chasing mules, hoping to scatter the ones they couldn't steal. In blind panic, the mules that weren't tethered found a broken down part of the corral wall and ran into the camp. They kicked wildly, not caring who they hit. Soldiers had to worry more about being killed by their mounts than the enemy. More tents were destroyed. Enemy soldiers whooped in triumph. Those who weren't killed at least.

"Damn it to hell," Gil hissed. He ran into the corral between most of the mules and the wall and waved his arms wildly. "No, baby, not this way. No! Stupid bloody animal."

Whether the animals trusted him or just didn't want to deal with an obviously crazy person, they changed direction until they were huddled against the stone walls, most of them safe for the moment. Gil ran side to side, gasping, cursing and sweating, saving as many of the beasts as he could. His back was exposed and with every breath, he clenched and shut his eyes, expecting to feel a bullet in his back.

Eventually, the gunfire tapered off into sporadic bursts. Barely able to see for the grit in his eyes, Gil took the time to look around. Men squatted on the ground, catching their breath, begging for water. The enemy was in retreat.

A maniacal laugh accompanied the last of the machine gun fire. Gil looked over to see Dupre slumped exhausted against the wall, while Jean LaForce stood behind his Maxim, firing off round after round at the retreating enemy, laughing and whooping. The macabre victory dance drew worried looks from the other soldiers. Some people enjoy killing more than others. Everyone knew to keep their distance. That kind of maniac could get you killed as easily as save you.

Becker's huge hand clamped down on LaForce's shoulder. "Private. Private! Enough. Stop! Don't waste your ammo."

LaForce's eyes were huge as dinner plates, and he couldn't stop laughing. "Did you see? We taught them, didn't we? Woohoo!"

"Stop it! Calm down, boy. Breathe." The sergeant didn't let go until the lad calmed down. Gil found it hard to believe the straggly-bearded maniac was his sweet, mild-tempered friend. Whatever remnants remained of Jacques Manot lay in pieces on the ground among the spent brass and dead bodies, both enemy and Legionnaire.

A courier shouted for Lieutenant Coste. The young officer pulled himself together, re-buttoning his uniform and trying to mold his handlebars back into place.

"I'm Coste."

The courier saluted. "Captain Vautier requests you at the command tent, sir."

Picking his braided kepi off the ground, Coste slapped the dust from it and placed it on his head. "Very well, lead the way."

The courier took three steps when a single shot rang out. A Berber, presumed dead, had rallied enough to take a shot at the officer in the pretty hat. Coste stopped, his face the very picture of annoyance. He placed a hand on his chest, groaned once, and dropped to his knees. After a moment, he collapsed face down in the dirt.

Two soldiers shouted and thrust their bayonets into the attacker, this time well and truly dead.

It was too late for Lieutenant Coste, the last French casualty of the Battle at Menhaba.

CHAPTER 32

With a bellyful of stone-hard bread and fly-bitten sausage, Gil wandered through the scattered remnants of the campsite. All around him, dazed men picked up litter and examined the scraps for anything useful. Most had few personal possessions to worry about. The more worrisome problem was that their uniforms were torn, shot at, ripped and occasionally soiled and pissed-in. Out in the desert, you couldn't wait for the quartermaster's office to open. You had to scrounge what you could. In a few hours, the ragamuffins from the village would come by with boots, hats, belts, and weapons. No one questioned their provenance.

Eighteen dead. No, nineteen. Gil still saw the perturbed look forever frozen on Lieutenant Coste's face. Nearly ninety legionnaires wounded. Vautier called it a victory in his report to Commandant Lyautey. Gil supposed it was, since the Mahdi lost about a hundred men that day. He looked over toward the village on the other side of the oasis. The enemy had an endless supply of recruits, unlike the Legion. It was the same on the Veldt. Kill one, and two more sprung up.

More to get them out of the way than because it made sense, someone had gathered the dozens of collapsed tents and simply rolled them tightly, leaving them stacked like cannonballs. Gil sorted through, dragging one off the pile, rummaged through it, then re-rolled it with little hope of finding his gear.

Then he saw the printing. Six. Five. Four. The serial numbers were stenciled at the bottom of each square of canvas that made up their tents. In moments of boredom, he'd memorized the numbers on his tent. Gil couldn't quite believe there would be anything worth salvaging, but smiled anyway. At least he'd found his belongings. Thank God for bureaucracy. He wouldn't have to sleep under anyone else's stains and filth.

He reached for it at the same time as another filthy pair of hands. He shouted in English, "Oi, that's my tent!"

The exhausted man spat blood and flakes of his chapped lips as he spoke. "Says who?"

Gil pointed to the serial number. "Four, five, six, five, four. That's my—our—tent." He briefly wondered where Meier was, and whether he was among the dead or wounded.

The bantam-rooster sized legionnaire shrugged. "It's just a piece of canvas. One's as good as another."

"Not. To. Me." Gil leaned close, locked eyes with the interloper, and pulled it away. The man thought about responding, but the potential murder in Gil's eyes won. He put his hands up in surrender.

"Fine, Christ. Take it."

Gil did. He tugged on the corners of the material, pulling it off the pile. It felt heavier than he expected and stumbled backwards. Without a look at the other soldier, he dragged the tent and its contents to an open patch of ground and frantically opened it up.

To his amazement, the bedrolls and both packs were inside. Because they'd been properly rolled and stored, his things survived better than Meier's. He smugly laid his goods on the ground and began repacking.

First his bedroll. Gil stood and shook it out as best he could. The wind blew the dust and dirt back into his face. Cursing, he turned his back to the wind and tried again. When the dirt, stones and most of the vermin were gone. He crushed a spider like a cigarette butt with the toe of his boot, then carefully laid the bedding out and re-rolled it with mathematical precision. On the second try, he was satisfied and tied it tight.

Perfect. Or as good as it was going to get out here in the middle of the *Sud Oranais* Nowhere.

Then he grabbed a rock big enough to sit on, rolled it into position and squatted on it. He carefully removed the contents of the pack and laid them on the ground. Most everything was still there. He even found the tribal knife from his first battle. Taking his thumb, he traced the beautifully carved symbols and vicious steel edge. Then, with loving care, it went to the bottom of the pack, along with the second ornate razor he kept for non-grooming purposes. It was hard to march with it in his boot, and he felt no need to as long as they were moving. This weapon was for maintaining order. He saw no irony in the fact it was only needed in civilized towns and peacetime. Order had to be maintained.

Piece by piece, he reorganized and perfectly rebuilt his pack.

"Was there anything left?" Meier stood there, leaning on his Lebel. From the look of him, he might have been one of the nineteen dead and nobody'd told him yet.

"Jesus, you're alright." Gil stood, almost embraced his tent-mate, then pointed to the rock seat. "Sit, You look like hell."

Meier groaned but obeyed. He attempted a smile. "I must look better than I feel." He dropped his head in his hands then took several deep breaths, then lifted his head as though coming up from deep water. "Anything salvageable?"

Gil looked at his perfectly restored pack, then at Meier's goods scattered inside the tent. "Mostly, I think. We were lucky."

He picked up a couple of pieces of the other man's clothing, but Meier waved him off. "I'll get it. It doesn't frigging matter."

Gil stared at him. Didn't matter? Of course, it bloody mattered. War was madness and chaos. Everything was. Civilian life was merely a different collection of insane circumstances. The only thing permitting anyone to survive was imposed order.

He grabbed Meier's bedroll and shook it out. Maybe if he started cleaning up, Meier would snap out of his funk.

"Stop that. You're not my mother."

"I don't mind, really." Imposing his own will on Meier's mess would make him feel better, was the point.

Quick as his aching body permitted, Meier staggered to his feet and slapped the blanket from Gil's hands. "It doesn't matter. Stop that. Can't you get it through your thick head that nobody gives a rat's ass?"

Gil stared at Meier, who was building up to a full tantrum, if not a nervous breakdown. The Alsatian stomped to his pack and kicked it. His shaving kit flew a few inches away. Meier lined up like a football player and kicked it, sending it into arching into the air.

From somewhere, a deep voice shouted, "Hey, thank you!"

Meier didn't seem to care he'd just lost his toiletry kit. His voice rose and became shriller. "What are we doing here?" Gil knew every soldier asked that question from time to time. Mostly it was rhetorical. Meier shouted like he expected answers. "Look at us. We're in the middle of God-damned nowhere. For what? Tell me."

"Because you're in the Legion, you horse's ass!" A voice called out and Gil realized Meier's outburst had drawn a crowd. A small, tight circle of men watched, wondering what madness was developing.

Cheeks burning with embarrassment, Gil turned to Meier, palms raised. "Why don't we get the tent up? You, we- both need a good night's sleep, and things will be better in the morning, yeah? What you need is rest."

"What I need is to go home. Somewhere the rain falls, and everything isn't gray or brown. What was I thinking?"

Gil wanted to help, but didn't want to be associated with the embarrassing outburst. He looked around, saw two abandoned tent poles, picked them up and held them out to Meier. "Here, let's get our tent set up. You'll feel better."

Meier knocked the poles from his hand. Gil watched dumbfounded as the sticks bounced on the ground. "You don't understand. There is no rest. There will never be rest. It'll be like this until we die, then it will be some other poor asshole's turn."

The gawking of the other soldiers bothered him more than anything Meiers said. He needed to get the tent up just so he'd have a place to escape to. He picked up the pole and gently took Meier's arm. A tantrum was… disorderly. "Help me here."

The ranting man stood mostly useless, staring at the tent pole in his hand while Gil got the canvas draped over it. Then he threw his own bedroll and pack inside. Slowly, like leading a recalcitrant child, he took Meier's belongings and gently placed them under the shelter.

He couldn't resist peeking. Everything was jammed into the pack with no rhyme or reason. A sheet of paper turned out to be a hand-drawn map of the Atlas Mountains and the coastline of Morocco, with mysterious Xes placed sporadically. Gil folded it and tucked it along the side of the bag.

All the poison apparently shouted out of his system, Meiers meekly followed him into the tiny tent. Gil handed the pack over and watched it fall to the ground at the foot of his bedroll.

Gil stripped to his undershirt and pulled his boots off, knowing he'd probably regret it in the morning if his feet swelled too much. Then he laid out Meier's blanket and helped him shrug out of his filthy johnet. There were thick brown bloodstains on it, but it didn't seem to belong to Meier. Whether it was shock, sunburn or simple exhaustion, he groaned with each movement.

"This will all be better in the morning. Good night, Meier."

"Marcus."

Gil blinked. "Excuse me?"

"My first name. It's Marcus. You didn't know that, did you, Gil?" There was an acidic edge to his voice as he over-enunciated the English name. "Not that it matters, does it?"

Gil folded the bloody jacket carefully and laid it beside Meier's bedroll. It didn't feel right calling him Marcus. Meier laid back on his bed, an arm thrown over his eyes.

A crumpled piece of paper had fallen from one of their pockets. Gil picked it up and casually glanced at it. Then he read it again.

Men of the Legion,

Why die for France?

There was no need to read the rest of it. He shoved the note into his own pocket and lay down. He'd mention it to Meier in the morning. Weariness rolled over him like a stone, and he was dead to the world in seconds.

CHAPTER 33

For three days after the battle, Gil was perfectly happy in his routine. Up at dawn. Feed, water, and shovel up after the mules. Some animals suffered scrapes or damaged hooves and were more skittish than ever. Gil patiently helped them. They were still an oasis of sanity and good company compared to his fellow troopers.

Meier, blessedly, was assigned to KP duty to keep him out of the sun until he healed up and was no longer shedding skin like a snake. Gil had nearly gagged watching white dry flakes drop into his soup. They never saw each other except for the start and end of each day. Sullen belligerence had replaced his normal quiet. What words he did utter dripped with sarcasm, venom and, Gil couldn't help but feel, accusation.

On the fourth day, after the final respects were paid to the fallen and the amnesia that settles over a troop when the shooting stops took effect, the inevitable happened.

Gil was in the corral. At some point over the last days, he'd quit greeting the animals with a string of curses and insults. Instead, he'd walk from nose to nose, patting them and offering greetings, receiving mostly nuzzles and the occasional half-hearted nip for his efforts. Fritz got a special greeting and the occasional piece of carrot or parsnip liberated from the soup pot and was the only one called by name.

He'd almost finished watering them when a bugle blew Assembly. "Oh, Christ," he muttered.

"What is it?" Jo Baldewijns asked. He'd assigned himself to the mules and Gil was grateful for both the help and the good-natured company. They walked together to the outer ring of men gathered around a water wagon turned stage.

Captain Vautier, dressed in a somehow spotless white uniform, braid gleaming on his kepi, marched back and forth with his hands behind his back. His eyebrows looked like they'd been brushed and groomed for the occasion. "*Mes braves*, we are breaking up this little picnic. Some of you will remain to help pacify the village." Pacify, of course, meant punishing the locals for their collaboration with the Mahdi's men. Gil fervently hoped he wasn't in that bunch.

Vautier continued, "Most of you will go on to Morocco to help establish order among our new, uh, countrymen." This was met by a mix of groans and laughter that was quickly cut off by a lift of those brows.

"The rest of the Twenty-Fourth will go to Fort Béchar to relieve the troops there. Your sergeants will tell you more. We know you'll do your duty as legionnaires." He spun on his heels and walked off, leaving the men no wiser than they'd been a moment ago.

Becker stepped forward. His dust-covered uniform and muck-encrusted moustache painted a different picture than the commander. "Listen up! If you're with me, you are going to Béchar. We leave at first light."

Gil realized he'd been holding his breath, but could now release it. Returning to the fetid, cramped fortress was the best of a series of poor options. He could stay and take part in whatever retaliation was planned for the people of the Menhaba oasis, men, women and children. He'd seen enough of that in South Africa, thank you.

Marching into the wilds of unsettled, perhaps unconquerable mountain tribes and sleeping on rocky ground while waiting to be ambushed in his sleep was too much chaos to contemplate. At least the fort had real cots.

"Vincente!" The sergeant's voice pulled him from his woolgathering.

"*Oui, Sergent.*"

Becker stepped closer, and Gil saw the exhaustion in his bloodshot eyes. "You've done a fine job with the mules."

Gil didn't bother to thank him, just stood at ease looking straight ahead. He already knew where the conversation was headed and dreaded it less than he would have in the past.

"We're taking most of the animals to Béchar. We need them in as good shape as possible." Gil nodded, but otherwise remained stoic. Truthfully, he was becoming fond of the bloody things, and more time with the animals meant less with people. Not a bad trade. Then he flashed on Gauthier, hiding out in his wood shop. How did that turn out?

"Yes, sir." He hesitated, then chose just to ask the question out loud. "Uh, what about Meier?"

Becker bit his lower lip before answering. "You're stuck with him til you get to Béchar. Then we'll assign him somewhere he can be of use, assuming he stays in the shade. You're staying with the livestock." He leveled his gaze and looked Gil in the eye. There was no point in complaining, so a simple nod was the response. It meant he'd be at the fort for a while. A routine. Order. Small likelihood of a random bullet. He thought about Meier's black looks and truculence. Of course, the odds were never one hundred percent.

Dawn the next day found thirty mules, four eighty-millimeter guns, and a hundred men marching northwest through the desolate frontier. The Atlas Mountains to the west and foothills to the south and east may as well have been prison walls with steep rock on the West and rising desert hills to the east. The only way was forward.

Meier took his turn riding Fritz while Gil *hup-hup-hup-hupped* alongside. Up ahead somewhere were Dupre and LaForce. And their Maxims. The kid had taken to sleeping alongside his new toy. Every soldier had a purpose, and it looked like Johnny Strong found his. He'd look better without that ridiculous stringy beard, but that wasn't any of Gil's concern.

A day away from their objective, they met another troop heading for the base. This one was mostly supplies. Grub for the fort offered false hope that they'd eat better than on the trail. If Gil's memory served, the cooks at Béchar could turn filet mignon into wallpaper paste, but he didn't feel a need to bust anyone's bubble. One thing lifted his, and everyone's, spirits.

Payroll.

Two grim-looking men led a scrawny, mangy mule laden with provisions and one more important piece of cargo. A blue hinged box bounced on its back. Every legionnaire knew they were due a piece of that treasure when they arrived at Béchar, which was now only one uncomfortable night's sleep away.

"I see they have our blood money for us," Meier groused as he unloaded Fritz and dropped their bags and goods to the ground. His eyes kept drifting to the center of the camp. To the payroll and its guardians. Gil winced and nearly complained as his worldly goods thudded to the ground. Then he thought twice about irritating a clearly unhappy armed man.

"About time. We haven't been paid since we left Sidi. Not that there's been anything to spend it on."

"Is there anything there at all? Liquor at least? Women?"

Gil cast his memory back. As he recalled, liquor, at least the homemade kind, flowed freely. As for feminine solace, Rose would have been the May Queen of Fort Béchar. The only women he remembered were crones, servants, and washerwomen. Wise tribespeople hid their pretty daughters far from the reach of French soldiers for as long as they could.

"I have to go make sure the mules are properly bedded down."

"Going to sing them a lullaby?" Meier asked.

"You're the singer. I just shovel shit and try to keep idiots from ruining the Legion's livestock." Gil stretched, then carefully moved his pack and placed it out of the way of any traffic.

Meier threw the tent poles to the ground, then tugged and several saddlebags slid off Fritz's back onto the dirty ground. "I'll set up the tent and try to grab some sleep. I'm on watch tonight. Second bloody watch."

"Look at it this way, you can't get a sunburn at night." It was meant as a joke, but Gil could tell it wasn't warmly received.

Gil pegged Fritz's hobble to the earth. "Do you need a hand with the tent?" he asked, already knowing the answer.

"I've got it. Go play farm boy." That was all Gil needed to hear. He scratched Fritz's ears and headed out on his rounds.

After a dinner of thinner-than-usual gruel and rock-hard biscuits, Gil sacked out. He didn't hear Meier leave, but was vaguely aware he was alone in the tent. He allowed himself to spare a thought for Rose, took advantage of the empty tent, then went right back to sleep.

Until the shouting started.

Gil jerked awake and reached for his weapon. There was no shooting yet, so he allowed himself the luxury of putting his boots on. Something was out of place. It was the middle of the night, but there was no way of knowing the exact time. A flash of annoyance ran through him. Then his face flushed as he saw his pack overturned and the items on the top falling out. Damn Meier and his petty grievances.

Gil emerged from the tent and realized immediately that Fritz was missing. Had the idiot taken the mule on guard duty? That seemed unlikely, but the knot around the peg had been neatly untied, and the hoof prints showed no signs of hurry. They just led off to the edge of the camp.

Nobody raised an alarm like that for one mule. He followed the confused, grumbling men deeper into the camp, to where the payroll guard's flea-bitten mule stomped in anger and confusion.

As Gil looked through a gap in the circle of legionnaires, it took him a minute to make sense of the scene. Two men lay on the ground in a thick puddle of blood. Deciphering the surrounding chatter, it seemed nobody had shouted out.

He looked, along with everyone else, making no sense of such a scene. Three details wormed their way from Gil's eyes into the deepest fear-riddled parts of his brain. First, the men's throats had been cut in long, neat slices. Since nobody screamed, probably in their sleep.

Second, the strongbox holding the payroll for the men at Fort Béchar was missing.

What riveted Gil to the ground was the third sight. His beautiful, personal, lethal razor, covered in gore, lay beside one of the soldiers.

CHAPTER 34

Gil stood rooted to the ground as Becker and another sergeant pushed their way through to the bodies. He bent over the corpses, checking for signs of life, although the deep gashes where their throats should have been and what looked like gallons of blood told him it was a fool's errand. The other sergeant, built like an ox and half as bright, picked up Gil's precious razor and held it up.

"Whose razor is this? Huh?"

Nobody answered while Gil held his breath and did some quick reckoning. Who knew he carried a razor? Anyone who'd been in the barracks at Sidi with him.

Who knew it was his razor? Certainly, the old legionnaire he pulled it on the night of the fight at Le Chat Noir, assuming he wasn't too terrified to remember. Dupre and LaForce. Maybe Gomez, who was marching somewhere in the Moroccan wilds. He held his breath for what seemed an eternity.

Nobody spoke. They had bigger concerns.

"Where's the money?"

"Does this mean we don't get paid tomorrow?"

"Who says we don't get paid?" The night devolved into shouting and ac-cusations against everyone, from bandits to tent-mates of dubious reputation. As chaos ruled the circle of soldiers, Gil stepped away. He gripped his stomach, trying to quell the growing panic in his gut. His head was a swarm of angry hornets.

Desperate to make sense of everything, he turned from the fire, stepped away, and squeezed his eyes shut. It was one thing to rob the payroll guards. Killing the soldiers was horrific enough, but his razor had done similar work in the past. He found himself staring at his hands as he remembered the robbery in La Barasse. Yes, it was his razor. But it was *his* razor. Someone had rifled through his pack.

Not someone. Meier.

Gil felt bile rise in his mouth at the thought of that imbecile rifling through his perfect, personal, prized possessions. He wandered in small circles, ignored by everyone but becoming more frantic.

"Christ. Oh Christ. Bloody Meier. You fucking..." What else had the idiot taken? Gil screamed into his hands and bolted back to their, screw that, his tent.

Running so hard, he ducked in and nearly knocked the poles aside. Somehow, he managed not to bring the tent down on his own head. Gil dumped his pack and sorted through it . Most of his things were untouched, although his newest pair of socks was gone. The knife he had taken from the Berber was still hidden at the bottom of his pack. Gil turned it over and over in his palm. What did that mean?

Meier wasn't after weapons so much as he was trying to shift the blame to Gil.

Prick.

Inventory didn't take long. A pair of socks, the razor. A small magnifying glass for starting fires. He knew precisely what was in that pack and where it belonged. Muttering to himself, Gil began shoving his things into place and then stopped. This called for order. No time to make poor decisions.

He dumped his pack completely onto his bedroll and began again. The knife. His ratty holey socks and underwear. Most things were where they belonged, but damn Meier for taking his new pair of hole-less socks.

Order was paramount in situations like this, when the world seemed out of kilter. Then he looked around and realized his saddle bags were missing. Ammo, tinder.

The picture became clearer. Meier stole his things. He'd killed fellow soldiers.

And he took Fritz. The poor innocent mule didn't deserve to be an accessory to murder and robbery. Meier took him to haul away the goods. It certainly wasn't for speed. Nobody had ever seen the gray mule at a trot, let alone anything faster than a slow, loping shuffle. But where was he going?

The scrap of paper still lay on the ground. Soldiers of France, and all that. The Germans were helping cowards and the disenchanted desert, but there were no Germans in Algeria.

The prick was headed to Morocco.

Casablanca was the only foothold the Kaiser had there, if one could believe the rumors, but what else was there to go on?

West, then. Into the mountains. On a slow mule and loaded with gear. Travel by night was potentially fatal without guides or a clear path. Meier would have gotten as far as he could, then would have to settle in for the night and continue at dawn. When the sun was up.

Gil hoped the cretin's brain would fry in the sun, the pasty-faced bastard.

His temper built from his gut to his skull, where it threatened to blow the top of his head off like a volcano. The son of a bitch Meier defiled his pack. He stole from the troop. Orel's screed about betraying your fellows added to the pounding in Gil's brain.

A thief *and* a deserter. They'll catch him and hang him. The thought lowered Gil's blood pressure a little. But justice written large wouldn't mean much. He wanted his pound of flesh.

He wanted, no needed, to be there when Meier got caught. He ached to see the shamed look in that stupid, criminal, disgusting face. To show that the feeble attempt to set him up failed.

Gil was well aware of what he should do. Let the *Police Militaire* find him and deal with the consequences. Let Orel the Eagle hunt him down like a rabbit. That made him smile a bit, but only momentarily. The feral need for payback, for vengeance, to restore order and stop the out-of-control spinning in his head was too hard to deny. His old self, the Lion, master of the streets of Marseille, pounded on his ribs to get out.

He'd felt like this before, when he followed those gamblers to La Barasse. When he sliced that goon's ear off and opened his throat. When he took the money from the shocked gambler's hand and laughed while fanning through it. On the last night *Gilbert le Lion* roared.

He'd get Meier himself. Hell, he could probably track the fool down and bring him back before lunch. One way or the other. Dead or alive.

The lion in his brain whispered to him. They'd probably give him a medal. It would at least get him out of tending mules and let him be a real soldier again. A promotion wouldn't be so bad. after all, he'd more than earned it. And a raise.

Order would be restored.

The more Gil walked in circles, arguing with himself, the more sense it made. He was smarter than Meier. A better soldier. He was a better shot than the weasel and wouldn't wilt in the sun like a delicate flower. Gil Vincente was, he decided at last, much the better man.

But Meier had a head start, fueled by panic and his pursuers' confusion. True, he was on the Legion's slowest mule. Gil would need a more dependable mount, especially if he was going to bring back the body.

There was no way Meier was coming back alive. He'd violated too many rules and deserved what came to him. Gil burned to be there when it happened.

But how? If somebody had recognized the razor, he'd be in irons by now. The men were lost in the confusion and arguing amongst themselves. If he was going to do something completely mad, the time was now.

He threw his pack onto his back and checked his canteen. The gear weighed almost nothing without the tent, poles or bedroll. He was going to miss his lovely blade, but it was gone forever, and traveling light was the priority. Ammo, his Lebel, and his sidearm were the heaviest things he could take with him. And the most important if justice was going to be served.

Trying to be as inconspicuous as possible, he strode through the camp. His ears picked up snatches of conversation.

"Who was on watch tonight?"

"...can't believe the bastards would rob us right in the camp like this. We'll punish them even more than we just did."

"We're still getting paid, right?"

Gil allowed himself a vision of returning with the money, the conquering hero. Then he heard it. The annoyed whinny of Captain Vautier's monstrous black horse.

Gil offered a quick prayer of thanks to a god he didn't believe in. He fervently hoped that god believed in him.

CHAPTER 35

Gil strode deliberately through the chaos. Men argued and shouted, pretending to help find the murderers. Nobody noticed him or bothered asking why he had his pack shouldered. He knew damned well nobody would notice a soldier doing his job.

The officers huddled by the bodies, so the Capitaine's horse was unattended. It was a beautiful black gelding. Not a pure Arab, but as close as he'd seen in a while. Gil drank in the sight of it. He'd loved handling the officer's horses in South Africa, their strength and power symbolizing the might of the Empire. So much stronger and more beautiful than a bunch of ugly half-breeds.

He shook himself out of his reverie. Nobody was paying attention and Meier was getting further away by the minute. If he dared, he could be halfway to Morocco before anyone noticed. The rational man inside came up with a hundred reasons to stop before it was too late. The Lion inside roared the reasonable Gil into submission.

The horse had been left saddled. That was the last sign he needed. God, no call it Fate, was making it too easy. Gil undid the hobbles around its fetlock and ran an appreciative palm over its chest.

"Good lad. We're going to go for a ride, alright?"

Gil pulled the stirrup off the saddleback and put a boot in.

"Hey. What do you think you're doing?" The Captain's valet yelled at him.

Ignoring the last warnings of his saner self, he pulled up into the seat and wrapped the reins around his fist. In his most authoritative voice, he barked at the young officer. "It was Meier. Marcus Meier who did it. I'm going after him."

The young man grabbed for the bridle, but the horse, eager for action, tossed its head and the young officer missed. Gil stroked the animal's neck and looked down at the frustrated kid. "You're letting the murderer get away. I'm going after him before he gets too far."

"But- "

"Yawwww," He yelled and nearly trampled the adjutant as the horse took off. By now, he'd caught the attention of the rest of the camp. The animal spun in a wide circle as Gil shouted over his shoulder at the confused legionnaires, "Tell them I've gone after Meier. Catch up when you can!"

Then he snapped the reins and gave the horse its head. The huge animal reared, whinnied, and leapt forward. All eyes turned to follow the sound and the sight of a filthy, bedraggled private stealing the Capitaine Vautier's prized mount.

Snatches of conversation rode the wind. "Isn't he Meier's partner?"

"Maybe he was in on it."

"Maybe it's *le cafard*."

Gil heard, but none of the words registered. He was busy becoming the hero of this insane opera. He'd bring back that weasel's pelt as much for stealing the payroll as for violating what didn't belong to him. Those were Gil's things. Someone had to restore order.

He knew better than to gallop the horse in the dark, so he slowed to a trot as soon as the campfires were tiny pinpricks in the night air. It was too dark to see clearly and too many mule tracks had churned up the soil to pick Fritz's out. The narrow valley ran north-south. Assuming Casablanca was Meier's goal, there was only one direction he could have gone. The only pass through the mountains lay west and a little south, if that crude map could be believed.

It was the fastest route. If the Mahdi's men were tracking the troop's movements, the steep narrow gap was also where they'd be hiding. It was desperate. Short-sighted. It was stupid.

It was precisely where Meier would head, hoping no one would follow. The sunburnt sack of turds had never met Le Lion. Gil got off the nameless black horse, who immediately stomped and whirled towards the camp.

"Not yet, beauty. We've got work to do." Gil yanked the reins harder than he meant to. The horse stomped and tossed its head, a heavy hoof just missing the toe of his boot. "Shh, shh, I'm sorry. That was too hard. I'm sorry."

He stroked the horse's neck and mane until its eyes narrowed, and breathing returned to normal. "Good boy. Okay let's go." He stepped back up into the saddle and clicked his tongue. The black gelding stepped forward on the well-worn road with only one look back to the camp. Maybe it had enough of Vautier and his wicked eyebrows as well.

Gil pulled to the right, and the horse slowed. He'd clocked the vertical slit in the mountain wall on their way north. It would require a quick trek across the flat valley floor. With timid steps, the horse's iron shoes rang against the stones, not nearly as surefooted as a mule. The image of the beautiful animal with a broken leg flashed in his mind and for the first time, Gil second guessed himself.

The qualms he felt had become a full-force storm of contradictory thoughts. He was right. He was an idiot. They'd give him a medal. If he came back empty-handed, it was the brig and the Zephyrs at best. Deserting was secondary to stealing an officer's horse, which was way behind homicide. For that, he'd likely hang. There was no choice. He'd thrown the dice. He had to find Meier. Soon.

Either Fritz was moving faster than expected, and they were still ahead, or Gil guessed wrong, in which case, he was royally screwed. His head pounded, and he felt an overwhelming exhaustion push through his body. Twice he caught himself jerking awake but urged the horse on anyway.

The way ahead became clearer in the blue-grey pre-sunrise light. Spiky plants with their flowers still closed to the night, the bigger boulders well away from the path. With better instincts than Gil, the horse had found a goat trail sloping slightly upward towards the foothills. "Good boy. They can't have gotten far," he said, trying to convince both of them.

They were almost at the slot canyon that led to the path. The trail grew steeper. Scrappy patches of dried grass grew where dew formed against the rocks and trickled into small pools. Gil's stomach growled. Hard as he tried, it was impossible to argue with his complaining stomach. He had a little biscuit stored away in his pack. He always kept his canteen filled, so water wasn't as much of a concern. What he didn't bring was horse feed.

Looking at the dry, dusty path through the canyon, he stopped and dismounted. The horse, Gil couldn't remember what Vautier called it, snorted loudly. Gill pulled the bit from his mouth and draped it over the saddle. With a trembling hand, he patted its neck, pulling burrs and insects from its mane. "Go ahead, eat up. We still have work to do."

While he and the animal were getting along, he didn't trust the horse to stay put while he did some reconnoitering. He lifted the corner of a heavy stone, ran the end of the reins under it, and dropped it with a grunt. Then he knotted the reins so they couldn't slip under the rock. If it tried hard enough, the beast could probably get away, but that should be enough to keep in place for breakfast. Gil wouldn't be gone that long.

The rising sun pointed Gil's shadow to the narrow hole in the mountain's wall. With a look back at the horse, happily munching away, he placed a hand on the stone and listened carefully. The only sound was the early morning buzz and tick of insects. His ears detected something like the rustle of leaves, but that wasn't possible. There were no trees to speak of.

He walked about fifty meters further and heard it again. In a thin beam of bright sunlight that pierced the canyon's murky darkness, a bright white sheet of paper flopped and drifted across the path.

Stumbling after it, the target blew ahead of him, leading a merry chase until Gil raised a boot and stomped it to the ground.

Picking it up, he studied the neat rows of small print written on it, then choked out a single, "Ha," as he continued reading. A list of names and figures.

It was the payroll manifest. Meier had stopped to empty the strong box.

He ran back to where he left the horse munching contentedly. "*Allez*, big boy. We've got him now."

CHAPTER 36

Ignoring his complaining gut, he led the reluctant horse at a walk through the rock maze that formed the entry into the canyon. Now that the sun was above the horizon, he had a better look at the well-beaten trail as he led the animal. The big black gelding followed unwillingly. Gil's ears tried to sort through the buzzing, humming, squawking of birds and insects for any sign of Meier.

Another piece of paper was caught in a thorn bush. Gil plucked it, scratching his hand. He sucked at the wound and cursed, then folded the sheet and stared at it. This had to be inside the strongbox with the money. The silly bastard had taken the time to break the case open. Something blue stood out against the gray-green plants and sandstone, flapping in the cool morning breeze.

A five franc note. Gil examined it, disbelieving. Nearly a month's wages in one dark blue scrap of paper. This was what a well-ordered life was worth.

The Legion took pride in paying legionnaires their pittance in cash, as opposed to military scrip. That meant the strong box would have been bursting with cash, albeit in small denominations given that the average soldier made less than seven Francs a month.

A sharp bend in the trail led to a flat rocky shelf with a view of the entire valley behind him. Heart in his throat, Gil stepped to the edge, shaded his eyes and looked over. He half expected to see soldiers pursuing him and Meier. Instead, all he saw was flat arid land. He thought he could make out the distant line of the road they had traveled from Menhaba, but that might have been an illusion.

Gil felt mild disappointment that no one had chased after him. Then he calmly ran through the scenarios in his mind. If no one gave chase, what was going on? Surely Vautier would have insisted someone go after them, if only to get his horse back. The men would have insisted on vengeance for the stolen money. But they'd only had a couple of gendarmes on the march. Meier killed the two guards charged with protecting the money.

With his razor.

The troop was only a few hours' march from Fort Béchar. Clearly, they hotfooted it to the fortress for help. They were likely almost there. That meant he and Meier would have a day's start, but the pursuers would bay for blood like hounds. If they caught him alone, they wouldn't ask questions.

He needed to get Meier himself. Explain what had happened. Be the hero.

A franc note flipped and floated onto the trail, and Gil quickly pocketed it. Why had Meier opened the box in the middle of nowhere? And how far ahead was he?

A sandy spot on the trail provided the answer. A set of perfectly preserved mule prints were pressed into the powdery ground. The wind hadn't yet blown sand over it, so the print was fresh. An hour or two perhaps. Gil hadn't stopped for longer than it took the horse to eat, so odds were Meier hadn't either. In his weakened condition—and let's face it, at full strength, the man was no Hercules—it meant Gil should be able to catch him if he hurried.

Against the horse's loud protests, he climbed onto its back. The metal shoes made the trail treacherous for the animal, but it was a risk he was prepared to take. The horse disagreed and bounced and writhed, trying to shake its illegitimate rider.

"Come on, you big bastard. Play nicely." Gil pulled the reins tight, the bit biting into the corner of the horse's mouth until it calmed down and proceeded forward. He saw a drop of blood at the corner of the soft mouth and winced. He knew better.

"Sorry about that, mate." Gil spoke in English, and the ridiculous thought occurred to him that the poor beast didn't understand him. Then he laughed, stroked its mane and repeated himself in French. A kick of his boot heels into the withers launched them down the trail at a clip too slow for Gil's taste, but faster than poor Fritz had ever gone in his life.

They'd only gone a minute when he saw something wedged between two rocks just off the path. It was blue, metal and about two feet by three feet. The strongbox.

It lay gaping open on its side in the rocks and brush. More payroll papers and a few banknotes fluttered and tumbled in the breeze. Gil clicked his teeth at how clumsy Meier had been. Clearly, the man had no plan beyond the robbery itself. And what a waste of money. He jumped down and jammed what he could find in his pockets, promising to repay it when he recovered the rest of the payroll.

There was a wet reddish-brown splatter on the metal latch. A nearby stone had the same bloodstains. Gil pictured the scene in his mind's eye- Meier smashing the lock with the rock, cutting himself in the process. The thief moved as much of the money as possible into something easier to carry and putting a smaller target on his back if found by bandits. The fact so many bills were left on the ground made Gil wonder exactly how much cash there had to be in that box.

He felt optimistic for the first time since sunrise. Meier was sloppy, Gil was orderly. The thief was injured, although how badly Gil didn't know for sure. Gil was hungry, but had plenty of water and time was on his side.

"Come on, let's get him." He clicked his tongue against his teeth, kicked gently behind him and the horse set off at a trot that was probably too fast for the trail, not nearly hasty enough for its rider's needs.

The sun felt like a branding iron on Gil's neck, even through the flap on the back of his kepi. If he was uncomfortable, Meier must have been miserable.

Good. Serves him right, the thieving bastard.

That's when he heard Fritz's familiar, annoying bray. The horse froze, surprised to hear another animal. It lifted its head and sniffed loudly. Gil slipped off and wrapped the reins in his fist. Foolishly laying his finger to his lips, he signaled the horse to be quiet.

One foot carefully in front of the other, walking heel-toe, he navigated the stony path as quietly as possible. It sloped at a sharp angle down into a gully, and he couldn't avoid kicking the occasional stone. He hoped no one heard.

His ears were peeled for any sounds. One loud honk wasn't enough for him to judge how far away his query was. Then he heard Meier's tenor voice, completely out of place in the most barren of African mountain passes, singing in German.

In dem Duft, Duft, DuftDieser Luft, Luft, Luftja, ja, ja, jaBerlin! Hör' ich den Namen bloß!

The cocky bastard. Warbling away like he didn't have a care in the world. He was clearly oblivious to the fact that Gil, and the judgment he carried with him, was so close.

Dropping the reins, Gil crouched low, inching closer. He poked his head over an outcrop and looked down into a shady gulch. Meier was singing and eating something. Gil's stomach protested the unfairness of it. Food. The thief planned this all more carefully than he gave the bastard credit for. Meier brought food with him. How long had he been planning the betrayal? That alone was worthy of grudging respect. He'd had Fritz loaded and ready to go. There was the map, and the coded desertion flyer. He'd stowed at least a couple of day's rations. The rest of what he needed, he stole from Gil. No easy feat.

Flashes of blue paper waved from the edges of the saddlebags. Those were Gil's bags- full to bursting with the money from the strongbox. Hunger and exhaustion were forgotten as he looked at the money. So much more than he'd ever seen. Even after La Barasse.

Quietly, he slipped his pack off and dumped it beside the sweaty, spooked, and confused horse. He loaded the Lebel, fastened Rosalie onto the muzzle, and then made sure his sidearm was good to go.

Gil looked skyward, took a long deep breath, then poked his head over the rock to get a good look at his prey. Meier was blissfully unaware of what was coming after him. It would be so easy to just pick him off, but he'd prefer to take him in alive. That's what Orel would do.

Then that stupid mule let out a warning honk.

"Bloody traitor," Gil hissed at Fritz and leaned over the rock. His rifle pointed down at the shocked fugitive. Meier's song died in his throat.

CHAPTER 37

"*Der schiss,*" Meier said, scrambling for his rifle. His eyes widened, and he frantically scanned the rocks around him for the source of the noise. The muzzle of his Lebel waved back and forth. In German he rasped out, "*Wer bist du?*" He repeated the question in French, demanding to know who was there.

The frightened, feral look on Meier's face made Gil reconsider his approach. Ideally, he wanted to bring the man in alive. But what sounded perfectly plausible, bouncing on horseback alone with his thoughts, became a different matter altogether when faced with an angry, frightened, well-armed opponent. His eyes fell on the pink scar running across his left wrist. It wasn't the first time he'd done something half-cocked without thinking it through. He called himself thirty kinds of idiot, then dropped behind a boulder to think.

Gil watched as a long, dark shadow stretched in front of him and up the side of the rock he leaned against. The rising sun burned orange and yellow behind his back. That would help. Meier had to look directly into the blinding morning light and couldn't see clearly. That advantage would probably only last another hour, then the sun would be too high to provide decent camouflage.

"Who's there?" Meier demanded again. He stepped backwards, gun pointing in Gil's general direction, putting the oblivious Fritz between himself and the danger lurking at the top of the gully.

Gil cursed himself, Meier, and that damned Judas mule. His eyes burned, and he wiped his arm across them, which didn't really help. The morning breeze was laden with sand and pollen. The captain's black horse whinnied, which set Fritz honking again. Meier now knew that whoever was after him was up and to his left.

He yelled again, "Who's there? Show yourself." If he wanted Gil to poke his head up, he did the worst possible thing. He fired a bullet that shot wide and kicked up a rock chip off to Gil's left.

Gil nestled into his rocky shelter. Taking a deep breath, he laid his rifle on the rock and stuck his head up, trying to get Meier in his sights. Shooting him wouldn't be ideal, but would solve a lot of problems.

First, a dead body was easier to handle. He could toss Meier's carcass over Fritz's back and return triumphant with the murderer, the money and the mule plus the Captain's horse. A loud rumble shook his stomach. There was also the issue of food. The rat bastard had been hoarding food for this moment and wasn't likely to share just because Gil asked nicely.

As quietly as he could, Gil set himself up in a sniper's nest. First, he found a niche in the rocks that would nicely cradle the Lebel's muzzle. He aligned himself with his back to the rising sun's rays. There wasn't much time to take advantage of the light and shadows. He'd have to move quickly.

Slowly, he raised his head just enough to sight down the barrel to where Meier stood, still scanning for signs of his pursuer. It was a long way downhill. Gil squinted and placed his finger on the trigger.

Meier took two steps back to get a better angle uphill. Fritz's enormous head was now in the way of any shot Gil might have. He didn't mind shooting his treasonous tent-mate, but an innocent animal was at risk.

"Goddammit," Gil muttered. What was it going to take to get him out in the open? He waited, an invisible clock *tick-tocking* in his mind. When he couldn't stand the silence any longer, he shouted, "Me-Marcus. We have you; give up."

Meier's face was blank, then a sneer crossed his lips. "Vincente? Is that you?"

He risked poking his head over the rock to see what Meier was doing. "Yeah. It is."

The other man shook his head. "I really hoped they'd have you in irons by now. And who in Christ's name is 'we,'? Who's with you?"

The horse let out a well-timed whinny. Meier swiveled his head side to side, looking for the source of the sound. Gil nodded his thanks to the animal, then yelled down the hill. "I've got two military policemen with me. You're surrounded."

Meier took another step back. He'd located the sound of Gil's voice. "Horse shit. If you had the Military Police with you, I'd be talking to one of them. You came by yourself, didn't you, dumbass?"

Gil had no time to think of anything more clever than to shout, "Screw your mother."

Meier threw his head back and laughed. "And where'd you get a horse? Did you steal it?"

Gil cupped his hands over his mouth and yelled, "Commandeered it so I could catch you and bring you back."

"No, you didn't. You took off half-cocked, and now they think you murdered the guards, took the money, and stole a horse. You're fucked. Ha!" He let out a barking laugh.

"Screw you!" Gil sighted and fired. He missed high, and Meier squatted down, now completely hidden behind Fritz, who shuffled uncomfortably. Gil could swear the blasted animal turned its big, friendly face up the hill at him.

What kind of coward hides behind a poor animal? Gil's anger flared, and he tried to get another shot off, but couldn't find an obvious line of sight. "Move your arse, ya bloody idiot," he muttered through his teeth. He fired another shot, this one lower but too far right.

All this time, Meier had been clocking Gil's position. In a flash, he raised his rifle and fired up the hill. Chips of sandstone flew past Gil's ear. Then Meier, still squatting behind his living barricade, gathered the remnants of his lunch, shoved it into his pack and took Fritzy by the reins. "*Komm schon, Fritz*," and he clicked his tongue. Fritz followed reluctantly.

Gil's anger and helplessness made his head He couldn't let Meier get away, yet couldn't really do anything to stop him. Returning empty-handed was no option at all. He'd be arrested, probably hung. Visions of Gauthier's blue, lifeless face swinging like a pendulum appeared in his mind's eye.

He frantically rubbed his eyes to dispel the vision. "Idiot. You ruddy idiot. You've buggered it all up again." He didn't realize he was screaming out loud until he heard Meier's mocking laughter.

"What's wrong, Englishman? Here. This should help get you to Casablanca. The Germans are helping us get out of this dung heap of a country. Consider it a present." He grabbed a handful of bills from the saddlebag—Gil's saddlebag—and threw them in the air. Then he yanked on Fritz's reins and led him further down the labyrinthine gully, looking back to make sure the Englishman wasn't following.

Gil watched through a head swirling with anger, frustration, and self-loathing. He'd been an idiot. His plan was stupid, completely lacking in order or discipline. Now he'd pay. Again. But there was nowhere to go.

The bridge to Marseille had long been reduced to ashes with no hope of return.

If he failed to bring Meier and the money back, he'd hang.

Orel's thick Cossack accent reverberated in his mind. *Nothing is lower than someone who betrays his brothers.* If he fled, he'd be a deserter.

He'd gone off half-cocked with no food or water. Odds were already good he'd die out here, a miserable failure with no one to mourn him.

Gilbert the Lion joined the Legion for order. For the world to make sense. For the discipline to cope with the world's madness. Instead, it was all going to hell.

There was only one thing to do.

With shaking hands, he affixed Rosalie to his rifle, loaded a fresh cartridge, and shoved another into his jacket pocket. Barely audible, he hissed something like a prayer, "You can do this. You can do this. You stupid horse's arse, you can do this."

Without another second's thought, he stood, fired and headed down the steep path, zigzagging and firing as he went. By the time he reached the flat bottom of the gulley, Meier had disappeared around a corner.

Gil held his weapon steady, step by step, approaching the corner. Then, he pressed his back to the rock wall and listened. He had no clue if Meier had gotten the hell out of there or was waiting in ambush. It didn't matter. This was the moment.

As he took a step into the trail, prepared to shoot whatever he saw, he heard two things. First, the horse he'd abandoned at the top of the trail let out a piercing, terrified whinny. The second was a gunshot from up high. How the hell had Meier gotten up there?

He hadn't. Gil looked behind him to see two robed figures running down the hill after him. The fleeting thought occurred to him. Did he want to be killed by a comrade or a bandit? Those were the options unless he could find a way out.

CHAPTER 38

Choosing the devil he didn't know, Gil ran from the attackers. He zigzagged through the towering boulders and steep sandstone, unsure of where he was headed. Behind him, he heard the shrieking of the Captain's horse, no doubt those bastards' property now. Male voices yelling in the local dialect urged each other on.

Over his own ragged breathing, Gil thought he detected four voices. The local Berbers kept scouting and raiding parties small both for speed and to reduce losses. If he was wrong, he was dead. Sporadic gunfire echoed off the gully walls.

They were trying to flush him out.

He was never afraid of a fight, but dying needlessly held no appeal. Escape was the only thing on his mind at that moment. He had no way back. His choices were reduced to either capturing Meier, Fritz, and the money or die in the middle of nowhere for no reason. That Vautier's gorgeous black gelding was now in Berber hands was a problem he would address if he survived.

Bursting onto a dry creek bed from the rocky maze, his target was about two hundred yards ahead. The man was tugging frantically but with no success on the mule's reins, while Fritz dug his forefeet into the gravelly soil. The mule let out a honk and shook its head, nearly pulling Meier from his feet.

Gil was too winded to shout, but Meier must have heard him, because he raised his head and yelled something in German. It was impossible to tell from this distance if he was cursing the mule or him. Somewhere behind him, a bullet rang off stone. Gil lifted his arms and waved frantically.

"Bandits! There are—" A scream and a shot from somewhere behind and above him drowned out his warning. Meier looked up, his eyes wide with fright and confusion. He yanked even harder on Fritz's reins, and the mule relented and moved forward a few steps. Meanwhile, he fumbled with his sidearm, waving it at Gil while moving backwards, his eyes scanning the upper rocky ridges.

In a fog, Gil looked for some sort of cover on the flat surface. To Meier's left, a five-foot-high boulder might provide enough cover.

If he could get there.

Cutting sharply, he veered off course and ran as fast as he could. A couple of dust clouds kicked up to either side, but there were far fewer shots than he expected. Then he realized why. He wasn't the target. One lone soldier meant nothing. Meier had what they wanted most—the mule loaded with potential loot.

Once he was crouched in the shady lee of the rock, he risked checking on Meier. The thought occurred to him that they'd be doing him a favor by killing the bastard. Then the reality of his situation washed over him. Life wasn't that simple.

It didn't matter if Meier died, particularly, although no real legionnaire should die alone at the hands of barbarians. But a dead *Ferengi* was a bonus. Franc notes were of limited use in mountain villages, but the propaganda value alone, the moral victory of stealing the Infidel's precious treasure, would embolden the rebels. Gil remembered their focused mad attack at Menhaba. How much braver, and more dangerous, could they get?

Several deep breaths helped clear his mind. What the hell should he do now? If they killed Meier, they'd get everything. Gil would be left in the wilderness, alone, to die. Everyone would believe him to be a deserter. That wasn't the only problem. If he lost the gear and Fritz, he'd be good as dead. If the bandits didn't kill him, heat and thirst likely would. If by some miracle the search party from

Béchar found him, he was still a corpse, only there'd be a week or two's delay before they hung him and finished the job.

He watched two figures descend from the heights. One thief was up there with the horse, or more likely halfway to the nearest camp. He wished the gelding well.

"Bollocks," he said to himself and checked the Lebel. Then he stood, aimed at the closest Berber, and fired. The target dropped, although he was still alive and not mortally wounded, judging from the screaming and cursing.

Click. Click. Gil threw the bolt and fired another shot. This one dropped the second man in his tracks. Gil swung the barrel a hundred and eighty degrees around him. He saw Meier staring. Fritz shook his head and shuffled in place.

Something moved on the rock face above and behind Meier. Meier fired his sidearm, missing wildly. Gil calmed himself, then pulled the trigger. He missed Meier by a mile, but the shot found its mark. A third bandit fell from the rocks directly behind Meier and Fritz and crashed lifelessly to the ground. Meier gaped like an idiot, his mouth open in shock as if the body had fallen from the sky.

The gully was now quiet except for the hum of insects. Remembering the fate of the unfortunate Lieutenant Coste, Gil approached the wounded man, who'd gotten to his feet. Blood flowed freely down his leg, staining the bottom half of his trousers. He was severely wounded in one leg but held a viciously sharp curved blade in one hand. The gibberish he yelled was clearly a challenge to fight like a man.

Gil didn't oblige him. Pulling his own sidearm, he stood well out of the blade's reach, then shot the man between the eyes. He looked at the demonic hate etched on the dead man's face, but noticed something far more important. His waterskin and food bag. Gil ripped it from the brown cotton belt. He took a huge swig of water and poured some over his face and rubbed furiously. Then he tied the bag to his own sash, where it bounced off his leg.

"Do you expect me to thank you?" Meier shouted in French.

Gil turned towards him and stepped forward. His head spun with hunger, thirst and the after-effects of adrenaline. In a voice full of bravado and bullshit, he yelled back, "It would be nice, you ungrateful Bosche prick."

He hoped Meier couldn't see how shaky and close to collapsing he was. It wouldn't be long before he would be unable to support his own weight, so he made himself walk to a stone halfway between the body and Meier and sat down, never taking his eyes off the other soldier.

"Thank you, then. I won't kill you, but I'm leaving you here. Take that bushy-eyed bastard's horse and go home."

That would not happen. It couldn't.

Gil scanned the area for more attackers. It didn't look like there was anyone other than the two of them. Meier's gaze was fixed on him. Fritz stared neutrally from one of his riders to the other, appearing uninterested in the coming duel.

Meier's exhaustion was plain in his croaking voice. "Just let me go. Hell, come with me." He slapped at the bulging saddlebags hanging from Fritz's back. "There's plenty. We can split it when we get to Casablanca."

For a heartbeat he considered the offer, but he'd lived a life without order. He couldn't do it again. On top of that, he needed to put his life back to rights. If he could capture, or more likely kill Meier, he would return the money and prove his innocence. There were no other choices.

"I know you think I'm an arsehole, but I'm not an idiot," Gil answered. He slowly approached with one hand on his weapon. With the rifle in his other hand, he couldn't swat away the stinging clouds of flies circling his head. It was all he could do to walk a straight line.

Meier glared back, keeping Fritz between them.

Gil's jaw tightened. What kind of coward hides behind a helpless animal? More than anything else, that made Gil's mind up for him.

Fritz took two steps forward and then back, shuffling nervously and looking from one of his riders to the other as if demanding an explanation. "Easy boy, it's alright," Gil told the animal.

"The hell it is! I'm not going back to that shithole. I'm going to Casablanca, and the Germans will put me on a boat to a civilized country, with enough money to start again. Something safe. Maybe a butcher shop."

Meier paced as he babbled on. Keeping Fritz between them, he shouted, sometimes at Gil, sometimes to the sky. He waved his gun wildly, punctuating each thought by shaking it at Gil.

In Marseille, Gilbert the Lion lived by the rule: don't ever lose your bearings. When you became so emotional you couldn't think, bad things happened. His wrists had the scars to prove it. He was dancing on that knife edge, but Gil wondered how close Meier was to that line himself. The only way to find out was to push harder.

"Being a butcher wasn't so safe for your uncle. He died anyway."

"He was murdered by that son of a whore. Literally a whore. Did he tell you that about his mama? Your friend Jean?"

With false confidence, Gil shouted back. "I don't believe you. He's a good kid. A better soldier than you by a mile." Whether or not he believed Meier was irrelevant. He had his doubts about LaForce, but Gil was focused on keeping the other man off balance. Uncertainty led to stupid mistakes. He knew that for a fact.

His plan didn't appear to work. Meier's hand was even steadier now, his glare darker and more focused. He stood straighter, and a sneer crawled across his face.

Gil's heart sank. If he was trying to rattle the thief, he'd failed. Disastrously.

"I don't want to shoot you, but I will." Meier moved a little to improve his shot but stayed behind Fritz. His pistol was raised and leveled right at Gil. Gil forced himself to keep inching forward. Step by step, wincing with each footfall, he came forward expecting a bullet at any second.

"Stop. I mean it."

Gil took five more steps, treading carefully but inexorably towards Meier. The Alsatian shrilly yelled, "Why do you even care? It's not your money. These aren't your soldiers. It's not your country."

He recalled the words of Colonel Orel: "But they are my brothers. And you killed them." He was a little surprised at his own words, damned if they weren't true. That wasn't the only reason, of course. His voice grew stronger and his head swam as he continued, "And you did it with MY RAZOR! Mine! And you touched it. You stole our pay." Gil felt himself losing control, and hated himself, but couldn't stop. All the rage, disorder, madness that had built up for months spewed out of his parched mouth.

He continued drawing ever nearer. "Don't you see? This is all your fault. And I have to set it right."

"You're mad as a hatter." Meier shook his head, then fired.

The bullet missed, but Gil dove to the dirt anyway. Wiping his eyes, he looked up. The normally placid Fritz was now fidgeting and huffing nervously. Meier stepped out directly behind the mule. He grinned at the sight of his opponent pinned to the ground. He moved directly to his right. There was a clear line of fire to Gil. Meier took aim and shot again. This one sailed high, but there was no follow-up.

Gil lay in the stony dirt, paralyzed by what he saw. Fritz, startled at the explosive gunfire, kicked viciously backward and caught Meier in the temple. The man crumpled to the ground, thrashed like a fish for a second, then lay still.

"Mother of God," Gil whispered. He got to his feet and staggered towards Meier but knew from the way the body lay folded in on itself it was too late to help. Even if he wanted to.

He and Fritz looked at each other as he stood over the carcass. The right side of Meier's head was staved in, blood and bits of brain staining the gully floor. The bloody ground was already thick with ants. Gil fought the urge to puke his empty stomach out, then reached out a hand and stroked Fritz's soft nose. Never taking his eyes off the body, he heard himself chuckle.

"Good lad. That's a good boy."

CHAPTER 39

For Christ only knows how long, Gil stood stroking Fritz's mane and stared at the lifeless body on the ground. Meier's dull, dead blue eyes looked back. A mask of betrayal, whether aimed at him or the mule, was forever painted on the remains of that broken, caved-in face.

The adrenaline faded, as did the nausea. It was replaced with a body-enveloping hunger. Gil led Fritz to a shaded spot where the animal could graze on thorny bushes while he took care of his own needs. He ripped open the Arab's food bag. Dried fruit and meat never tasted so good, even washed down with warm brackish water that left his mouth tasting of copper and mud.

The food sat like a stone in his stomach, but the hunger passed. His mind stopped swimming for the moment. There was finally time to think. There had been too little of that since he took off after Meier a full day, maybe more, ago. It was midday of whatever bloody day this was.

He looked up to the sky for guidance that never came, then began talking to himself, trying to make sense of what to do next. It hadn't been a complete disaster. Meier was dead. Gil felt an odd relief that he wasn't the one responsible, but it did not make things less complicated. Odd that he felt worse than Fritz did.

The thought of hauling the body for two days or more through the desert filled him with dread, more for the work and mess it would entail than any qualms about the corpse itself. But how else was he to prove the man was dead?

He remembered Orel taking the identification tags and books from the deserters in the canyon. Grunting and slapping his knees, he walked over to the corpse, nudged it with the toe of his boot and then began searching the body, beginning at the boots.

Meier's feet were far too big for his boots to be of use to Gil, and he took such little care of his equipment and uniform that they were best left for rags. Brushing the ravenous, biting insects aside, he found little of use.

Most important was Meier's identification. That, along with the stolen money and gear, would back up the story he was forming in his mind. The thieving arsehole planned and executed the robbery and the murders, attempting to jam up Gil with that razor. A quick search of the pockets revealed one of those notes. "Soldiers of France..." Gil shoved it into his pocket, imagining his triumphant return to the troop.

"Look," he'd tell them. "Poor Meier fell prey to the treacherous German attempts at suborning desertion." He basked in their imaginary gratitude. Catching a thief and a deserter. Hell, maybe breaking up a ring of deserters. After all, someone had given Meier that flyer, and the code might reveal who it was. That and returning the payroll would atone for a multitude of sins.

The only fly in the ointment was the loss of Vautier's gelding. Bringing Fritz back would hardly atone for that quality horseflesh, but that was a minor quibble. Surely, his victory would atone for a minor sin against an officer.

Somewhere in the back of his mind, he wondered if his story was as watertight as he imagined. The longer he was missing, the more suspicion would fall on him as at least an accomplice to the crime. Of course, that he was headed towards the search party would work in his favor. What kind of arsehole criminal runs back to his pursuers?

Perfect.

Time to head back.

He led Fritz to within a few feet of the body. The mule snorted and turned its head away as Gil conducted a thorough inventory. The stolen saddlebags were full of cash. He didn't bother to count it, just made sure the bags were closed as tight as possible, and whatever fell out went into his pockets for safekeeping. Meier's bags contained food he must have been squirreling away for days. That, with the bag he took from the bandit, gave him enough food and more variety than he'd experienced in weeks.

He picked up the man's Lebel and sidearm along with a nearly empty case of ammunition. Who knew what dangers he faced on the way back? He'd take all the help he could get, and returning Meier's weapons would only add to his credibility.

Meier's pack contained a scrawling, piss-poor map that showed the major trails and rough locations of every trail between Fort Béchar and Casablanca. The port on the Moroccan coast was circled in black ink, leaving no doubt about Meier's intentions.

Gil ran a finger over the map. A well-marked road led back to the fort. That's what he needed to do. Get back to the Twenty-Fourth as fast as he could, the conquering hero. It looked like a winding, high trail but had a couple of "X"s that were likely wells or watering holes. There'd be plenty of water and likely grass for Fritz, who was never picky.

Doubts circled his brain like horseflies, distracting and occasionally painful. The story fit together. It was orderly. It made sense. But what if they didn't believe him?

He wouldn't dwell on that. Things were falling into their orderly places. His plan was solid, and a solid plan won every time.

Even though the sun was high, he couldn't wait a minute longer. It was time to head back. He stowed the food, the map, and Meier's identification carefully into his pack and then slid his arms into it and adjusted it for comfort.

"Come on, Fritz." It occurred to him that was the first time he'd ever called the mule by name. Of course, the mule had saved his life. It seemed the least he could do.

It took the better part of an hour to climb up the steep trail to the spot he'd left Vautier's gelding. The ground was torn up, but there was no sign of blood or violence. He wished nothing but the best for the Captain's horse. At least he hadn't gotten it killed. That had to count for something.

By mid-afternoon, the sun radiating off the rocks was too much to bear. He found a shady spot between the rocks with a soft sandy bottom. He could rest, hydrate, and still have a few hours of daylight. Traveling in such terrain in the dark would be a terrible idea, and Fritz could surely use the rest. You wouldn't know it to look at the old boy, though. He stood as stoic and bored-looking as ever while Gil grunted and laid a blanket on the soft dirt.

"You have the first watch, my friend."

Hearing no objection from his companion, Gil fell fast asleep.

He woke with a start. A cool breeze on his sweaty mud-tracked face told him it was closer to sundown than he expected. He woke slowly, but jolted to attention when he found a gray Velvet Spider taking shelter in the moist dark lining of his collar.

"Christ, nasty thing," he grunted, knocking it to the ground and crushing it with more force than necessary. "Don't laugh, you'd be next." Fritz didn't seem concerned.

Wolfing down a few dried dates, he took the reins and led his mount along the track, walking in companionable silence. About nightfall, he reached the crossroads of the path he'd taken and the shortest route to the fort. Checking the map while there was still light, he saw a watering hole should be a short walk ahead. The tiniest ember of hope flared in his chest.

"This is it, my friend. Smooth sailing from here. We'll get you a drink and some supper, settle in for the night, then head for home in the morning." The mule surprised him by nuzzling his shoulder, and Gil rewarded him by offering him some of the precious water.

Even Fritz agreed things were looking up.

CHAPTER 40

Gil slept like the dead. He woke just as the thin white line of dawn defined the horizon between sky and flat desert plain. Dried sweat and dust hardened into clay at the corners of his eyes. Unable to just blink it away, he poured water into a cupped hand and scrubbed his face. Then he lifted it up and let the cool breeze dry his skin.

Fritz honked a greeting and lifted his head, tugging on the thorn bush he was tied to.

"In a hurry? Got somewhere to go?" Gil shared his mount's impatience. The sooner he reached Fort Béchar, the sooner this would all be over. The conquering hero and his equine companion. There'd be Satan's own hell to pay over Vautier's horse, but his story held up. As he led Fritz down the trail, he rehearsed his story.

The traitorous bastard Meier killed the couriers and stole the payroll. Hopefully, nobody knew that was his razor, but if they did, he'd just swear Meier stole it. *It was a frame-up, Mon Capitaine.* Yes, he took the horse, and it's likely in the hands of the bandits who attacked us as I was about to arrest the miscreant. I have proof the bastard's dead. I'm returning the money and the mule. *Look at this face. Do I look like a thief?* He'd sleep the sleep of the just.

Gil was going over his testimony for the third time, trimming some of the embellishments, so it was both more believable and less braggadocious. Humility was best, especially if he wanted leniency for commandeering the horse.

Fritz heard it first. His nostrils flared, and he sniffed loudly, then halted and began backing up. Gil grabbed the reins. "Where do you think you're going?" He stood stock-still but followed the animal's wide eyes up the trail, trying to discern the source of the trouble. He quietly mumbled, *"Shh-shh,"* and stroked the mule's fuzzy nose.

A long bend in the trail obscured his view of what lay ahead, so he took slow, careful steps. A flash of blue caught his eye, but the sun was directly in his face, and it took a moment to figure out what it was.

A stocky, rough-looking sergeant stood with his back to the trail, fumbling with the buttons on his pants. At last, he got them fastened and whistled through his teeth. A sad, skinny mule stepped into view.

The animals smelled each other at the same time and honked greetings in unison. The legionnaire, startled, whirled around to see the source of the noise. Gil and the man, by the markings on his uniform Military Police, stared at each other in stunned silence. The sergeant, working on a better night's sleep and less moldy food, no doubt, snapped into action first.

"Hold it right there!" He grabbed his Lebel from the back of the mule. The bayonet was firmly in place and pointed at Gil's stomach. "Who are you?"

Gil relaxed the muscles in his face and mustered a smile. "Private Gil Vincente. *Le Vignt-quatrieme Regiment Monté.* He walked towards his rescuer with his hand out.

The sergeant barked, "Hold it right there!" Gil heeded the command and raised his palms as he watched the rifle pointed at his chest. "We've been looking for you," the sergeant said.

"I bloody hope so. It's been what, two nights? Three? I got it. All of it." He slapped the saddlebag full of cash, smiled and took a couple of more steps forward.

"I said hold it." There was no arguing with the tone, so he put his hands up in a half-hearted gesture of surrender.

Gil's cheeks flushed at the blatant disrespect, but held his voice steady. If he maintained his calm, this would all come out in the wash. "Is this really necessary? I have the money, all of it right here. Meier is dead. Damn his thieving soul."

"Drop your weapons and move over against the rock." Gil choked back a response and obeyed. Couldn't this idiot see he was on their side?

He threw his rifle and sidearm to the ground and stepped back, a friendly look on his face despite the anger welling inside. "Who else is with you?"

"Captain Orel and another man. A private."

His shoulders sagged, and he rotated them to his ears and down. Then he stretched his neck and faked a grin. "Perfect. I know Orel. We'll get this all sorted." He was a little insulted that the search party was so small, but he'd found Meier, they'd found him. All's well that ends well. He reached for his canteen but a headshake from the sergeant put an end to that. "What, I can't even get a drink?"

"When you're in irons, you can have a drink. For now, just sit your arse down."

Gil couldn't help taking an angry two steps forward. "Irons? That's not-" He was cut off by the Click-clack of the bolt thrown on the other soldier's weapon.

The suspicious soldier squinted down the barrel of his weapon. "What else do you do to thieves and murderers?"

Gil hoped he couldn't hear the outrage in his voice as he clenched his teeth and asked, "Murderer? I didn't kill anyone."

"You telling me that wasn't your razor killed those men?"

Crap.

He winced and took a calming breath. "Meier stole that from me. Probably so someone like you would think I did it."

"We'll see."

Sweat dripped down the back of his neck and pooled under his armpits. It was more than the heat that bothered him. They recognized his razor. Who told them? This was going to make things more complicated. Good thing Orel was coming. The man liked Gil and would listen to reason.

"Step forward. Slowly. Hands up!" The Sergeant waved him forward.

"Is this really—"

"Hands up!" Gil shot his hands high in the air. Best to play nice until someone more reasonable showed up.

"Step forward. Three steps. Keep them up."

One step. Two. Three. "Happy?" The soldier grunted and Gil kept talking. "Do you have a name at least? I'm Gil."

Laying his Lebel against a rock, bayonet pointing skyward, the soldier ran his rough hand over Gil's neck. "*Hulot. Sergent Hulot.*" He slapped Gil between the shoulder blades and roughly searched each pocket. Gil watched helplessly as a wadded up blue Franc note fell to the ground.

Gil let out a friendly chuckle. "I picked that up off the ground. Couldn't just leave it lying around, could I?"

"Shut the hell up. I thought you said everything was in the saddlebags."

Gil felt a rough hand slap upside his head. Heat rose in his chest and rushed to his cheeks. He knew police like this. Soldier or not, this whore's son was no better than the patrolmen in Marseille. Reason was no weapon against them. But fighting back when he was so close to being home free...

"I was bringing it back. I swear."

"I said, shut up." Hulot shoved a rough hand into the pocket and its contents fell to the ground. Several more banknotes, a half-eaten piece of dried apricot, and a piece of white paper fell to the pebbly ground.

Gil's heart sank to the bottom of his gut as the sergeant bent and opened the paper ball. The man's piggish eyes widened as he read.

"Fuck me," Gil whispered. It was the German invitation to deserters. "I picked that up from Meier. He was heading for—" His words were cut off by a backhanded slap across the face.

"Traitorous pig. You'll hang for this." The legionnaire's face was bright red, and he was snorting like a bull.

Gil held his hands up, palms out. "No. No. This is all a misunderstanding. Captain Orel will help sort this out."

"Don't bloody move," the sergeant ordered. He turned to Fritz and began ham-handedly rummaging through the saddlebags.

"It's all there, I swear." Gil's voice had a tinge of desperation he knew wasn't helping make his case. "There's no need to- "

"I said shut up!" Hulot roared as he threw one set of bags to the ground and roughly poked through the gear still loaded on Fritz's back.

Gil felt a shout build in his throat, but managed to swallow as he watched the clumsy, destructive search. All his carefully stowed gear was scattered across the desert floor. Blood pounded in his temples. Lava flowed through his body. A red haze came over his eyes as anger boiled.

Hulot was a man possessed. He grabbed Gil's pack and, with his eyes locked on Gil's, pulled items one by one and threw them to the ground.

"Please. No, you don't have to do that. Please..." Gil watched helplessly. It was all so unnecessary. Hulot laughed as he threw Gil's belongings around. No order. No reason.

"What else are you hiding here?" He grabbed the last pack, and what remained of Gil's things hit the ground. The last of his clean socks, the bandit's ornate knife, his tinderbox. The shaving kit was quickly opened and tossed to the ground.

Gil found himself shouting incoherently. It was stupid, he knew, but there was no need to treat a fellow legionnaire like this. He'd chased a killer with no help. He was returning the money. He'd done everything this clumsy ogre demanded. Why would he do this?

He couldn't help himself. He bent and scooped up some of his clothes, shaking the dust from it.

"Drop it!"

"Screw you. You didn't have to do this." Righteous anger filled his lungs to bursting, and only screaming relieved the pressure.

He felt cold steel against his throat. Hulot held his rifle tight, the blade of his bayonet against Gil's throat. "Hold still. I'm not telling you again."

Gil heaved a sigh of relief as the soldier withdrew the weapon, then felt the air leave his body as a sucker punch caught him in the solar plexus, driving him to his knees. Gasping like a fish in a boat, his empty lungs refused to obey. He dropped to the ground, hands clutching at the gravel. Hulot stood over him laughing.

He looked up at the horse's ass of a sergeant. The bully, the bastard. Slowly, he rolled to his hands and knees. The air slowly reentered his body. He looked up through cloudy eyes in time to see the sole of Hulot's boot catch him in the cheek and drive him into the desert.

"I said, stay down!"

It was advice Gil couldn't take. In his helpless fury, his hands scrambled for something, anything, he could use to strike back. Sun glinted off the spotless blade of the Berber's curved knife. Shaking, filthy fingers gripped the carved handle.

Hulot leaned over and shouted in Gil's face. "You don't listen worth a shit, do you? I said—"

The words were cut off by the wicked steel blade puncturing his guts. Scalding hot blood squirted as Gil pulled the knife out and thrust again. The sickening butcher shop sound of a blade striking meat was drowned out by Gil's furious shrieking.

"You shouldn't have touched... my... things." His vision cleared only when the sergeant pitched face-first into the rocky trail.

Hulot's mule lowered its head and stomped on the ground. Fritz calmly stepped between his master and the stranger. Big black eyes turned to the hysterically laughing man.

Gil wrapped his arms around his waist and shuffled in a circle. Christ, what had he done? This was bad. How would he explain this? His carefully crafted story was in worse shambles than his belongings.

"Hawkins, you bloody goddamned idiot. You're such a useless tit." This wasn't right. It was all so very, very wrong. He punched himself in the head. And again.

Snot ran from his nose and mingled with the tears and sweat already staining his face. His beautiful plan. It was so solid. Orderly.

Now it had all turned to shit. Orel and the others would be here any minute. What was he going to do? Gil saw the body lying on the trail in a quick-drying pool of blood. Even if he hid the body, there was no concealing what had taken place.

Every soldier knew the difference between killing and murder. The beautiful blade of the dagger stuck accusingly from Hulot's chest. It looked so out of place among all the soldier's gear spread around it.

Gil scooped up his gear and clothes and shoved them into the kit. More than anything, he wanted to take the time to stow it all properly. And he would when he got back to Fort Béchar. Where he'd go to prison unless...

A thought hacked through the fog in Gil's mind. The scene didn't look like two soldiers fought. It looked more like the arrogant bastard wound up on the wrong end of a bandit's blade. The tiniest ember of hope glowed in his chest.

The scene came into focus. He and Fritz were triumphantly returning from getting vengeance on Meier. They stumbled on Hulot and his mule as they were attacked by bandits. He came, valiantly of course, to the Sergeant's aid. Too late for the brave legionnaire. Gil chased off the heathen buggers and barely escaping with his own life.

It made sense to his scrambling mind. The story could work.

It had to.

His heart stopped, threatening to burst through his chest. His vision cleared. Thoughts passed through his brain in a more orderly manner. The bandit knife buried in Hulot's gut was compelling evidence for his tale. The scattered gear as well.

Ignoring the insulted honking from Hulot's mule, Gil grabbed gear and threw it haphazardly around. It would have to look convincing. In his fear, he wondered when Orel and the others would show up.

If there was any justice, it wouldn't be for a few minutes more.

When he was done, the scene surely looked to innocent eyes like the gallant Sergeant Hulot had been attacked by bandits who skittered off when a second brave son of France arrived. Just to make it more convincing, Gil took both mules by the reins and walked them back and forth, leaving hoofprints everywhere that the rocky soil permitted. That eliminated boot prints, but also the imprint of sandals. No one could tell exactly what had transpired.

When the scene met his approval, he reached down and scooped up the dirt and blood collecting under the body and smeared it over his capote and some on his neck. A bloody hand through his hair completed the look. His face throbbed where he'd been slapped, and he smiled. To think that Hulot himself made it seem like Gil took a beating while trying to rescue the sergeant.

When his darting eyes couldn't find a detail out of place, Gil Vincente calmly took Hulot's Lebel, bolted a bullet into place, and fired a shot in the air. That should attract help. He cupped his hands and shouted up the trail as loud as he could, *"Au secoure?* Help. Legionnaires, where are you?"

Then Gil sat on a rock, took a pull from his canteen, and waited for the search party to arrive.

CHAPTER 41

Sitting on the rock, waiting for help, Gil fought to keep his demons under control. He wouldn't panic again. He couldn't.

His story about chasing Meier and returning still held up. He came across a bandit ambush and rushed to help. Too late for Sergeant Hulot, but that's war.

It would work.

It had to.

The longer he sat there, the more cracks he saw in the façade he built. Accusing voices in his head mocked him. He wasn't smart enough to pull this off. He'd end up on the wrong end of a rope. The scars on his wrists showed clean and pink through the filth on his body. Better he'd died back in Marseille. Most of the voices had his father's Geordie accent.

No. Screw them. He could do this.

He was still in control.

Order could still be returned.

If help didn't come soon, though, he wasn't sure he could hold it together.

A gunshot from somewhere up ahead jolted him from his self-flagellation. Gil leapt to his feet, grabbed his own rifle, and fired off a welcoming shot. "Help. Over here!"

Voices and the clomping of hooves on stone drew nearer. Around the far bend came a large man riding a familiar mule. Anya brayed, and Fritz responded in kind. Captain Pavel Orel and another soldier Gil couldn't identify from that distance approached. Seeing the body in the middle of the trail, Orel kicked his heels into Anya's flanks and trotted up. He reached down and pulled his pistol.

Gil rose on shaking legs and saluted with a shaking hand. "Sir! Private Vincente, sir."

A shocked Orel pulled Anya up short and stepped to the ground. He kept the pistol pointed at Gil as his eagle eyes took in the scene.

"What in Christ's name happened?" The captain monitored the still-saluting private while checking Hulot's corpse.

"Bandit sir. I chased them off, but it was too late—"

Orel was on one knee beside the body, looking up at Gil. He ran a hand over the Berber dagger's handle. Then, he studied the ground around the body. His eyes locked on Gil's. "What the hell are you doing here?"

All the rehearsals for this moment and Gil had never spoken the words out loud. They poured out of him like a geyser. "Sir, I was on my way back to Fort Béchar. I caught Meier. I have the money. See?"

Orel stood and crossed his arms. "Slowly, Private. Tell me exactly what happened."

Gil felt a moment of relief. He gulped in enough air to recite the story he'd so carefully rehearsed.

"Yes sir. So, like I said, I was on my way back to the base when I heard a shot. Two bandits were attacking Sergeant..." Gil paused like he didn't know the stupid bastard's name.

"Hulot. Sergeant Hulot. A good man," Orel prompted.

Gil managed a sad nod. "Hulot, sir. They took off when they saw it was a fair fight. They bolted like the cowardly heathens usually do."

"Meier?"

He was ready for the question. "Dead sir. May I?" Gil gestured to his pocket.

Orel nodded, and Gil pulled out the dead man's identification. Handing it over, he added, "I tried to bring him in alive."

The captain snorted and waved him off. He slipped Meier's identification card into his capote's inner pocket. "And you were returning the money to the fort?" He conducted a cursory search of the saddlebags. Seeing the amount of money, he appeared satisfied. "What about the Captain's horse?"

Gil bit his lip hard enough to make it tremble, but it killed the grin he felt forming. "Gone sir. The locals took him." He hoped he looked properly ashamed of his behavior. "I shouldn't have done it, but I thought I could catch Meier..."

Orel held up a palm to shut him up.

"Sir?" A familiar voice came from behind the captain. Gil looked and couldn't believe his luck as a body stepped out of the shadows. It was Jean LaForce.

"Oh God. What happened?" The young man stopped when he saw Hulot's fly-covered body.

Gil grinned. "Johnny Strong! What the Christ are you doing here?"

Jean walked forward, his eyes on the body. "Came to see if you were alright. I couldn't believe you'd be wrapped up in all this."

Gil nodded. "And to see Meiers dead?"

The kid shrugged. "Is he?"

Gil smiled warmly. "Yes. Yes, he is."

"Did it hurt?" LaForce asked.

"Probably not enough." Gil thought two hooves to the head likely hurt like hell, but it would never be enough for LaForce's purposes.

Orel slapped the dirt off his hands and looked around. "Are they still around?"

Gil was perplexed. "They, sir?"

Orel's impatience flared behind those eagle eyes. He took off his kepi and wiped the sweat from his bald head. "These bandits of yours. Where'd they go?"

Gil pointed behind him. "South sir. I think there's a village about an hour's ride."

Orel stared at the ground for long enough that alarm bells rang in the back of Gil's head. Finally, he grunted and waved at the body. "LaForce, get him onto his mule. We'll take him home."

"And the money. Johnny, I got the money" Gil's breathing was deeper now that his chest wasn't so tight. He gave the saddlebags a playful slap. Fritz honked in protest.

Orel looked deep in thought, and he snapped his fingers. "Come on, LaForce. Get to it." He turned to Gil. "You too. Let's go."

Jean didn't respond. He stood over the body, looking down with confusion in his innocent blue eyes. Suddenly, he stepped to the left and faced Gil. Slowly he raised and pointed his rifle.

Gil knitted his brows. "Johnny, what's wrong?"

Jean LaForce stared at Gil. His smile vanished. "Sir?"

Orel already had a leg in the stirrup to climb onto Anya, then stopped. "What is it, Private?"

"Sir, I... I recognize that knife."

LaForce swung his weapon towards a stunned Gil Vincente.

CHAPTER 42

Captain Orel ran a thumb over the carved symbols in the handle. "Whose is it?"

Gil's whole body tensed. He studied Jean LaForce's face. The lad had trimmed his beard, making him look less pubescent. His boyish frame was no longer gaunt. A man's muscles filled out the uniform that once hung on him like a scarecrow. There was a new confidence in the way he cradled that rifle in the crook of his elbow.

LaForce gestured with his chin. "It's his, sir. Vincente."

Orel pursed his lips. "Like the razor we found."

"Like the razor, sir," came the monotone reply.

The response croaked out of Gil's mouth, an octave too high. "Meier took my razor. Uh, *ahem*, that's not mine." With his eyes, Gil entreated the lad to believe him as he pointed at the knife. "I mean, they all carry those things. Can't tell one from the other." He followed that with a half-hearted chuckle.

Orel stepped away from the body, triangulating himself to both Gil and LaForce. He pointed a thick finger at Gil. "You. Shut up." Then he pointed to the younger man. "You. How do you know this is his?"

"He took it off a local, sir, before we left Sidi. Never goes anywhere without it. "

Gil opened his mouth to protest, but it came out in a near-whimper. "That one's not mine. Sir... Johnny, what are you saying?"

"Shut up!" The kid was sweating, his face a mask of something Gil couldn't nail down. Maybe it was hatred, more likely crippling disappointment. "I didn't think it was you. I swear on my mother, I didn't believe it."

"Because I didn't do it, you backstabbing little son of a bitch. Meier used my razor to put suspicion on me. Sir, he'd planned this for a while."

"And what happened to Sergeant Hulot? How did this mysterious knife of yours wind up in his belly?"

"It didn't sir. It's not mine."

Orel moved to Gil's pack on the ground and kicked at a pair of socks. "This yours?"

Gil's chapped lips scarcely managed to form words. "Yes, sir."

"So, if we go through it, we'll find your knife in the bag?" Orel bent to pick up the pack, and Gil's hand shot out to grab that wiry arm. Orel turned, fury in his eyes. "Remove your hand or lose it, Private."

Gil pulled away like he'd scorched his palm on a stove. "I'm sorry, sir. It... it's not there. I... I lost it. Meier probably took it when he took the razor."

The captain looked to a shaken LaForce, who shook his head. Those blue eyes were cloudy with tears. "I'm sorry, Gil. I truly am."

Orel pulled his pistol and waved Gil to the middle of the trail. "Private Vincente, you are under arrest for accessory to the murder and robbery of two couriers, and the murder of Sergeant Hulot. Oh, and horse theft."

"But I'm going to the fort! Look, I'm bringing the money back. Why would I—"

Orel's thumb cocked his pistol. "I'd advise you to be quiet. Don't make it worse. A court martial will determine what happens to you."

Gil thought twice about responding. He gulped, hung his head, and meekly nodded. At least there'd be a trial. He could lay out his story, exactly how he planned. They'll believe it. Orel always assumed the worst, that everyone was a traitor. He wasn't a traitor. He was the hero of this tale.

He had to be.

"LaForce, pick up his things, please."

Jean hustled to obey. He grabbed Gil's pack and started shoving clothes and gear into it, but not before rummaging around. "No knife here, sir."

Gil winced with each thrust. The boy knew how important order was, but it's like he didn't care at all. What happened to that little puppy that used to follow him around? Suddenly, ignoring the lad all these months felt like a tragic mistake.

The younger man got on his knees and scooped up the spilled money. He turned his face up to Gil. "I came because I knew you didn't do it! I wanted to make sure you were alright." He picked up a franc note, then another. He nearly missed the wrinkled ball of white paper hidden behind a stone.

"What's that?" Orel gestured with his chin.

"That's not mine. It's Meier's," Gil blurted out.

LaForce handed it over to an impatient Captain. Orel opened it and Gil watched his eyes go dark and steely.

It was the invitation by the Germans to desert. To come to Casablanca. It also had the handwritten code Meier would use to make contact.

Gil was fucked.

Orel took two measured steps towards him. They were about the same height, but the Russian's commanding aura overwhelmed the Englishman. "You traitorous piece of shit. You would desert the Legion? Your comrades? Your friends? I should kill you where you stand."

Gil knew the man meant it. He fought with his bladder, willing it to hold. There had to be a way out of this. Everything was chaos.

He needed time.

Time to think.

Time to get his story straight.

He knew how bad this looked, but it was all a series of honest mistakes. He needed just a little more time to impose order.

"Private, take him into custody. But first, get Hulot's body onto his mount. We'll take him home for the honors. Vincente, make yourself useful."

Gil took a big sniff and nearly choked on the dusty snot. Raising his hands, he said, "I'm coming. It's okay."

Without looking at each other, Gil and Jean LaForce laid Hulot's body over the saddle of his sad, sullen mule. The animal seemed confused at the lifeless cargo, but obeyed the command to stand still.

A thousand hornets swarmed in Gil's mind, each accusatory question a fiery sting. What if he hadn't left Her Majesty's Army? What if he'd stayed in Marseille? What if he'd married Colette?

What if he wasn't such a monumental loser?

His thoughts were interrupted by Orel's iron grasp on his elbow. Gil didn't hear exactly what was said. It didn't matter. In his fury and confusion, he wheeled around and shook the Captain off him. "Leave me alone, you bastard. I said I was coming. Don't fucking touch me."

Blindly, he shoved the captain away from him, then threw a weak punch that landed on Orel's chin, sending the officer staggering back but doing no real harm.

First, Orel rubbed a hand over where Gil had struck him. Then he stepped forward, spittle flying from his thin lips. "You're dead. You know that? You're a dead man!" A vise - like hand gripped Gil's throat.

Something took over. The world was composed only of black and red shapes. No details. Nothing identifiably human. Gil swung wildly at the biggest, nearest shape. Somewhere, people were shouting. Blows rained down on him, but he didn't care. The disorder would not take him.

One sound registered through the cyclone of anger and confusion.

A gunshot.

The world snapped back into focus. Gil was on his ass on the dusty trail. His chest was on fire. He looked down to see a spreading crimson spiderweb stain his capote.

Ten yards away, Jean LaForce held his rifle in shaking hands. It was still pointing at the man on the ground. A wisp of smoke drifted upward from the barrel.

"You bloody shot me." It was a statement of fact, not an accusation.

He was no longer in the dusty desert. Images of Newcastle, then the camp in the Veldt. Good times in Marseille, a bloody night in La Barasse. Colette wept. Rose laughed.

His eyes rolled up to the clear blue and white African sky. Gil Vincente, Gil Hawkins, Gilbert le Lion, all closed their eyes and everything turned black.

Jean LaForce calmly lowered his weapon. He was surprised to find his tongue bleeding from where he'd bitten it, but otherwise remained cool. "Are you alright, sir?"

Orel nodded. "Yes, thank you, Private." He looked at Gil's lifeless body, the eyes staring up at the sky. He didn't bother closing them. The German note in his hand went into a pocket. He muttered under his breath in the language of his Cossack ancestors.

"Take Hulot, and let's go," Captain Orel finally said.

"What about... Vincente? Sir."

"Gather his gear and identification. We'll take it with us. Make sure the money is secure."

LaForce felt his hand shaking and shoved it into his pocket. "What about the body?"

"Leave him for the vultures. Or the Arabs. He's no longer a true legionnaire. I don't care what happens to him. Neither should you."

Orel turned his back and walked over to Anya. He rubbed her muzzle, buried his nose in her mane, and whispered in her ear. LaForce couldn't make out what he said. It probably didn't matter.

After picking up as much gear as he could cram into Gil's pack, he looked down at the body. Without a word, he grabbed what was left of Gil by the hands and dragged the limp body off the trail into a brushy patch. He left it facing up as he stood over it for a few seconds, then turned and walked to the mules.

As Orel watched, Jean LaForce took a blanket from Fritz's back, returned to the corpse, and carefully covered it up to the neck. He knelt quickly and crossed himself.

Then Johnny Strong made sure the corners were tucked under just so.

Without another word, he took Fritz's reins, along with his own mule and Hulot's. Staring straight ahead, he followed Anya and Orel back up the hill towards Fort Béchar.

Fin

HISTORICAL NOTES AND OBLIGATORY AUTHOR STUFF

B efore I give you the notes, thank you for reading The Deserter. This is the part where I beg you for reviews. In a crazy sales environment for books, it's the raw number of reviews that helps an author sell books, not just the kind words.

Please take a moment to let the world know what you thought of my seventh (!) novel. Amazon, Facebook, Twitter, Bluesky, Instagram, corner strangers in Starbucks, whatever. It would mean a lot.

I'll wait.

Okay, now on to the historical notes. Hard as it is to believe, there was a time when the French Foreign Legion had a prominent place in pop culture. PC Wren's novels, especially Beau Geste and Beau Sabeur, were read around the world. Pulp magazines such as Argus were packed with tales by authors like Theodore Roscoe. The movies in particular loved the Legion. The first silent film version of Beau Geste was in 1926, and it has been remade in one form or another over half a dozen times. By one count, more than 70 films have been made in the sand and sword genre, and that's just in English. Eventually, the idea of soldiers in the desert devolved into such a cliché, it became fodder for Charlie Chase, Laurel and Hardy, the Three Stooges and Marty Feldman. (For an amazingly researched look at the Foreign Legion in pop culture, check out Frank Thompson's incredible work, "The Compleat Beau Geste.")

If memory serves, my first exposure to the Foreign Legion may have been a Pepe Le Pew cartoon (ask your parents). The first desert movie I saw one afternoon, home sick from school, was "Under Two Flags," with Ronald Coleman and Claudette Colbert (ask your parents.) Not Oscar-bait, but I was hooked.

As with most historical periods caught on film and in genre literature, the idea of the *Legion Étranger* was more important than the reality. The notion of a military force as a last chance, a refuge for men with dark secrets and a need to face their demons, appeals to a lot of us. Stir in exotic locales, easily identified bad guys, a little casual racism and toxic masculinity, *et voila*.

As a fighting force, especially in the desert, they were formidable for a time, but as famous for the battles they lost as the campaigns it won. Defeat at Camaron led to Cinco de Mayo celebrations, and Dien Bien Phu is known for being the reason for America's involvement in the Vietnam War if we remember France being there at all. (Don't get me started on how Americans learn history—or don't.)

Like westerns for a long time, the genre fell out of favor but always had a place in my "boy's adventure stories" heart next to the Three Musketeers and Treasure Island. I kept looking for an excuse to write this story until it worked its way to the usable part of my brain. Admittedly this isn't the sanitized, Gary Cooper version. It's more like Beau Geste directed by Sam Peckinpah but as I always say, YOU try living in my brain for a while.

Historical fiction is tricky to get right, and I hope I've captured the tone and most of the relevant facts.

The Battle of Menhaba occurred on April 14-16, 1908. The actual fighting on the Moroccan-Algerian frontier played out pretty much as described in the book. It was mule-mounted troops, particularly the 24th Mounted Company, who took the brunt of the attack. Lieutenant Maurice Coste, moustache and all, was the last recorded casualty on April 16.

About that time, the Germans began suborning desertion from the Legion to aid their own (largely futile) colonial ambitions. There was a hilarious disaster in Casablanca Harbor that I would have loved to write about, but came too late for the timeline to work in this book.

Life in Sidi Bel Abbès is well recorded. I've tried to be factual down to the layout of the fort and location of certain buildings and the street names. Le Chat Noir is made up, but it doesn't take much to imagine a dozen other establishments just like it really existed. I hope Rose married well.

Gil's background as a soldier in the Boer War and his experiences manning the concentration camps on the Veldt are drawn from multiple sources. It is hard to write about the European experience in the early 20th century without stepping into sensitive territory. British and European colonialism had its horrors (still does) and it had to have played on the minds and consciences of those involved. Some of them, at least.

Many of the details in the story came from online sources (I don't read French worth a damn, and even if I did, military records are only so available. Or trustworthy.) A big thanks to Douglas Porch and his magnum opus, "The French Foreign Legion- A Complete History of the Legendary Fighting Force."

The Legion Etranger exists to this day, although it's a shadow of its former self. Aren't we all?

My thanks to everyone who helped bring this book to life. In particular, my friends and colleagues at the Sin City Writers group in Las Vegas, most of whom had never heard of the Foreign Legion when I started bringing in chapters. Have I mentioned I'm feeling old and Americans don't know history?

Beta readers included talented authors Cam Torrens, Dave Buzan and Frank Thompson, my resident expert on all things Legion (seriously, read them) as well as Kevin Keefe and PB Ray. Anything that's slipped through the cracks is on me. A huge special thanks to my writing buddy (read her work!) Jill Hand, who not only caught a lot of little things, but found a huge mistake that might have ruined the book completely and shattered what little credibility I have. She has a great eye for detail and a knack for ticking off the right people.

That brings me to whoever is reading this at the moment. Thank you for supporting my work. I hope you'll check out the rest of my books.

This is my return to historical fiction after a three-book detour into urban fantasy with the Werewolf PI series. It's good work, and I'm glad I wrote it, but also happy to be back in my natural habitat. Obviously, there's no sequel planned to The Deserter (do I have to say "Spoiler Alert," at the end of a book you just read?) I don't know what's next, but I plan on doing stand-alone stories, I'm not sure I have another full series in me and there are too many great stories to tell.

Last but not least, thank you to The Duchess, Her Serene Highness, Mad Max, most manly of poodles, and my family in Canada.

In case you're curious, I do not know where my brain will take me next. I just hope you'll join me wherever it is. Follow me at WayneTurmel.com, or on Facebook, Bluesky or Instagram. And don't be afraid to let me know what you think and interact with me. It lets me know someone's actually out there.

Don't let the weasels get you down.

WWT

Also by Wayne Turmel

Historical Fiction

The Count of the Sahara (1920s Archaeology and biography)

The Lucca Le Pou Stories : (Adventure set in the Crusades)

Acre's Bastard (Part 1)

Acre's Orphans (Part 2)

The Deserter: A Tale of the Foreign Legion (Algeria and Morocco, 1908)

Urban Fantasy

The Werewolf PI Series

Johnny Lycan & the Anubis Disc (Part 1)

Johnny Lycan & the Vegas Berserker (Part 2)

Johnny Lycan & the Last Witchfinder (Part 3)

Follow me at WayneTurmel.com

www.ingramcontent.com/pod-product-compliance
Lightning Source LLC
Chambersburg PA
CBHW030619120726

47904CB00006B/1962